YESTERDAY'S SPY

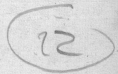

Len Deighton

YESTERDAY'S SPY

2914

ARROW BOOKS

Arrow Books Limited
20 Vauxhall Bridge Road, London SW1V 2SA

An imprint of the Random Century Group

London Melbourne Sydney Auckland Johannesburg
and agencies throughout the world

First published in Great Britain by Jonathan Cape 1975
Triad Grafton edition 1976
Arrow edition 1991

Printed and bound in Great Britain by
Cox & Wyman Ltd, Reading

ISBN 0 09 985730 8

1

'The Guernica network!' said Steve Champion, holding up his glass.

I hesitated. White's Club – *sanctus sanctorum* of Establishment London – seemed an inappropriate place to indulge in revolutionary nostalgia.

'Let's just drink to Marius,' I said.

'Marius,' said Champion. He drank, and wiped his blunt military-style moustache with the back of his glove. It was a gesture I'd noticed that time we'd first met – Villefranche, landing from a submarine, one night when the war was young. It was as wrong for him then as it was now. In those days Regular Army captains of the Welsh Guards did not wipe the froth off their faces with the back of their hand. But then Regular captains of the Brigade of Guards, sent to France to set up anti-Nazi Intelligence networks, were not expected to meet newly arriving agents with a girl on each arm and an open bottle of champagne.

'Marius,' I said. I drank too.

'What a comical crew we were,' said Champion. 'Marius the revolutionary priest, you straight from training school, with your terrible accent and your pimple ointment, and me. Sometimes I thought we should have let the Nazis catch us, and watched them die of laughing.'

'It was Marius who reconciled that network,' I said, 'the Communists and the deserters and the hot-heads and us professionals. It was Marius who held the network together. When he went, we all went.'

'He was past his prime by then,' said Champion. 'He'd

had too much of it. He wouldn't have lasted much longer anyway. None of us would have.'

'Marius was young,' I said. 'Almost as young as I was.'

'Marius died in a torture chamber,' said Champion. 'He died within six hours of being arrested . . . it was incredibly brave and he deserved the medal . . . but he could have saved himself by giving them some useless information. He could have deciphered some ancient codes and given them the names of people who'd already gone back to London. He could have bought a few days, and in a few days we could have rescued him.'

I didn't argue. Even after all this time it was difficult to be objective about the death of Marius. His energy and his optimism had kept us going at times when it seemed that all was lost. And his reckless bravery had more than once saved us.

For Champion it was even more difficult. He'd always blamed himself for the young priest's death. Perhaps that was partly why he'd married Marius's younger sister. And perhaps it was partly why the marriage had now fallen apart.

We both watched the far end of the room, where two Socialist Cabinet Ministers exchanged jokes about their golf handicaps and tips about the stock exchange. Champion reached into the waistcoat of his beautifully cut chalk-stripe suit. He flipped back the cover of the gold hunter that had belonged to his father and his grandfather, looked at the time, and then signalled a club servant to bring more drinks.

'The divorce came through,' he said. 'Caty and me – it's all over. Nowadays I live all the time in France.'

'I'm sorry,' I said.

'Why?' said Champion.

I shrugged. There was no point in telling him that I liked them both, and enjoyed what had once been their happy marriage. 'Those weekends at the house in Wales,' I said. 'Where will I go now to get French cooking like Caty's?'

'Well, Caty still lives there,' said Champion. 'And she'd love to see you again, I'm sure.'

I looked at him. I would have expected him to invite me to his new house in France rather than to that of his ex-wife in Wales, but Steve Champion was always unpredictable. Even more so since he'd become a wealthy businessman. He lit a fresh cigarette from the dog-end of his old one. His hand trembled; he had to steady it with the one on which he always wore a glove – to hide the absence of the fingertips he'd left behind in an interview room of St Roch prison in wartime Nice.

'You never thought of going back?' he said.

'To live in France?' I said.

He smiled. 'To the department.'

'Hah! It's a thought, isn't it?' I said. 'I didn't, Steve, and I'll tell you why.' I leaned a little closer to him, and he glanced round the room with no more than a flicker of the eye.

I said, 'Because the department never asked me to, Steve.'

He smiled soberly.

'And I'll tell you something else, Steve,' I added. 'There are people who say that you never left the department. Whenever we get together like this in London I wonder whether *you* are going to try recruiting *me*.'

'Now you're laughing at me, boyo,' said Champion, in his stage Welsh accent. He reached into his pocket and produced a clear plastic envelope. Inside it were five picture postcards. Each depicted an airship or a balloon, and in the foreground were men in straw hats and women in leg-of-mutton-sleeved dresses, inhabitants of an innocent world that had not quite learned to fly. On the other sides of the cards was a tangle of greetings to long-forgotten addressees, and curious old postage stamps.

'A philatelic auction in Bond Street,' said Champion. 'That's why I came to London. I just couldn't resist these.'

I looked at his purchases. By now Champion should have realized that I was a lost cause as far as his obsession with airmail stamps was concerned. 'And Billy?' I asked. I handed his airships back to him.

'Yes, I'm seeing a lot of Billy this week,' said Champion, as if visiting his young son was no more than an afterthought. 'Caty has been very good about letting me see Billy.'

He went through the postcards one by one and then put them away with exaggerated care. 'The night Billy was born,' he said, 'I was up to the neck in bank loans, promissory notes and mortgages. I was sure I'd done the wrong thing . . . did I ever tell you how I started: with the uncut diamonds?'

'I've heard stories,' I admitted.

He inhaled carefully on his cigarette. 'Do you know Accra?'

'No.'

'The arse-hole of West Africa. I was flat broke, and working hard to buy a ticket home. I was translating export permits for cocoa traders and wangling customs forms for importers – all of them Arabs. My Arabic has always been good, but by the time I finished working with those jokers I could have done the sports reports for Radio Cairo. When I think of it!' He clasped his hands tight as if to stretch the joints. 'I took the bumpf down to the customs sheds one day – June, it was, and bloody steamy, even by Accra standards. I made the usual golden obeisance to the officials and loaded ten crates of Renault spares on to the truck I'd hired. But when I uncrated them back in the cocoa warehouse, I find I'm knee-deep in French MAS 38s, complete with cleaning kits, and spares and instruction booklets.'

'Sub-machineguns,' I said.

'Go to the top of the class.'

'But could you get the Long cartridge?'

'Am I glad you weren't involved, old boy! No, you *couldn't* get them. But the kids who bought them were too young to remember the MAS 38, so they think they are MAT 49s, for which there is 9 mm stuff ready to be nicked from a local police or army unit. Right?'

'Right.'

'But I'm getting ahead of the story. Imagine me – the only man in Accra who'd sooner have Renault spares than sub-machineguns, sitting on ten cases of them. All of them customs cleared, rubber stamped and signed for. It *was* tempting.'

'But you didn't succumb?'

'Oh, but I did.' He took a drag on his cigarette and waved the smoke away. 'Two hundred and thirty-five dollars each – American dollars – and I could have doubled it, had I sold them to the loudmouths with the fuzzy-wuzzy haircuts.'

'Ten to a case?' I said. 'About ten thousand pounds profit.'

'I had to stop my client going down to the customs and raising hell about his Renault spares. I owed a bit of money, I had to get an exit permit, and clearance from the tax office: it all costs money.'

'You came home?'

'I went to buy my air ticket from a crooked little Portuguese travel agent. I started bargaining with him, knowing that he could unload my US dollar bills at a big premium. To cut a long story short, I ended up giving him all my American money in exchange for a bag of uncut diamonds from Angola and a boat ticket to Marseille.'

'You went to Marseille?'

'Old man Tix had just died, his whole set-up was for sale. Caty's sister told me about it. But the Algerian fighting was still on, and the Tix fruit and vegetable importing was no more than a ream of headed notepaper and a couple of fleabitten offices in Constantine.'

'And the quarry was defunct.'

'The quarry – yes.' Champion smiled. We'd both hidden in the quarry during a big German round-up, when old man Tix had chased a German officer out of the house shouting 'Sale Boche' at him, crossing himself as he did so. 'The quarry was finished. They'd mined, too, but it was costing so much to dig that the old boy did better on unemployment benefit.'

'But you sold your diamonds and bought the Tix place from his widow?'

'That was only a down payment,' said Steve, 'but Madame Tix wanted me to have it. She waited a long time for the rest of the money. It was a gamble for all concerned. We were betting on a peaceful settlement of the Algerian war.'

'You were always a good guesser, Steve,' I said.

'The peace between France and Algeria meant immigrant labourers – that got the mine back into profit.'

'Lower wages,' I said.

'But still higher than any they could get in their own country.'

'But you closed the mine and the quarry – you sent the men home.'

Champion smiled. He said, 'It was the *idea* of cheap labour in the mine. That's what enabled me to get my capital. Avaricious little hairdressers with their hands in the till . . . contractors fiddling their tax, and hard-eyed

14

old bastards from the merchant banks. They came to see my quarry and the Arabs sweating their guts out. They liked it – that was the kind of investment those little sods could understand. That was the way their grandfathers – and their friends' grandfathers – had made a fortune in Africa a hundred years ago.'

'And you put that money into the fruit and veg.'

'Much more than money . . . soil analysis, a professor of botany, a programme of seeding techniques, long-term contracts for the farmers, minimum price guarantees for seasonal workers, refrigerated warehouses, refrigerated transport and contracted refrigerated shipping. I put a lot of money into the Arab countries.'

'And now they have oil as well.'

'Oil is a one-crop economy,' said Champion.

'A gilt-edged one,' I said.

'That's what they said about coffee and tea and rubber,' said Champion. 'I truly believe that North Africa must trade with Europe, right across the board. The Arab countries must have a stake in Europe's well-being. The economics must link, otherwise Africa will let Europe die of inflation.'

'I never thought of you as a crusader, Steve.'

Champion seemed disconcerted at the idea. He picked up his glass to hide behind it.

Two men came downstairs: one was a famous poet, the other a peer of the realm. They were arguing quietly and eruditely about the lyrics of an obscene Eighth Army song about the extra-marital activities of King Farouk.

A club servant came to tell Champion that a lady was waiting at the entrance. 'Come along,' said Champion. 'This is someone I'd like you to meet.'

A servant helped Champion into the lightweight vicuna coat, designed like a British warm, and handed him the bowler hat that made him look like a retired general.

15

Someone unseen gave a perfunctory brush to the shoulder of my dirty raincoat.

The snow obliterated the view through the doorway, like static on an old TV. Outside in St James's Street, London's traffic was jammed tight. Champion's girl gave no more than the nod and smile that manners demanded. Her eyes were devoted to Champion. She watched him with the kind of awe with which an orphan eyes a Christmas tree. It was always the same girl. This one had the same perfect skin that Caty had, and the same soft eyes with which Pina had looked at him. Except that decades had passed since Caty or Pina had been this kid's age.

'Melodie,' said Champion. 'It's a nice name, isn't it: Melodie Page.'

'It's a lovely name,' I said, in my usual sycophantic way.

Champion looked at his watch. 'It's a long time since we jawed so much,' he told me. 'My God, but you would have been bored, Melodie. We must be getting old.' He smiled. 'Melodie and Billy are taking me to the theatre tonight. They are going to repair one of the gaps in my musical education.'

The girl hit his arm in mock anger.

'Rock music and pirates,' Champion told me.

'A potent mixture,' I said.

'Billy will be glad I've seen you. You always remember his birthday, he told me.'

'Yes,' I said.

'That's damned nice of you.' Champion patted my arm.

At that moment, exactly on schedule, a black Daimler drew level with the entrance. A uniformed driver hurried across the pavement, opening an umbrella to shelter Champion and the girl from the weather. He opened the door, too. As the girl slid into the real leather seating,

Champion looked back to where I was standing. The snow was beating about my ears. Champion raised his gloved hand in a regal salute. But when only three of your fingers are able to wave, such a gesture can look awfully like a very rude Anglo-Saxon sign.

2

I could see my report about Champion on Schlegel's desk. Schlegel picked it up. He shook it gently, as if hoping that some new information might drop out of it. 'No,' said Schlegel. 'No. No. No.'

I said nothing. Colonel Schlegel, US Marine Corps (Air Wing), Retired, cut a dapper figure in a lightweight houndstooth three-piece, fake club-tie and button-down cotton shirt. It was the kind of outfit they sell in those Los Angeles shops that have bow windows and plastic Tudor beams. He tapped my report. 'Maybe you can shaft the rest of them with your inscrutable sarcasm and innocent questions, but me no likee – got it?'

'Look,' I said. 'Champion was just seeing his kid, and buying stamps – there's no other angle. He's a rich man now: he's not playing secret agents. Believe me, Colonel. There's nothing there.'

Schlegel leaned forward to get a small cigar from a box decorated with an eagle trying to eat a scroll marked *Semper Fidelis*. He pushed the box to me, but I'm trying to give them up.

'He's in deep,' said Schlegel. Puckered scar tissue made it difficult to distinguish his smiles from his scowls. He was a short muscular man with an enviable measure of self-confidence; the kind of personality that you hire to MC an Elks Club stag night.

I waited. The 'need-to-know' basis, upon which the department worked, meant that I'd been told only a part of it. Schlegel took his time getting his cigar well alight.

I said, 'The story about the machineguns fits with

everything I've been told. The whole story – the stuff about the uncut diamonds providing the money to start the mine, and then the fruit and vegetable imports – that's all on non-classified file.'

'Not all of it,' said Schlegel. 'Long after the file closes, Champion was still reporting back to this department.'

'Was he!'

'Long before my time, of course,' said Schlegel, to emphasize that this was a British cock-up, less likely to happen now that we had him with us on secondment from Washington. 'Yes,' said Schlegel, 'those machine-guns were shipped to Accra on orders from this office. It was all part of the plan to buy Champion into control of the Tix set-up. Champion was our man.'

I remembered all those years when I'd been drinking and dining with the Champions, never suspecting that he was employed by this office.

Perhaps Schlegel mistook my silence for disbelief. 'It was a good thing while it lasted,' he said. 'Champion was in and out of Egypt, Algeria and Tunisia, arguing about his melons, carrots and potatoes, keeping his eyes open and dropping a few words to the right people, doing us all a power of good. And the *way* that Champion had scored – selling cannons to some freaky little terrorist outfit – all helped.'

'So what was the fadeout?'

Schlegel blew a piece of tobacco off his lip, with enough force to make the bookcase rattle. 'The feedback of information began to sag. Champion said the French were starting to lean on him, and it was getting too dangerous. It was a top-level decision to let him go. It was the right decision. You Brits are good at bowing out gracefully and you'd done all right out of Champion by that time.'

'And now?'

'A guy in German security trying to make a name for himself. He's dug out some stuff about Champion's financial affairs. They are asking questions about the guns at Accra.'

'Bonn gets hysterical – and we have to join in the screaming?'

'If the Champion business becomes a big scandal, they'll say we were careless when we let him go.'

'Perhaps it was a little careless,' I suggested.

'Well, maybe it was,' said Schlegel. He picked up my report exonerating Champion. 'But your whitewash job isn't going to help matters.'

'I'll take another shot at it,' I said.

He slid my report across the polished desk. Then from a drawer he got Perrier water and a tiny bottle of Underberg bitters. He shook the bitters into the mineral water and stirred it with a ballpoint pen to make it a delicate brown. 'Want some?'

'That's just for hangovers,' I said. 'And even then it's got to be a pretty damn bad hangover.'

'I like it,' said Schlegel, and drank it slowly, savouring each sip.

I took the report and stood up to leave. Schlegel said, 'This is going to be a lousy rotten miserable bummer. I hate these jobs where we are shaking down our own. So you don't have to give me a bad time, or give yourself a bad time for not covering up for him.'

'I had that lecture at Indoctrine Four, when I went to the CIA Communications symposium in 1967,' I said.

'Champion saved your life,' Schlegel reminded me. 'If you can't hack it, just say you want out.'

'I know what kind of out I'd get,' I said bitterly.

Schlegel nodded. 'And I'd countersign it,' he said. In a way, I preferred Schlegel's New World directness: the

20

others would have tried to persuade me that such a request would have had no effect on my career.

Schlegel stood up to look out of the window. It was still snowing. 'This isn't just some kind of fancy positive vetting job,' he said. 'This is a hot one.' Schlegel scratched his behind, and reflected.

'Someone across the street could lip-read you,' I warned him.

He turned to look at me pityingly. It was Schlegel's often expressed belief that we'd get more done here in London if we worried less about such details. 'The Germans are sending one of their people down to Nice to investigate Champion,' he said thoughtfully.

I didn't respond.

'Have you been taken suddenly drunk or something?' said Schlegel.

'I didn't want to disturb your deductive processes,' I said. I polished my spectacles and blinked at him.

'Damned if I understand it,' he said.

'You're in Europe now, Colonel,' I said. 'This German scandal has come just when the Bonn government are warming up for an election. When their security people discovered that Champion had once been a British agent it was the answer to all their problems. They wrote "Passed to British security" in the margin and fired it across here. Now the German Defence Minister can refuse to answer any questions about the scandal on the grounds that it would prejudice the security of their British ally. It will give them all they need to stall until the election is over. When they are elected again it will be "Minister requested" and that's the last we'll see of it. I've been through all this before, Colonel.'

'Well, you know more about all this European Mickey Mouse than I'll ever understand,' said Schlegel. It was a double-edged compliment and he bared his teeth to let

21

me know it. 'We'll hold it for the three-month cycle,' he offered, as if trying to come to terms with me.

'Don't do me any favours,' I told him. 'I don't give a good goddamn if you publish it as a whole-page ad in *Variety*. I've done what I was asked. But if the department expected me to return with the synopsis for World War Three, I'm sorry to disappoint. If you want to send me back to spend the rest of the year drinking with Champion at the department's expense, I'll be very happy to do so. But Champion is no dope. He'll tumble what's going on.'

'Maybe he already did,' Schlegel said slyly. 'Maybe that's why you got nothing out of him.'

'You know what to do, then,' I told him.

'I already did it,' he said. 'A short dark kid. Looks ten years younger than she really is: Melodie Page. Been with the department nearly eight years!'

3

'William, come to Mother, darling, and let me give you a kiss.' Champion's failed marriage was all there in that imperious command. An elegant French wife who persisted in calling their small son Billy 'William', and who gave him kisses, instead of asking for them.

She gave Billy the promised kiss, pulled a dead leaf off the front of his sweater and then waited until he'd left the room. She turned to me. 'All I ask is that you don't remind me how keen I was to marry him.' She poured fresh hot water into the teapot, and then put the copper kettle back on the hob. It hummed gently with the heat from the blazing logs. There was a stainless-steel kitchen only a few steps along the carpeted corridor, but she had made the tea and toasted the bread on the open fire in the lounge. From here we could look out of the window and watch the wind ruffling the river and whipping the bare trees into a mad dance. The black Welsh hills wore a halo of gold that promised respite from the dark daylight.

'I didn't come down here to talk about Steve, or about the divorce,' I protested.

She poured tea for me and gave me the last slice of toast. She spiked a fresh piece of bread on to the toasting fork. 'Then it's surprising how many times we seem to find ourselves talking about it.' She turned to the hearth and busied herself with finding a hot place in the fire. 'Steve has this wonderful knack,' she continued bitterly, 'this wonderful knack of falling on his feet . . . like a kitten.'

It was an affectionate analogy. The rejection had hurt, I could see that. I buttered my toast and put some of Caterina's homemade jam on it. It was delicious and I ate it without speaking.

'This damned house,' she continued. 'My sister wrote to tell me how much it would be worth if it was in France. But it's not in France, it's in Wales! And it costs a fortune to keep the slates on, and mend the boiler, and cut the lawn . . . and heating oil has nearly doubled in price just since the last delivery.' The bread started to smoke. She cursed softly, broke the scorched piece off and threw it away into the flames before toasting the other side. Caterina could cope with things. That was her misfortune in a way. She wanted to be cosseted and looked after but she was ten times more efficient than any of the men who wanted to do it. 'So Steve gets rid of the house, burdens me with all its problems and expenses, and everyone tells me to be grateful.'

'You're not exactly poor, Caty,' I said.

She looked at me for a moment, deciding if I knew her well enough to make such a personal remark. But I did know her well enough.

'You know what the arrangement was . . . If he's going down to the river, I'll kill the little devil.'

I followed her gaze to where her small son was dragging a toy cart across the lawn. As if sensing that he was being watched, he changed direction and started back up towards the smart new sauna again. Caterina went back to her tea and toast. 'He's changed a lot, you know . . . I swore to my father that Steve had come through the war unmarred, but it took ten years to take effect. And then the last few years have been hell . . . hell for both of us, and little William, too!'

'He had a lousy war, Caty,' I said.

'So did a lot of other people.'

I remembered the day in 1944 when I went into Nice prison just a few hours after the Gestapo had moved out. I was with the forward elements of the American Army. There was another Englishman with me. We asked each other no personal questions. He was wearing Intelligence Corps badges, but he knew Steve Champion all right, and he was probably sent directly from London, as I had been. The Germans had destroyed all the documents. I suppose London were sure they would have done, or they would have sent someone more important than me to chase it.

'Look at that,' said this other officer, when we were kicking the cupboards of the interrogation room apart. It was a shabby room, with a smell of ether and carbolic, a framed engraving of Salzburg and some broken wine bottles in the fireplace. He pointed to a bottle on the shelf. 'Steve Champion's fingertips,' said my companion. He took the bottle and swirled the brine around so that through the mottled glass I saw four shrunken pieces of dark brown organic matter that jostled together as they were pushed to the centre of the whirling fluid. I looked again and found that they were four olives, just as the label said, but for a moment I had shivered. And each time I remembered it I shivered again. 'You're right, Caty,' I said. 'A lot of people had it much worse.'

Overhead the clouds were low and puffy, like a dirty quilt pulled over the face of the countryside.

'There was all that "we Celts" nonsense. I began to believe that Wales was little different from Brittany. Little did I know . . . My God!' said Caterina. She was still watching Billy in the garden. 'The banks of the river are so muddy this last week . . . the rain . . . one of the village boys was drowned there this time last year.' She looked up at the carved wooden crucifix on the wall above the TV set.

'He'll be all right.' I said it to calm her.

'He never dares to go down as far as the paddock when Steve visits. But he just defies me!'

'Do you want me to get him?'

She gave a despairing smile. 'I don't know,' she said. She tugged at her hair. I was a 'friend of Steve's': she didn't want me to get any kind of response from Billy that she had failed to get. 'We'll watch from here,' she said.

'That's probably best,' I agreed.

'You English!' she said. I got the full blast of her anxiety. 'You're probably a fully paid-up subscriber to the Society for the Prevention of Cruelty to Animals.'

'That wouldn't necessarily make me a child-beater,' I said. 'And it's the *Royal* Society.'

'No one can live with a man who is racked with guilt. And Steve is racked with guilt.'

'You're not talking about the war?' I asked.

'I'm talking about the marriage,' she said.

'Because Steve has no need to feel guilty about the war,' I told her.

'My mother told me about Englishmen,' said Caterina. She raised her hand in a gesture more appropriate to an Italian market than to an English drawing-room. And now her voice, too, carried an inflection of her birth ties. 'You don't have to have something to feel guilty about!' Her voice was high and almost shrill. 'Don't you understand that? Guilt is like pain – it hurts just the same whether it's real or imagined!'

'I'll have to think about that,' I said defensively.

'You think about it, then. I'll go and fetch William.' She pushed the silk cosy down over the teapot to keep the tea warm while she was gone. But she did not go. She kept her hands round it and stared into the distance. Or perhaps she was staring at the silver-framed photo of her

26

brother Marius, the young priest who'd died in that carbolic-smelling basement. Suddenly the sun stabbed into the room. It wasn't real sun, there was no warmth in it, and precious little colour. It spilled over the embroidered traycloth like weak lemon tea, and made a rim round Caty's hair.

They were both like their mother, these Baroni girls. Even as children they'd looked more like visiting towns-people than like village kids. Tall and slim, Caty had that sort of ease and confidence that belied the indecision she expressed.

'I won't stay here,' she said, as if her thoughts had raced on far beyond our conversation. 'My sister wants me to help with her boutique in Nice. With the money I get from the house, we could start another shop, perhaps.'

The sun's cross-light scrawled a thousand wrinkles upon her face, and I was forced to see her as she was, instead of through the flattering haze of my memories. Perhaps she read my thoughts. 'I'm getting old,' she said. 'Steve's getting old, too, and so are you.' She smoothed her hair, and touched the gold cross that she wore.

She was still attractive. Whatever kind of post-natal exercises she'd done after Billy's birth had restored her figure to that of the trim young woman Steve had married. She used just sufficient make-up to compensate for the pale English winters she'd endured for so long. Her nails were manicured, and long enough to convince me that she didn't spend much time at the sink, and her hair was styled in the fashion that requires frequent visits to the hairdresser.

She smoothed the striped silk pants across her knee. They were stylish and tailored. She looked like an illus-tration that American *Vogue* might run if they ever did an article about English crumpet. I wondered if she spent many elegant afternoons sitting by the log fire in her fine clothes, pouring herself lemon tea from a silver teapot.

'Do you know what I think?' she said.

I waited a long time and then I said, 'What do you think, Caty?'

'I don't believe you just *bumped into* Steve. I think you were sent after him. I think you are still working for the Secret Service or something – just like in the war. I think you are after Steve.'

'Why would anyone be after him, Caty?'

'He's changed,' she said. 'You must have noticed that yourself. I wouldn't be surprised what he was mixed up in. He has this sort of schizophrenia and an obsession with secrecy. I don't know if you get like that in the Secret Service, or whether the Secret Service choose that sort of man. But it's hell to live with, I'll tell you that.'

'I think you still love him,' I said.

'You've always hero-worshipped him,' she said. 'He was your big brother, wasn't he? You just can't imagine that some boring little housewife like me would have the effrontery to be glad to get rid of your wonderful Steve Champion. Well, I am glad. I just hope like hell that I never see him again, ever.'

I don't know how she expected me to react, but whatever she expected, I failed her. I saw a look of exasperation. She said, 'I tried, believe me, I tried very hard. I even bought new things and wore false eyelashes.'

I nodded.

'I thought Steve had sent you . . . to get William.'

'No,' I said.

'He'll stop at nothing to get him. He told me that. But I'll fight him, Charles. You tell Steve that. He'll never get William from me.'

She picked up Billy's favourite toy rabbit and went to the door. She looked back at me as if I was a Solomon

28

who would decide Billy's future. 'If I thought he would be happy with Steve, I wouldn't mind so much. But William is not like his father – he's a gentle child and easily hurt.'

'I know he is, Caty.'

She stood there for a moment, thinking of things to say, and not saying them. Then she went out of the room.

I saw her as she passed the window. She was wearing a riding mac and a scarf over her head. She had Billy's rabbit under her arm.

4

That Champion's Master File had been brought from Central Registry was, in itself, a sign of the flap that was in progress. It was seldom that we handled anything other than the Action Abstracts and they were a three-hour task. This Master would have stacked up to a five-feet-tall pile of paperwork, had the Biog, Associative, Report, Vettings and year by year Summaries been put one upon the other.

The papers had yellowed with age, the photos were brittle and dog-eared. The yellow vetting sheets were now buff-coloured, and the bright-red Report dossier had faded to a brownish-pink.

There was little hope of discovering anything startling here. The continuing triple-A clearance, right up to the time that Champion stopped reporting to the department, was in itself a sign that men more jaundiced than I could ever be had given Champion a clean bill of health. Since then the department had shown little interest in him.

I looked at his Biographical entries. Champion's father, a Welsh Catholic, had been a senior lecturer at the Abbasiyah Military Academy, Cairo. Young Champion came back to England to attend public school. From there he won a place at the Royal Military Academy, Sandhurst. For a boy who grew up to table-talk of tactics, battles and ballistics, Sandhurst was a doddle. Champion became an under-officer, and a well-remembered one. And his scholarship matched his military expertise: modern history, four languages and a mathematics prize.

It was Champion's French-language skills that earned

for him a secondment to the French Army. He went the usual round of military colleges, the Paris Embassy, Maginot Line fortresses and Grand General HQ, with occasional glimpses of the legendary General Gamelin.

Champion had only been back with his regiment for a matter of weeks when a War Office directive automatically shortlisted him for a Secret Intelligence Service interview. He was selected, trained and back in France by 1939. He was just in time to watch General Gamelin's defence system surrender to the Nazis. Champion fled south and became 'net-officer' for what was no more than a collection of odds and sods in the unoccupied zone. His orders were to stay clear of the enthusiastic amateurs that London called their Special Operations Executive, but inevitably the two networks became entangled.

It was Champion who greeted me in person that night when I landed from the submarine at Villefranche. I was assigned to SOE but Champion kidnapped me and got it made official afterwards. If I'd gone up to Nîmes as ordered, my war service would have ended two or three months later in Buchenwald.

But Champion used me to sort out his own network and I stayed with him right up to the time the network crumbled and Champion was taken prisoner. Eventually he escaped and was flown back to London. He got a DSO and a new job. Even before D-Day, Champion was assigned to peacetime network planning. He demanded choice of personnel, and got it. His first request was to have me as his senior assistant. It wasn't easy for me now to look at Champion's file with an objective eye.

When you read old files, you realize how the paperwork itself decides the progress of an inquiry. Schlegel gave Bonn's report a twelve-week life cycle, so the coordinator decided not to give it a file number. He attached it as an appendix to Champion's abstract. Then I had to do a written report, to glue it all together. With everyone satisfied, the file would have gone over to Current Storage and then gone sliding down the priorities until it ended in a tin archive box in Hendon.

But it didn't.

It was activated by an alert slip that came from the officer who was 'running' Melodie Page. She failed to report for two cycles. This would normally have meant the opening of an orange Caution File with its own file number. But with Champion's abstract signed out to me, it caused the girl's alert slip to be pinned on to my desk diary.

Suddenly the Champion file was wearing red stickers in its hair, and everyone concerned was trying to think of a 'Latest action' to pin to it, in case the Minister wanted to read it himself.

'I don't like it,' said Schlegel.

'Perhaps she's fallen for Champion,' I said.

He looked at me to see whether I meant it. 'That's all I need,' said Schlegel. 'You coming in here inventing new things for me to worry about.'

'And you want me to go to this flat that Champion is supposed to have kept as some kind of bolt-hole?'

'It's a ten-minute job. Special Branch will send Blantyre and one of the Special Branch break-in specialists. Just take a look round, and file a short report tomorrow. No sweat – it's only to show we're on our toes.'

'Are you sure I'm experienced enough to handle something like this?'

'Don't go touchy on me, bubblebrain. I want a piece of paper: something recent, with a senior operative's signature, to put in the file before it leaves here.'

'You're right,' I said.

'Goddamn! Of course I'm right,' he said in exasperation. 'And Mr Dawlish will be looking in there on his way back from his meeting in Chiswick.'

The top brass! They really expected questions in the House, if Dawlish was going to do an I-was-there piece for them.

Steve Champion's hideaway, in Barons Court. Well, I don't have to tell you what kind of house it was: Gothic horror comes to town! Depressing place, with no sign of any tenants, and a dented metal grille that asks you who you are, and buzzes when it opens the lock.

That bugger Blantyre was already there, chatting away merrily with his 'break-in specialist' who'd already splintered the paintwork on the outer door and left a wet footprint in the hall, and who, on closer inspection, turned out to be Blantyre's old buddy Detective-Inspector Seymour.

There they were, striding all over the clues and pouring each other double portions of Champion's booze.

'I didn't know you were coming,' said Blantyre.

'So I see.'

Blantyre held up his glass and looked at it, like one of those white-coated actors in TV commercials about indigestion. He said, 'We were wondering whether to send samples to the lab.'

'Send a whole bottle,' I said. 'Order a case from Harrods, and give them his Diner's Card number.'

Blantyre's face reddened, but whether in shame or anger I could not be sure. I said, 'Good. Well, if I'm not disturbing you two, I'll take a look round while there's still some evidence left.'

Blantyre gave me both barrels of a sawn-off twelve-bore, sighed and left the room wearing a sardonic smile. His drinking companion followed him.

I'd hardly started having a look round when Dawlish arrived. If Schlegel was hoping to keep our break-in inconspicuous, I'd say that Dawlish screwed up any last chance, what with his official car and uniformed driver, and the bowler hat and Melton overcoat. To say nothing of the tightly rolled umbrella that Dawlish was waving. Plastic raincoats are *de rigueur* for the rainy season in Barons Court.

'Not exactly a playboy pad,' said Dawlish, demonstrating his mastery of the vernacular.

Even by Dawlish's standards that was an understatement. It was a large gloomy apartment. The wallpaper and paintwork were in good condition and so was the cheap carpeting, but there were no pictures, no books, no ornaments, no personal touches. 'A machine for living in,' said Dawlish.

'Le Corbusier at his purest,' I said, anxious to show that I could recognize a cultural quote when I heard one.

It was like the barrack-room I'd had as a sergeant, waiting for Intelligence training. Iron bed, a tiny locker, plain black curtains at the window. On the windowsill there were some withered crumbs. I suppose no pigeon fancied them when just a short flight away the tourists would be throwing them croissants, and they could sit down and eat with a view of St James's Park.

There was a school yard visible from the window. The rain had stopped and the sun was shining. Swarms of children made random patterns as they sang, swung, jumped in puddles and punched each other with the same motiveless exuberance that, organized, becomes war. I closed the window and the shouting died. There were dark clouds; it would rain again.

'Worth a search?' said Dawlish.

I nodded. 'There will be a gun. Sealed under wet plaster perhaps. He's not the kind of man to use the cistern or the chimney: either tear it to pieces or forget it.'

'It's difficult, isn't it,' said Dawlish. 'Don't want to tear

it to pieces just to find a gun. I'm interested in documents
– stuff that he needs constant access to.'

'There will be nothing like that here,' I said.

Dawlish walked into the second bedroom. 'No linen on
the bed, you notice. No pillows, even.'

I opened the chest of drawers. There was plenty of
linen there; all brand new, and still in its wrappings.

'Good quality stuff,' said Dawlish.

'Yes, sir,' I said.

Dawlish opened the kitchen cupboards and recited
their contents. 'Dozen tins of meat, dozen tins of peas,
dozen bottles of beer, dozen tins of rice pudding. A
package of candles, unused, a dozen boxes of matches.'
He closed the cupboard door and opened a kitchen
drawer. We stared at the cutlery for a moment. It was all
new and unused. He closed it again without comment.

'No caretaker,' I said. 'No landlady, no doorman.'

'Precisely,' said Dawlish. 'And I'll wager that the rent
is paid every quarter day, without fail, by some solicitor
who has never come face to face with his client. No
papers, eh?'

'Cheap writing-pad and envelopes, a book of stamps,
postcards with several different views of London – might
be a code device – no, no papers in that sense.'

'I look forward to meeting your friend Champion,' said
Dawlish. 'A dozen tins of meat but three dozen bars of
soap – that's something for Freud, eh?'

I let the 'your friend' go unremarked. 'Indeed it is, sir,'
I said.

'None of it surprises you, of course,' Dawlish said,
with more than a trace of sarcasm.

'Paranoia,' I said. 'It's the occupational hazard of men
who've worked the sort of territories that Champion has
worked.' Dawlish stared at me. I said, 'Like anthrax for
tannery workers, and silicosis for miners. You need

35

somewhere . . . a place to go and hide for ever . . .' I indicated the store cupboard, '. . . and you never shake it off.'

Dawlish walked through into the big bedroom. Blantyre and his sidekick made themselves scarce. Dawlish opened the drawers of the chest, starting from the bottom like a burglar so that he didn't have to bother closing them. There were shirts in their original Cellophane bags, a couple of knitted ties, sweaters and plain black socks. Dawlish said, 'So should I infer that you have a little bolt-hole like this, just in case the balloon goes up?' Even after all these years together, Dawlish had to make sure his little jokes left a whiff of cordite.

'No, sir,' I said. 'But on the new salary scale I might be able to afford one – not in central London, though.'

Dawlish grunted, and opened the wardrobe. There were two dark suits, a tweed jacket, a blazer and three pairs of trousers. He twisted the blazer to see the inside pocket. There was no label there. He let it go and then took the tweed jacket off its hanger. He threw it on the bed.

'What about that?' said Dawlish.

I said, 'High notch, slightly waisted, centre-vented, three-button jacket in a sixteen-ounce Cheviot. Austin Reed, Hector Powe, or one of those expensive mass-production tailors. Not made to measure – off the peg. Scarcely worn, two or three years old, perhaps.'

'Have a look at it,' said Dawlish testily.

'Really have a look?'

'You're better at that sort of thing than I am.' It was Dawlish's genius never to tackle anything he couldn't handle and always to have near by a slave who could.

Dawlish took out the sharp little ivory-handled pen-knife that he used to ream his pipe. He opened it and gave it to me, handle first. I spread the jacket on the bed

36

and used the penknife to cut the stitches of the lining. There were no labels anywhere. Even the interior manufacturer's codes had been removed. So I continued working my way along the buckram until I could reach under that too. There was still nothing.

'Shoulder-pads?' I said.

'Might as well,' said Dawlish. He watched me closely.

'Nothing,' I said finally. 'Would you care to try the trousers, sir?'

'Do the other jackets.'

I smiled. It wasn't that Dawlish was obsessional. It was simply his policy to run his life as though he was already answering the Minister's questions. You searched all the clothing? Yes, all the clothing. Not, no, just one jacket, selected at random.

I did the other jackets. Dawlish proved right. He always proves right. It was in the right-hand shoulder-pad of one of the dark suits that we found the paper money. There were fourteen bills: US dollars, Deutsche Marks and sterling – a total of about twelve thousand dollars at the exchange rate then current.

But it was in the other shoulder-pad that we found the sort of document Dawlish was looking for. It was a letter signed by the Minister Plenipotentiary of the United Arab Republic's Embassy in London. It claimed that Stephen Champion had diplomatic status as a naturalized citizen of the United Arab Republic and listed member of the Diplomatic Corps.

Dawlish read it carefully and passed it across to me. 'What do you think about that?' he asked.

To tell you the truth, I thought Dawlish was asking me to confirm that it was a forgery, but you can never take anything for granted when dealing with Dawlish. I dealt him his cards off the top of the deck. 'Champion is not on the London Diplomatic List,' I said, 'but that's about the only thing I'm certain of.'

Dawlish looked at me and sniffed. 'Can't even be certain of that,' he said. 'All those Abduls and Ahmeds and Alis . . . suppose you were told that one of those was the name Champion had adopted when converted to the Muslim faith. What then . . . ?'

'It would keep the lawyers arguing for months,' I said.

'And what about the Special Branch superintendent at London airport, holding up the aeroplane departing to Cairo? Would he hold a man who was using this as a travel document, and risk the sort of hullabaloo that might result if he put a diplomat in the bag?'

'No,' I said.

'Precisely,' said Dawlish.

A gust of wind rattled the window panes and the sky grew dark. He said nothing more. I took my coat off and hung it up. It was no good pretending that I wouldn't be here all day. There's only one way to tackle those jobs: you do it stone by stone, and you do it yourself. Dawlish sent Blantyre and his associate away. Then he went down to the car and called the office. I began to get some idea of the priorities when he told me he'd cancelled everything for the rest of the day. He sat down on the kitchen chair and watched me work.

There was nothing conclusive, of course: no dismembered limbs or bloodstains, but clothes that I'd seen Melodie Page wearing were packed in plastic carrier-bags, sandwiched neatly between two sheets of plasterboard, sealed at every edge, and integrated beautifully into the kitchen ceiling.

The wallpaper near the bed had deep scratches, and a broken fragment of fingernail remained embedded there. There was the faintest smell of carbolic acid from the waste-trap under the sink, and from there I managed to get a curved piece of clear glass that was one part of a hypodermic syringe. Other than that, there was only evidence of removal of evidence.

'It's enough,' said Dawlish.

From the school yard across the street came all the exuberant screams that the kids had been bottling up in class. It was pouring with rain now, but children don't mind the rain.

5

Schlegel likes Southern California. Sometimes I think it's the only thing he does like. You take Southern California by the inland corners, he says, jerk it, so that all the shrubbery and real-estate falls into a heap along the coast, and you know what you've got? And I say, yes, you've got the French Riviera, because I've heard him say it before.

Well, on Monday *I'd* got the French Riviera. Or, more precisely, I'd got Nice. I arrived in my usual neurotic way: ten hours before schedule, breaking my journey in Lyon and choosing the third cab in the line-up.

It was so easy to remember what Nice had looked like the first time I saw it. There had been a pier that stretched out to sea, and barbed wire along the promenade. Armed sentries had stood outside the sea-front hotels, and refugees from the north stood in line for work, or begged furtively outside the crowded cafés and restaurants. Inside, smiling Germans in ill-fitting civilian suits bought each other magnums of champagne and paid in mint-fresh military notes. And everywhere there was this smell of burning, as if everyone in the land had something in their possession that the Fascists would think incriminating.

Everyone's fear is different. And because bravery is just the knack of suppressing signs of your own fear, bravery is different too. The trouble with being only nineteen is that you are frightened of all the wrong things; and brave about the wrong things. Champion had gone to Lyon. I was all alone, and of course then too stupid not to be thankful for it. No matter what the movies tell you, there was no resistance movement visible to the naked eye. Only Jews could be trusted not to turn you over to the Fascists. Men like Serge Frankel. He'd been the first person I'd contacted then, and he was the first one I went to now.

It was a sunny day, but the apartment building, which overlooked the vegetable market, was cold and dark. I went up the five flights of stone stairs. Only a glimmer of daylight penetrated the dirty windows on each landing. The brass plate at his door – 'Philatelic Expert' – was by now polished a little smoother, and there was a card tucked behind the bell that in three languages said 'Buying and Selling by Appointment Only'.

The same heavy door that protected his stamps, and had given us perhaps groundless confidence in the old days, was still in place, and the peep-hole through which he'd met the eyes of the Gestapo now was used to survey me.

'My boy! How wonderful to see you.'

'Hello, Serge.'

'And a chance to practise my English,' he said. He reached forward with a white bony hand, and gripped me firmly enough for me to feel the two gold rings that he wore.

It was easy to imagine Serge Frankel as a youth: a frail-looking small-boned teenager with frizzy hair and a large forehead and the same style of gold-rimmed spectacles as he was wearing now.

We went into the study. It was a high-ceilinged room lined with books, their titles in a dozen or more languages. Not only stamp catalogues and reference books, but philosophy from Cicero to Ortega y Gasset.

He sat in the same button-back leather chair now as he had then. Smiling the same inscrutable and humourless smile, and brushing at the ash that spilled down the same sort of waistcoat, leaving there a grey smear like a mark of penitence. It was inevitable that we should talk of old times.

Serge Frankel was a Communist – student of Marx, devotee of Lenin and servant of Stalin. Born in Berlin, he'd been hunted from end to end of Hitler's Third Reich, and had not seen his wife and children since the day he waved goodbye to them at Cologne railway station, wearing a new moustache and carrying papers that described him as an undertaker from Stettin.

During the Civil War in Spain, Frankel had been a political commissar with the International Brigade. During the tank assault on the Prado, Frankel had destroyed an Italian tank single-handed, using a wine bottle hastily filled with petrol.

'Tea?' said Frankel. I remembered him making tea then as he made it now: pouring boiling water from a dented electric kettle into an antique teapot with a chipped lid. Even this room was enigmatic. Was he a pauper, hoarding the cash value of the skeleton clock and the tiny Corot etching, or a Croesus, indifferent to his plastic teaspoons and museum postcards of Rouault?

'And what can I do for you, young man?' He rubbed his hands together, exactly as he had done the day I first visited him. Then, my briefing could hardly have been more simple: find Communists and give them money, they had told me. But most of life's impossible tasks – from alchemy to squaring the circle – are similarly concise. At that time the British had virtually no networks in Western Europe. A kidnapping on the German–Dutch border in November 1939 had put both the European chief of SIS and his deputy into the hands of the Abwehr. A suitcase full of contact addresses captured in The Hague in May 1940, and the fall of France, had given the *coup de grâce* to the remainder. Champion and I were 'blind', as jargon has it, and halt and lame, too, if the truth be told. We had no contacts except Serge Frankel, who'd done the office a couple of favours in 1938 and 1939 and had never been contacted since.

'Communists.' I remembered the way that Frankel had said it, 'Communists', as though he'd not heard the word before. I had been posing as an American reporter, for America was still a neutral country. He looked again at the papers I had laid out on his writing table. There was a forged US passport sent hurriedly from the office in Berne, an accreditation to the New York *Herald Tribune* and a membership card of The American Rally for a Free Press, which the British Embassy in Washington recommended as the reddest of American organizations. Frankel had jabbed his finger on that card and pushed it to the end of the row, like a man playing patience. 'Now that the Germans have an Abwehr office here, Communists are lying low, my friend.' He had poured tea for us.

'But Hitler and Stalin have signed the peace pact. In Lyon the Communists are even publishing a news-sheet.'

Frankel looked up at me, trying to see if I was being provocative. He said, 'Some of them are even wearing the hammer and sickle again. Some are drinking with the German soldiers and calling them fellow workers, like the Party tells them to do. Some have resigned from the Party in disgust. Some have already faced firing squads. Some are reserving their opinion, waiting to see if the war is really finished. But which are which? Which are which?' He sipped his tea and then said, 'Will the English go on fighting?'

'I know nothing about the English, I'm an American,' I insisted. 'My office wants a story about the French Communists and how they are reacting to the Germans.'

Frankel moved the US passport to the end of the row. It was as if he was tacitly dismissing my credentials, and my explanations, one by one. 'The people you want to see are the ones still undecided.'

He looked up to see my reaction.

'Yes,' I said.

'The ones who have *not* signed a friendship treaty with the Boche, eh?'

I nodded.

'We'll meet again on Monday. What about the café in the arcade, at the Place Massena. Three in the afternoon.'

'Thank you, Mr Frankel. Perhaps there's something I can do for you in return. My office have let me have some real coffee . . .'

'Let's see what happens,' said Frankel. But he took the tiny packet of coffee. Already it was becoming scarce.

I picked up the documents and put them into my pocket. Frankel watched me very closely. Making a mistake about me could send him to a concentration camp. We both knew that. If he had any doubts he'd do nothing at all. I buttoned up my coat and bowed him goodbye. He didn't speak again until I reached the door. 'If I am wearing a scarf or have my coat buttoned at the collar, do not approach me.'

'Thank you, Mr Frankel,' I said. 'I'll watch out for that.'

He smiled. 'It seems like only yesterday,' he said. He poured the tea. 'You were too young to be a correspondent for an American newspaper, but I knew you were not working for the Germans.'

'How did you know that?'

He passed the cup of tea to me, murmuring apologies about having neither milk nor lemon. He said, 'They would have sent someone more suitable. The Germans had many men who'd lived in America long enough.

They could have chosen someone in his thirties or forties with an authentic accent.'

'But you went ahead,' I reminded him.

'I talked to Marius. We guessed you'd be bringing money. The first contact would have to bring money. We could do nothing without cash.'

'You could have asked for it, or stolen it.'

'All that came later – the bank hold-ups, the extortion, the loans. When you arrived we were very poor. We were offering only a franc for a rifle and we could only afford to buy the perfect Lebel pattern ones even then.'

'Rifles the soldiers had thrown away?' It was always the same conversation that we had, but I didn't mind.

'The ditches were full of them. It was that that started young Marius off – the *bataillon Guernica* was his choice of name – I thought it would have been better to have chosen a victory to celebrate, but young Marius liked the unequivocally anti-German connotation that the Guernica bombing gave us.'

'But on the Monday you said no,' I reminded him.

'On the Monday I told you not to have high hopes,' he corrected me. He ran his long bony fingers back into his fine white wispy hair.

'I knew no one else, Serge.'

'I felt sorry for you when you walked off towards the bus station, but young Marius wanted to look at you and make up his own mind. And that way it was safer for me, too. He decided to stop you in the street if you looked genuine.'

'At the Casino tabac he stopped me. I wanted English cigarettes.'

'Was that good security?'

'I had the American passport. There was no point in trying to pretend I was French.'

'And Marius said he might get some?'

45

'He waited outside the tabac. We talked. He said he'd hide me in the church. And when Champion returned, he hid us both. It was a terrible risk to take for total strangers.'

'Marius was like that,' said Frankel.

'Without you and Marius we might never have got started,' I said.

'Hardly,' said Frankel. 'You would have found others.' But he smiled and was flattered to think of himself as the beginning of the whole network. 'Sometimes I believe that Marius would have become important, had he lived.'

I nodded. They'd made a formidable partnership – the Jewish Communist and the anti-Fascist priest – and yet I remembered Frankel hearing the news of Marius's death without showing a flicker of emotion. But Frankel had been younger then, and keen to show us what his time in Moscow had really taught him.

'We made a lot of concessions to each other – me and Marius,' Frankel said. 'If he'd lived we might have achieved a great deal.'

'Sure you would,' I said. 'He would be running the Mafia, and you would have been made Pope.'

Flippancy was not in the Moscow curriculum, and Frankel didn't like it. 'Have you seen Pina Baroni yet?'

'Not yet,' I said.

'I see her in the market here sometimes,' said Frankel. 'Her little boutique in the Rue de la Buffa is a flourishing concern, I'm told. She's over the other business by now, and I'm glad . . .'

The 'other business' was a hand-grenade thrown into a café in Algiers in 1961. It killed her soldier husband and both her children. Pina escaped without a scratch, unless you looked inside her head. 'Poor Pina,' I said.

'And Ercole . . .' Frankel continued, as if he didn't want to talk of Pina, '. . . his restaurant prospers – they

46

say his grandson will inherit; and "the Princess" still dyes her hair red and gets raided by the social division.'

I nodded. The 'social division' was the delicate French term for vice squad.

'And Claude *l'avocat*?'

'It's Champion you want to know about,' said Frankel.

'Then tell me about Champion.'

He smiled. 'We were all taken in by him, weren't we? And yet when you look back, he's the same now as he was then. A charming sponger who could twist any woman round his little finger.'

'Yes?' I said doubtfully.

'Old Tix's widow, she could have sold out for a big lump sum, but Champion persuaded her to accept instalments. So Champion is living out there in the Tix mansion, with servants to wait on him hand and foot, while Madame Tix is in three rooms with an outdoor toilet, and inflation has devoured what little she does get.'

'Is that so?'

'And now that he sees the Arabs getting rich on the payments for oil, Champion is licking the boots of new masters. His domestic staff are all Arabs, they serve Arab food out there at the house, they talk Arabic all the time and when he visits anywhere in North Africa he gets VIP treatment.'

I nodded. 'I saw him in London,' I said. 'He was wearing a fez and standing in line to see "A Night in Casablanca".'

'It's not funny,' said Frankel irritably.

'It's the one where Groucho is mistaken for the Nazi spy,' I said, 'but there's not much singing.'

Frankel clattered the teapot and the cups as he stacked them on the tray. 'Our Mister Champion is very proud of himself,' he said.

47

'And pride comes before a fall,' I said. 'Is that what you mean, Serge?'

'*You* said that!' said Frankel. 'Just don't put words into my mouth, it's something you're too damned fond of doing, my friend.'

I'd touched a nerve.

Serge Frankel lived in an old building at the far end of the vegetable market. When I left his apartment that Monday afternoon, I walked up through the old part of Nice. There was brilliant sunshine and the narrow alleys were crowded with Algerians. I picked my way between strings of shoes, chickens, dates and figs. There was a peppery aroma of *merguez* sausages frying, and tiny bars where light-skinned workers drank pastis and talked football, and dark-skinned men listened to Arab melodies and talked politics.

From the Place Rosetti came the tolling of a church bell. Its sound echoed through the alleys, and stony-faced men in black suits hurried towards the funeral. Now and again, kids on mopeds came roaring through the alleys, making the shoppers leap into doorways. Sometimes there came cars, inch by inch, the drivers eyeing the scarred walls where so many bright-coloured vehicles had left samples of their paint. I reached the boulevard Jean Jaurès, which used to be the moat of the fortified medieval town, and is now fast becoming the world's largest car park. There I turned, to continue along the alleys that form the perimeter of the old town. Behind me a white BMW was threading through the piles of oranges and stalls of charcuterie with only a fraction to spare. Twice the driver hooted, and on the third time I turned to glare.

'Claude!' I said.

'Charles!' said the driver. 'I knew it was you.'

48

Claude had become quite bald. His face had reddened, perhaps from the weather, the wine or blood pressure. Or perhaps all three. But there was no mistaking the man. He still had the same infectious grin and the same piercing blue eyes. He wound the window down. 'How are you? How long have you been in Nice? It's early for a holiday, isn't it?' He drove on slowly. At the corner it was wide enough for him to open the passenger door. I got into the car alongside him. 'The legal business looks like it's flourishing,' I said. I was fishing, for I had no way of knowing if the cheerful law student whom we called Claude *l'avocat* was still connected with the legal profession.

'The legal business has been very kind to me,' said Claude. He rubbed his cheek and chuckled as he looked me up and down. 'Four grandchildren, a loving wife and my collection of Delftware. Who could ask for more.' He chuckled again, this time in self-mockery. But he smoothed the lapel of his pearl-grey suit and adjusted the Cardin kerchief so that I would notice that it matched his tie. Even in the old days, when knitted pullovers were the height of chic, Claude had been a dandy. 'And now Steve Champion lives here, too,' he said.

'So I hear.'

He smiled. 'It must be the sunshine and the cooking.'

'Yes,' I said.

'And it was Steve who . . .' He stopped.

'Saved my life?' I said irritably. 'Saved my life up at the quarry.'

'Put the *réseau* together, after the arrests in May,' said Claude. 'That's what I was going to say.'

'Well, strictly between the two of us, Claude, I wish I'd spent the war knitting socks,' I said.

'What's that supposed to mean?'

'It means I wish I had never heard of the lousy *réseau*, the Guernica network and all the people in it.'

49

'And Steve Champion?'

'Steve Champion most of all,' I said. 'I wish I could just come down here on holiday and not be reminded of all that useless crappy idiocy!'

'You don't have to shout at me,' Claude said. 'I didn't send for you, you came.'

'I suppose so,' I said. I regretted losing my cool if only for a moment.

'We *all* want to forget,' Claude said gently. 'No one wants to forget it more than I want to.'

The car was halted while two men unloaded cartons of instant couscous from a grey van. In the Place St François the fish market was busy, too. A decapitated tunny was being sliced into steaks alongside the fountain, and a woman in a rubber apron was sharpening a set of knives.

'So Steve is here?' I said.

'Living here. He lives out at the Tix house near the quarry.'

'What a coincidence,' I said. 'All of us here again.'

'Is it?' said Claude.

'Well, it sounds like a coincidence, doesn't it?'

The driver's sun-shield was drooping and Claude smiled as he reached up and pushed it flat against the roof of the car. In that moment I saw a gun in a shoulder holster under his arm. It wasn't an impress-the-girlfriend, or frightened-of-burglars kind of instrument. The leather holster was soft and shiny, and the underside of the magazine was scratched from years of use. A Walther PPK! Things must have got very rough in the legal business in the last few years.

He turned and smiled the big smile that I remembered from the old days. 'I don't believe in anything any more,' he confessed. 'But most of all I don't believe in coincidences. That's why I'm here.' He smoothed his tie again. 'Where can I drop you, Charles?'

50

6

Tuesday morning was cold and very still, as if the world was waiting for something to happen. The ocean shone like steel, and from it successive tidal waves of mist engulfed the promenade. The elaborate façades of the great hotels and the disc of the sun were no more than patterns embossed upon a monochrome world.

Trapped between the low pock-marked sky and the grey Mediterranean, two Mirage jets buzzed like flies in a bottle, the vibrations continuing long after they had disappeared out to sea. I walked past the seafood restaurants on the *quai*, where they were skimming the oil and slicing the *frites*. It was a long time until the tourist season but already there were a few Germans in the heated terraces, eating cream cakes and pointing with their forks, and a few British on the beach, with Thermos flasks of strong tea, and cucumber sandwiches wrapped up in *The Observer*.

I was on my way to Frankel's apartment. As I came level with the market entrance I stopped at the traffic lights. A dune buggy with a broken silencer roared past, and then a black Mercedes flashed its main beams. I waited as it crawled past me, its driver gesturing. It was Steve Champion. He was looking for a place to park but all the meter spaces were filled. Just as I thought he'd have to give up the idea, he swerved and bumped over the kerb and on to the promenade. The police allowed tourists to park there, and Champion's Mercedes had Swiss plates.

'You crazy bastard!' said Champion, with a smile. 'Why-didn't you tell me? Where are you staying?' The flesh under his eye was scratched and swollen and his smile was hesitant and pained.

'With the Princess,' I said.

He shook his head. 'You're a masochist, Charlie. That's a filthy hole.'

'She can do with the money,' I said.

'Don't you believe it, Charlie. She's probably a major shareholder in IBM or something. Look here – have you time for a drink?'

'Why not?'

He turned up the collar of his dark-grey silk trench coat and tied the belt carelessly. He came round the car to me. 'There's a sort of club,' he said.

'For expatriates?'

'For brothel proprietors and pimps.'

'Let's hope it's not too crowded,' I said.

Champion turned to have a better view of an Italian cruise-liner sailing past towards Marseille. It seemed almost close enough to touch, but the weather had discouraged all but the most intrepid passengers from venturing on deck. A man in oilskins waved. Champion waved back.

'Fancy a walk?' Champion asked me. He saw me looking at his bruised cheek and he touched it self-consciously.

'Yes,' I said. He locked the door of the car and pulled his scarf tight around his throat.

We walked north, through the old town, and through the back alleys that smelled of wood-smoke and shashlik, and past the dark bars where Arab workers drink beer and watch the slot-machine movies of blonde strippers.

But it was no cramped bar, with menu in Arabic, to which Champion took me. It was a fine mansion on the fringe of the 'musicians' quarter'. It stood well back from the street, screened by full-grown palm trees, and guarded by stone cherubs on the porch. A uniformed doorman saluted us, and a pretty girl took our coats. Steve put his hand on my shoulder and guided me through the hall and the bar, to a lounge that was furnished with black leather sofas and abstract paintings in stainless-steel frames. 'The usual,' he told the waiter.

On the low table in front of us there was an array of financial magazines. Champion toyed with them. 'Why didn't you tell me?' he said. 'You let me make a fool of myself.'

It was Steve who'd taught me the value of such direct openings. To continue to deny that I worked for the department was almost an admission that I'd been assigned to seek him out. 'True-life confessions? For those chance meetings once or twice a year? That wasn't in the Steve Champion crash-course when I took it.'

He smiled and winced and, with only the tip of his finger, touched his bruised cheek. 'You did it well, old son. Asking me if I was recruiting you. That was a subtle touch, Charlie.' He was telling me that he now knew it had been no chance meeting that day in Piccadilly. And Steve was telling me that from now on there'd be no half-price admissions for boys under sixteen.

'Tell me one thing,' Steve said, as if he was going to ask nothing else, 'did you volunteer to come out here after me?'

'It's better that it's me,' I said. A waiter brought a tray with silver coffee-pot, Limoges china and a sealed bottle of private-label cognac. It was that sort of club.

'One day you might find out what it's like,' said Steve.

'There was the girl, Steve.'

'What about the girl?'

'It's a Kill File, Steve,' I told him. 'Melodie Page is dead.'

53

'Death of an operative?' He looked at me for a long time. He knew how the department felt about Kill File investigations. He spooned a lot of sugar into his coffee, and took his time in stirring it. 'So they are playing rough,' he said. 'Have they applied for extradition?'

'If the investigating officer decides . . .'

'Jesus Christ!' said Steve angrily. 'Don't give me that Moriarty Police Law crap. Are you telling me that there is a murder investigation being conducted by C.1 at the Yard?'

'Not yet,' I said. 'There were complications.'

Champion screwed up his face and sucked his coffee spoon. 'So Melodie was working for the department?'

I didn't answer. I didn't have to.

Champion nodded. 'Of course. What a clown I am. And she's dead? You saw the body?'

'Yes,' I said.

'Level with me, Charlie,' said Champion.

I said, 'No, I didn't see the body.' Champion poured coffee, then he snapped the seal on the cognac and poured two large tots.

'Neat. Effective. And not at all gaudy,' said Champion eventually, with some measure of admiration. He waggled the coffee spoon at me.

It seemed a bit disloyal to the department to understand his meaning too quickly. 'I don't understand,' I said.

'You understand, old boy,' said Champion. 'You understand. But not as well as I bloody understand.' He paused while a waiter brought the cigarettes he'd ordered. When the waiter departed, Steve said softly, 'There's no dead girl – or if there is, your people have killed her – this is just a stunt, a frame-up, to get me back to London.' Champion moved his cigarettes and his gold Dunhill lighter about on the magazines in front of him, pushing them like a little train from *The Financial Times* and on to *Forbes* and *Figaro*.

'They are pressing me,' I said. 'It's a Minister-wants-to-know inquiry.'

'Ministers never want to know,' said Champion bitterly. 'All Ministers want is answers to give.' He sighed. 'And someone decided that I was the right answer for this one.'

'I wish you'd come back to London with me,' I said.

'Spend a month or more kicking my heels in Whitehall? And what could I get out of it? An apology, if I'm lucky, or fifteen years, if that suits them better. No, you'll not get me going back with you.'

'But suppose they extradite you – it'll be worse then.'

'So you say.' He inhaled deeply on his cigarette. 'But the more I think about it, the less frightened I am. The fact they've sent you down here is a tacit admission that they won't pull an extradition order on me.'

'I wouldn't bet on it.'

'Well, that's because you're too damned naïve. The department don't want me back in London, explaining to them all the details of the frame-up they themselves organized. This is all part of an elaborate game . . . a softening-up for something big.'

'Something that London wants you to do for them?' I asked. 'Is that what you mean?'

'Let's stop beating around the bush, shall we? The department has given me jobs from time to time. They do that with pensioned-off operatives because it keeps them signing the Act, and also because their pensions make them the most needy – and so the cheapest – people around.'

'Come back to London, Steve.'

'Can't you understand plain bloody King's English,

55

Charlie? Either the girl is *not* dead, and the department have put her on ice in order to finger me . . .'

'Or?'

'Or she's dead and the department arranged it.'

'No.'

'How can you say no. Do they let you read the Daily Yellows?'

'It's no good, Steve,' I said. 'The department would never do it this way and both of us know it.'

'The confidence you show in those bastards . . .' said Champion. 'We know only a fraction of what goes on up there. They've told you that Melodie was a departmental employee – have you ever heard of her or seen any documents?'

'The documents of an operative in the field? Of course I haven't.'

'Exactly. Well, suppose I tell you that she was never an employee and the department have wanted her killed for the last three months. Suppose I told you that they ordered me to kill her, and that I refused. And that that was when the row blew up.'

'Go on,' I said.

'The department made that contact for me. They said she was from the Palestinian terrorists. They told me that she was a nutty American student, the London contact for five hundred stolen Armalites and two tons of gelignite.' Champion was excited now and smiling nervously, as I remembered him from the old days.

He sipped his drink. 'They sent an American chap to see me. Is his name Schindler? Drinks that Underberg stuff, I remember. I wouldn't believe he was from the department at first. Then they sent a Mutual down to confirm him as OK. Is it Schroder?'

'Something like that,' I said.

'He mentioned the killing end. I didn't take him seriously at first. I mean, they must still have special people for that game, surely. But he was in earnest. Ten thousand pounds, he said. He had it all set up, too. He'd organized a flat in Barons Court stacked up with beer and whisky and cans of beans and soup. I'm telling you, it was equipped like a fall-out shelter. And he showed me this hypodermic syringe, killing wire and rubber gloves. Talk about horror movies, I needed a couple of big whiskies when I got out of there.' He drank some coffee. 'And then I realized how I'd put my prints on everything he'd shown me.' He sighed. 'No fool like an old fool.'

'Did they pay the bill for the tweed jacket we found there?'

'There was no reason to be suspicious,' said Champion. 'They told me to order the suits, and they paid for them. It was only when they sent a funny little man round to my place to take the labels and manufacturers' marks out of them that I began to worry. I mean . . . can you think of anything more damning than picking up some johnny and then finding he's got no labels in his suits?'

'There was money in the shoulder-pads,' I told him. 'And documents, too.'

'Well, there you are. It's the kind of thing a desk-man would dream up if he'd never been at the sharp end. Wouldn't you say that, Charlie?'

I looked at Champion but I didn't answer. I wanted to believe him innocent, but if I discounted his charm, and the nostalgia, I saw only an ingenious man improvising desperately in the hope of getting away with murder.

'How long ago are we talking about?' I said.

'Just a couple of weeks before I ran into you . . . or rather you sought me out. That's why I wasn't suspicious that you were official. I mean, they could have found out whatever they needed to know through their normal

57

contacts . . . but that girl, she wasn't one of them, Charlie, believe me.'

'Did you tell her?'

'Like fun! This girl was trying to buy armaments – and not for the first time. She could take care of herself, believe me. She carried, too – she carried a big ·38 in that crocodile handbag.' He finished his coffee and tried to pour more, but the pot was empty. 'Anyway, I've never killed anyone in cold blood and I wasn't about to start, not for the department and not for money, either. But I reasoned that someone would do it. It might have been someone I liked a lot better than her. It might have been you.'

'That was really considerate of you Steve,' I said.

He turned his head to me. The swelling seemed to have grown worse in the last half hour. Perhaps that was because of Champion's constant touches. The blue and red flesh had pushed his eye closed. 'You don't go through our kind of war, and come out the other end saying you'd never kill anyone, no matter what kind of pressure is applied.'

I looked at him for a long time. 'The days of the entrepreneur are over, Steve,' I told him. 'Now it's the organization man who gets the Christmas bonus and the mileage allowance. People like you are called "heroes", and don't mistake it for a compliment. It just means has-beens, who'd rather have a hunch than a computer output. You are yesterday's spy, Steve.'

'And you'd sooner believe those organization men than believe me?'

'No good waving your arms, Steve,' I said. 'You're standing on the rails and the express just blew its whistle.'

He stared at me. 'Oooh, they've changed you, Charlie! Those little men who've promised you help with your mortgage, and full pension rights at sixty. Who would have thought they could have done that to the kid who fought the war with a copy of *Wage Labour and Capital* in his back pocket. To say nothing of that boring lecture you gave everyone about Mozart's revolutionary symbolism in "The Marriage of Figaro".' He smiled, but I didn't.

'You've had your say, Steve. Don't take the jury out into the back alley.'

'I hope you listened carefully then,' he said. He got to his feet and tossed some ten-franc notes on to the coffee tray. 'Because if you are only half as naïve as you pretend to be . . . and if *you* have put your dabs all over some carefully chosen incriminating evidence . . .'

'Go on,' I said.

'Then it could be that London are setting us both up for that big debriefing in the sky.'

'You've picked up my matches,' I said.

7

'You'd sooner live in a dump than live in a nice home,' said Schlegel accusingly.

'No,' I said, but without much conviction. I didn't want to argue with him.

He opened the shutters so that he could see the charcuterie across the alley. The tiny shop-window was crammed with everything from shredded carrot to pig feet. Schlegel shuddered. 'Yes, you would,' he insisted. 'Remember that fleapit you used to have in Soho. Look at that time we booked you into the St Regis, and you went into a cold-water walk-up in the Village. You like dumps!'

'OK,' I said.

'If this place had some kind of charm, I'd understand. But it's just a flophouse.' For a long time he was silent. I walked across to the window and discovered that he was staring into the first-floor window across the alley. A fat woman in a frayed dressing-gown was using a sewing machine. She looked up at Schlegel, and when he did not look away she closed her shutters. Schlegel turned and looked round the room. I'd put asters, souci and corn-flowers into a chipped tumbler from the washbasin. Schlegel flicked a finger at them and the petals fell. He went over to the tiny writing table that wobbled unless something was wedged under one leg. My Sony radio-recorder almost toppled as Schlegel tested the table for stability. I had turned the volume down as Schlegel had entered, but now the soft sounds of Helen Ward, and Goodman's big band, tried to get out. Schlegel pushed the 'off' button, and the music ended with a loud click. 'That phone work?' he asked.

'It did this morning.'

'Can I give you a word of advice, fella?'

'I wish you would,' I told him.

For a moment I thought I'd offended him, but you don't avoid Schlegel's advice that easily. 'Don't stay in places like this, pal. I mean . . . sure, you save a few bucks when you hit the cashier's office for the price of a hotel. But jeeze . . . is it worth it?'

'I'm not hitting the cashier's office for the price of anything more than I'm spending.'

His face twisted in a scowl as he tried to believe me. And then understanding dawned. 'You came in here, in the sub, in the war. Right? I remember now: Villefranche – it's a deep-water anchorage. Yeah. Sure. Me too. I came here once . . . a long time ago on a flat-top, with the Sixth Fleet. Nostalgia, eh?'

'This is where I first met Champion.'

'And the old doll downstairs.' He nodded to himself. 'She's got to be a hundred years old . . . she was the radio operator . . . the Princess! Right?'

'We just used this as a safe-house for people passing through.'

'It's a brothel!' Schlegel accused.

'Well, I don't mind that so much,' I told him. 'The baker next door waves every morning when I leave. This morning, he winked.'

'Wouldn't you rather be in a hotel?'

'Well, I'm going to ask the Princess if the girls could be a little quieter with the doors.'

'Banging all night?' said Schlegel archly.

'Exactly,' I said.

'A cat house,' mused Schlegel. 'A natural for an escape chain. But the Nazis had them high on the check-out list.'

61

'Well, we won the war,' I said sharply. Schlegel would get in there, checking out the syntax of my dreams, if he knew the way.

'I'll call Paris,' he said.

'I'd better tell the Princess.'

'Do we have to?'

'We have to,' I said. 'Unless you want her interrupting you to tell you how much it's costing, while you're talking to the Elysée Palace.'

Schlegel scowled to let me know that sarcasm wasn't going to help me find out who he was phoning. 'Extension downstairs, huh?'

I went to the door and yelled down to the bar, at which the Princess was propped with *Salut les Copains* and a big Johnny Walker. 'I'm calling Paris,' I shouted.

'You called Paris already today, chéri,' she said.

'And now we're calling again, you old bag,' growled Schlegel, but he took good care to keep his voice down. Already she'd made him apologize to one of the bar girls for saying goddamn.

'That's right,' I told her.

'Just as long as you don't forget the money you're spending, my darling.'

'Darleeeng,' growled Schlegel. 'Will you believe that's the first hearing-aid I've seen with sequins on it?'

He picked up his plastic case, put it on the bed and opened it. At first glance it might have been mistaken for a portable typewriter, permanently built into its case. It was the newest model of acoustic coupler. Schlegel began typing on the keys.

I said, 'Anything fresh on the girl? Body been found, or anything?'

Schlegel looked up at me, sucked his teeth and said, 'I'll ask them what Missing Persons knows.' When Schlegel finished typing his message he dialled the Paris number.

He gave his real name. I suppose that was to save all the complications that would arise if he was phoning from a hotel that held his passport. Then he said, 'Let's scramble,' and put the phone handpiece into the cradle switch inside the case. He pressed the 'transmit' button and the coupler put a coded version of what he'd typed through the phone cables at thirty or forty characters a second. There was a short delay, then the reply came back from the same sort of machine. This time Schlegel's coupler decoded it and printed it on to tape in 'plain English'. Schlegel read it, grunted, pushed the 'memory erase' button and rang off.

'You ask those guys the *time*, and they'd tell you what trouble they're having from the Records Office,' he said. He burned the tape without showing it to me. It was exactly the way the textbook ordered but it didn't make me want to open my heart to him about Champion's version of the girl's death.

But I told him everything Champion had said.

'He's right,' said Schlegel. 'He knows we wouldn't be pussyfooting around if we had the evidence. Even if he enters the UK I doubt whether the department would let us hold him.'

'He must have killed the girl,' I said, with some hesitation.

'He didn't collect that shiner by walking into a lamp-post.'

I nodded. Champion's bruised face was just the sort of blow he might have suffered while overpowering the girl. And the two scratches on his cheek were just like the damage to the wallpaper near the bed. No matter how much I tried to push the idea away, Champion's guilt bobbed up again like a plastic duck.

'You tell me Champion was some kind of master spy,' Schlegel said. 'Well, I'm telling you he's a loser. So far he's fouled up every which way, so I'm not joining the fan club. Champion is a creep, an over-confident creep, and if he steps out of line we'll clobber him, but good!'

'That's the way it looks,' I agreed.

'You're telling me it's all a set-up?'

I shrugged. 'That's one of the new couplers, is it?'

Schlegel stroked the metal case that was intended to make it look like a cheap typewriter. 'I can plug that baby into any computer with terminals. Last week I used the CIA TELCOM from a call-box, and tomorrow I'll abstract from the London Data Bank.'

'London will ring you back?'

'But not here. Not secure enough. That old doll downstairs . . . no, I'll have to get going.'

'Meet her,' I said. 'Otherwise I'll get endless questions.'

'One drink,' he said.

'You could be right . . . about Champion, I mean. People change.'

We picked our way down the narrow creaking staircase before the time-switch plopped. I opened the door marked 'No Entry' and went through it into the bar.

Through the bead curtain I could see a patch of sunlight on the scaly brickwork of the alley. But inside, the room was as dark as night. An ornate table-lamp at one end of the bar made a golden spot on each of the bottles lined up behind the counter, and gave just enough light for the Princess to see the cash register.

'Come and sit here, Charlie darling,' she said, but her eyes were fixed on Colonel Schlegel. Obediently, I took the bar stool she indicated. Schlegel sat down, too. I put my arm round the Princess and gave her rouged and powdered cheek a circumspect kiss.

'Rapist!' said the Princess.

A girl appeared from out of nowhere and put her

64

hands on the counter to show us how willing she was to serve expensive drinks.

'Underberg,' said Schlegel, 'and soda.'

'And Charlie will have Scotch,' said the Princess. 'So will I.'

The girl served the drinks and, without discussing the subject, put it all on my bill. Schlegel had the coupler at his feet and I noticed the way he kept his shoe pressed against it to be sure it was not removed.

'Does your friend know that you were here in the war, Charlie?'

'Yes, he knows,' I said.

'What war was that, Charlie?' said Schlegel.

The Princess pretended not to hear Schlegel. She craned her neck to look in the fly-specked mirror behind the bar, so that she could make adjustments to her rouge and eye make-up.

'We had good times, didn't we, Charlie? We had good times as well as bad ones.' She turned to face us again. 'I can remember nights when we sat along this bar counter, with the German sentries walking along the sea-front there. Guns in my cellar and the wireless set in a wine barrel. My God! When I think of the risks we took.'

'You knew this guy Champion then?' Schlegel asked her.

'And I liked him. I still do like him, although I haven't seen him for years. A gentleman of the old sort.' She looked at Schlegel as he swilled down his Underberg and then crunched the ice-cubes in his teeth. 'If you know what I mean,' she added.

'Yeah, well, there's a lot of definitions,' said Schlegel affably, 'and most of them are obscene. So you liked him, eh?'

'Well, at least he didn't betray us,' said the Princess.

'Did anyone?' I said.

'That filthy little Claude betrayed us,' said the Princess.

'Claude *l'avocat*? I saw him only yesterday.'

'Here? The little swine is here?' shouted the Princess angrily. 'He'll get killed if he comes here to Villefranche.' She clasped her beads and twisted them against her neck, staring at me as if angry that I didn't understand. 'If only I'd kept the newspaper clipping.'

'About Claude?'

'He got a medal – an iron cross or something – he was working for the German police all the time. His real name is Claude Winkler, or some name like that. His mother was French, they say. He betrayed Marius and old Madame Baroni and poor Steve Champion, too.'

I drank my whisky. 'All that time and he was working for the Abwehr.'

'The Abwehr – how could I forget that word,' said the Princess.

'And they let us go on functioning,' I said. 'That was cunning.'

'Yes, if they'd arrested us all, others would have replaced us. It was clever of them to let us continue.'

'So Claude was a German,' I said. 'When I think of all those months . . .'

'And the RAF escape-route,' said the Princess. 'They let that continue, too.'

I nodded. 'As long as the flyers came through here, London would be convinced that all was well.'

'I would kill him,' said the Princess. 'If he came in this bar now, I'd kill him.'

'Claude Winkler,' said Schlegel, as the Princess got up from the bar stool in order to pour more drinks for us. 'Do you know what he does now?'

'Yes,' said the Princess. 'He still works for the Boche Secret Police.' She poured drinks for us. 'The nerve of the man! To come back here again.'

I put my hand over my glass. She poured whisky for herself, and this time Schlegel too had whisky.

'I'll kill him if he comes in here,' she said again. 'People think I'm a silly old woman, but I'll do it, I promise you.'

'Claude *l'avocat*,' I said. There were more tourists now, peering into the bars, reading the menus and looking at the crude daubs that the 'artists' sold on the waterfront. None of them came into this bar: it was a dump, just as Schlegel said. Fly-specked old bottles of watered-down cognac, and re-labelled champagne. Bar girls with fat legs and unseeing eyes. And upstairs, broken beds, dirty counterpanes and a 'badger man' who came in and shouted 'That's my wife!' before even your pants were down.

'So Claude betrayed us,' I said.

'Are you all right?' said the Princess.

'I'm all right,' I said. 'Why?'

'You look like you are going to be sick,' she said. If you work in a bar for thirty years, you develop a sharp eye for people who feel sick.

8

'We didn't just *want* to murder him; we planned the killing.'

Serge Frankel did not look up. He put the big magnifying glass over the envelope and examined the stamps carefully. Then he moved it to look at the franking marks. 'Yes, we planned it,' he said. He rubbed his eyes and passed the envelope to me. 'Take a look at that cancellation. What does it say?'

I leaned across the desk, careful not to disturb the trays and the tweezers and the small fluorescent lamp that he used to detect paper repairs and forgeries. I looked closely at the envelope. The stamping machine had not been applied evenly. One side of the circular mark was very faint. '"Varick St Sta . . ." Could it be Varick Street Station?'

'Can you make out the date?'

' May something nineteen thirty.'

'Yes, well that's what it should be.' He picked it up, using only the tips of his fingers. It was a foolscap-size cream envelope, with three large US stamps on it and a big diamond-shaped rubber stamp that said 'First Europe Pan-America Round Flight. *Graf Zeppelin*'.

'Is it very valuable?' I asked.

He slid it into a clear plastic sleeve and clipped it into a large album with others. 'Only for those who want such things,' he said. 'Yes, we planned to kill Claude *l'avocat*. That was in 1947. He gave evidence at one of the Hamburg trials. Pina saw it in a Paris newspaper.'

'But you did nothing.'

'Oh, it wasn't quite like that. Our bitterness was based upon our natural aversion for the betrayer – as yours is now. But Claude did not betray anyone. He was a German. He passed himself off as a Frenchman in order to help his own country . . .'

'Sophistry!'

'Can you remember Claude's accent when he was working with us?'

'He said he was from the north.'

'And none of us had travelled very much, or we might have detected quite a bit of Boche there, eh?'

'None of us had travelled enough – except for Marius. So he made sure that Marius died.'

'I think so,' said Serge calmly. 'But Claude's life was in danger all the time he was with us, did you ever think of that?'

'They were our people, Serge. And they died in squalid camps and torture chambers. Am I supposed to admire your calm and rational attitude? Well, I don't. And perhaps it would be better if you stopped being so godlike . . .'

'We Jews, you mean?'

'I don't know what I meant.'

'This is not in character, Charles. You are the one who stayed so calm. Without you we would have been out on the streets fighting, instead of silently building almost the only network that lasted till the end.' He cocked his head. 'Are you now saying that was wrong?'

I didn't reply. I picked up some of his valuable envelopes and went through the motions of studying them.

'You're fighting the wrong enemy,' said Serge. 'That's all over, that war! I'm more interested in what our friend Champion is doing with his import and export business with the Arabs.'

'Guns, you mean?'

'Who said anything about guns?' Behind him was the skyline of old Nice. The afternoon was dying a slow death, spilling its gory sunlight all over the shiny rooftops.

'You've resurrected the old network, haven't you?' I said.

He pointed to a large lamp that occupied most of the sofa upon which I was sitting. 'Move that infra-red lamp, if it's in your way. This weather is bad for my arthritis.'

'The Guernica network . . .' I said. He watched me as I pieced together my suspicions and the hints and half-truths that only now began to make sense to me. 'You're playing at spies . . . for money? . . . for old times' sake? . . . Because you all hate Champion? Tell me, why?'

He didn't deny it, but that didn't prove I was right, for he was not the sort of man who would leap in to correct your grammar – especially when there might be a deportation order awarded for the right answer.

'Curiosity – even nosiness – is not yet against the law, even in France,' he said.

'I saw Champion today,' I admitted.

'Yes,' said Serge, 'at the *Herren Klub*.'

It was a shrewd jibe, not because it described the club or its members, but because it provided an image of the *Fressenwelle* – Mercedes limousines, silent chauffeurs, astrakhan collars, the whiff of Havana and a muffled belch – I'd never before realized how well Champion fitted into such a scene.

'You are having him followed?' I asked.

Serge picked up an envelope and removed it from its clear plastic cover. 'I sent this to a customer last month. He complained that its condition was not good enough for his collection. Today I had it back from a second customer who says it looks too new to be genuine.' He looked up and smiled at me to make sure I shared the joke.

'Yes,' I said. It was no good pushing him.

'It's a pre-adhesive cover – 1847 – by ship from Port Mauritius to Bordeaux. It got that ship-letter cachet in southern Ireland. It was postmarked again in Dublin as a backstamp, and then got stamped at London and Boulogne before arriving in Bordeaux.' He held it close to the desk light. It was a yellowed piece of paper, folded and sealed so as to make a packet upon which the address had been written. On the back of the folded sheet there was a mess of rubber-stamped names and dates and a cracked segment of a red seal.

Serge looked at me.

'He thinks it's fake?' I said finally.

'He says the watermarks on the paper are wrong for this date . . . And the shape of the Dublin stamp . . . that too he doesn't like.'

'What do *you* say?' I asked politely.

He took it by the two top corners and pulled, so that the sheet tore slowly right down the middle. There was an almost imperceptible hesitation at the bottom and then the two halves separated, and the ragged edge flashed in the lamplight.

'He was quite correct,' said Serge. 'It was a forgery.'

'Did you have to destroy it?'

'If I kept it here, and a client wanted such a thing . . . How can I be sure I wouldn't yield to temptation?'

I smiled. It was not easy to think of this Spartan yielding to temptation.

'I was not even fifteen when I first joined the Communist Party. I was so proud. I slept with that card under my pillow, and in the daytime it was pinned inside my vest. I've given my whole life to the party. You know I have, Charles. You know I have.'

'Yes,' I said.

'The risks I ran, the times I was beaten with police

truncheons, the bullets in my leg, the pneumonia I caught during the Spanish winter fighting . . . all this I don't regret. A youth must have something to offer his life to.' He picked up the torn pieces of paper as if for a moment regretting that he'd destroyed the forged cover. 'When they told me about the Stalin–Hitler pact I went round explaining it to the men of lesser faith. The war you know about. Czechoslovakia – well, I'd never liked the Czechs, and when the Russian tanks invaded Hungary . . . well, they were asking for it, those Hungarians – I ask you, who ever met an honest Hungarian?'

I smiled at his little joke.

'But I am a Jew,' said Frankel. 'They are putting my people into concentration camps, starving them, withdrawing the right to work from anyone who asks to go to Israel. When these pigs who call themselves socialists went to the aid of the Arabs . . . then I knew that no matter what kind of Communist I was, I was first and foremost a Jew. A Jew! Do you understand now?'

'And Champion . . . ?'

'You come and visit me from time to time. You tell me that you are on vacation – I believe you. But I've always wondered about you, Charles. What sort of work does a man like you do in peacetime? You told me once that you were an economist, working for your government. Very well, but now you are asking me discreet questions about Champion, and all the others. So I ask myself if the work you do for your government is perhaps not entirely confined to economics.'

It was like taking a book down from one of these crowded shelves: you couldn't read the fine print until the dust settled. 'What is Champion up to, then?' I said.

'You mean, what am I up to?' said Frankel. 'Everyone knows what Champion is up to: he's an Arab.'

'And you?'

'I'm a Jew,' said Frankel. 'It's as simple as that.'

72

9

Geneva. Calvin's great citadel is perched precariously between the grey mountains of France and the grey waters of Lake Geneva. The city, too, is grey: grey stone buildings, grey-uniformed cops, even its money and its politics are grey. Especially its politics.

I looked out through the hotel's spotlessly clean windows, and watched the plume of water that is Geneva's last despairing attempt at gaiety. The tall jet fell back into the lake and hammered the surface into steel. The traffic moving slowly along the lakeside stopped, started and then stopped again. There was no hooting, no flashing headlights, no arguments, no complaining. The citizens of Geneva are as well adjusted as its clocks. It was 10 A.M., but the city was silent except for the rustle of banknotes and the ticking of a couple of billion wristwatches.

'You were a fool to come here. And so was I.' He pushed the bowl of cornflakes away untouched.

'You came because you knew I'd make plenty of trouble for you if you didn't come. I came because I had to.'

'You came for yourself! This isn't official; it's just for yourself. And it's bloody dangerous!' His upper-class voice was pitched high and slightly querulous, like some customer complaining about the caviare in Harrods.

'Well, it's too late now, Aziz.' I poured some tea for him and he gave me a wintry smile. Aziz was working for the World Meteorological Organization headquarters on the Avenue Giuseppe-Motta. His masters here in Geneva would have been astonished perhaps to discover that he was a senior analyst for Egyptian Intelligence. But certainly his masters in Cairo would have been devastated to hear that he'd been on London's payroll for nearly ten years. 'And anyway,' I said, 'this one is *going* to become official. Believe me, it is.'

'You said that in New York.'

'That was different,' I said. 'You got nineteen thousand dollars out of that one. This time it's free.'

'I'm glad you told me,' said Aziz. He sniffed. He was a bird-like little man, with thinning hair, large eyes and a nose like a ploughshare. His dark skin was inherited from the Sudanese peasant girl who bore him, while the chalk-stripe worsted, the hand-made shoes and public-school tie were worn with the aplomb he'd learned from the Egyptian mine-owner who acknowledged the boy as his son. The small turquoise pinned into his tie was taken from a mine that has been worked since the first dynasty of Egyptian kings. For such a man it is not easy to adapt to the stringencies of a nationalized land and high taxation. 'There will be no money this time?' He smiled. 'Surely you are not serious.'

'Champion,' I said. 'Steve Champion.' I gave him a few seconds to think about that. 'I need help, Aziz, I really need it.'

'You must be mad.'

I pushed him a little. 'London's request for the Libyan trade figures, the Sinai supplementaries, the Kissinger stuff and the analysis you did in December. That all came through me. You must have stashed away a quarter of a million dollars over the last three years, Aziz. And most of that stuff was a doddle, wasn't it? It's the easiest money you ever earned, Aziz. And all of that came through me.'

'What are you fishing for – a percentage?' He poured

himself more tea, and took a long time spearing the slice of lemon, but he never drank the tea. He toyed with the thin slice of lemon, and then dipped it into the sugar, popped it into his mouth and looked up guiltily. I smiled.

'You'd better let me phone the office,' he said. He looked at the gold quartz chronometer on his wrist, and touched his diamond cufflinks to make sure they were still in place. I suppose that must be the problem with diamond cufflinks, apart from the way they slash the red silk lining of your Savile Row suits.

'Go ahead,' I said. 'I don't care how long it takes. We'll have room service send lunch up here. I've spent half the night checking this room for electronic plumbing.'

He looked around the austere Swiss hotel room that cost as much per night as the average British worker received per week. He shuddered. 'It won't take that long,' he said.

'This time I've got more to lose than you have.'

He looked me up and down, from shoes to haircut. 'I don't think so,' he said finally. He sniffed again.

'Just Champion?' he said. All these people who sell us information are like that. They categorize it, and husband it, and let it go only grudgingly, as a philatelist disposes of bits of his collection, and tries to get rid of the dud stamps first. Aziz smoothed his hair across the crown of his head. There wasn't much of it, and he patted it gently. 'You've always played fair with me,' he said. 'I'd be the first to admit that.' I waited while he persuaded himself to tell me what I wanted to know.

'It's the same tedious story that we know only too well,' said Aziz, in his beautifully modulated English public-school accent. 'London put Champion into some of the rougher bits of the small-arms trade . . .'

'Terrorist weapons.'

'Terrorist weapons. And eventually Champion makes contact with our people.'

'Political Intelligence.'

'Political Intelligence,' repeated Aziz, and nodded. Why the hell he still called them his people, when he'd spent a decade selling them out, was strictly between him and his analyst, but I let him continue uninterrupted. 'London must have seen what would happen,' said Aziz. 'Ask yourself . . . Champion's father spent his whole life in Egypt. The Academy gave him a banquet when he retired. Nasser was a student of the old man, you know, as was Sadat. Even the younger Champion has better Arabic than I can put my tongue to.'

'Do you want to light that cigarette?' I said, 'Or do you prefer waving it around?'

He smiled and caught the matches I threw to him. He seemed surprised to find they burned as brightly as a gold lighter. 'We turned him, of course.' He blew smoke and took a piece of tobacco off his lip with a long fingernail. 'At first it was all quite straightforward; London knew he was a double, Cairo knew he was a double. It was a convenient method of communication between Egypt and you . . .'

'When was that?'

'Let's say until the summer before last. It was just before the Fleet exercises that he delivered the NATO wavelengths to us. That was not part of the plan – as far as London was concerned. They found out when Damascus got the wavelengths. London got a rocket from NATO, or so I heard. Yes, Champion burned his boats when he did that.'

'Champion did it for money?'

'My dear fellow . . .' he protested. 'What else?'

'You seem pretty certain about all this, Aziz. Even you have been known to make a mistake.'

76

'Have I?' He frowned. 'I certainly don't remember one.'

I got up and went back to the window to watch the lake again. I said, 'Are you just giving me the gossip from the Cairo Hilton?'

'This is all top-level stuff, old boy. There's a very limited circulation for Champion's material – top bloody secret, all the way.'

'How did you get it?'

'My brother-in-law, of course.'

'Of course,' I said. His borther-in-law was a one-star general in Cairo's Department of Political Intelligence that fills – and overflows from – a seven-storey building in Heliopolis.

Aziz was watching me closely as I turned away from the window. 'I can get you Xerox copies of anything special,' he offered. 'But it will take at least two weeks.'

'We'll see, Aziz.'

'Oh, yes, Champion's deep into it.' He stubbed out the cigarette and watched me as I figured out what to do next. 'It's upset you, hasn't it,' said Aziz, with more friendliness than I would have thought him capable of. 'I'm sorry about that, but Champion has gone a lot too far for London to be running him still – he's Cairo's man. He's ours.'

Ours, I thought, good old Aziz, consummate schizoid, that's the way to be. I sat down on the leather armchair and closed my eyes. 'There's got to be a better way than this to earn a living, Aziz,' I said. I had to be back in Villefranche that evening. It was a long drive and I was suddenly very, very tired.

'No doubt about that, old boy,' said Aziz. 'Trouble is . . . a chap's got to have a little bread, while he's figuring out what the better way is.'

10

He was wearing a short fur coat, and a black kerchief knotted cowboy-style, right against the throat. It was a measure of their subtlety that they sent along a man so unlike any policeman I'd ever seen. This youngster was completely different from the wrestlers of the Police Judiciaire in Marseille, or the hatchet-faced PJ boys who work in Nice. I'd noticed him the previous evening. He'd been drinking straight cognac at the far end of the bar when I went in to ask the Princess for the key of my room. It was a bad sign – cognac, I mean; I like my cops to stick to rot-gut.

He was in the same seat next morning, drinking coffee and smiling apologetically, as if he'd been there all night. 'Monsieur Charles Bonnard?' he said.

That was my wartime name: I thought I'd seen the last reel of that one, but now the nightmares came back. He didn't wait for my reply. 'My name is Fabre. Inspector Fabre, Renseignements Généraux, Lyon.'

'That's a relief,' I said. 'Just for a moment I thought you were from the Gestapo.'

He smiled again. 'We weren't quite sure what name you'd be using this time.'

'Well, I'm glad to hear someone wasn't,' I said.

'You'll have to come to Lyon, I'm afraid,' he said.

He could have been no older than twenty-five, but his youth, like his bizarre outfit, made him a likely recruit for the political undercover work of the RG. He was tall and broad-shouldered, but the slim hips would have suited a dancer or acrobat. His handsome bony face was white. In the north it would have gone unremarked, but here in the Riviera it seemed almost perverse that anyone should so avoid the sunshine.

He rubbed his fingers nervously. 'You'll have to come with us,' he said apologetically. 'To Lyon,' he told me again. He stopped rubbing his hands together for long enough to reach into an inside pocket for a tin of throat lozenges. He tore the silver wrapping from two of them, and popped them into his mouth in swift succession.

'You'll need overnight things,' he said.

I smiled. The Princess came in and put my coffee on the counter. She looked from one to the other of us and left without speaking. 'Why not pay your bill now?' he said. 'I'll make sure they hold your room for a few days. I mean, if you are not back tonight, why pay these hotel bastards?'

I nodded and drank some more coffee. 'Have you worked very long for the RG?' I asked.

He swallowed his throat lozenges. 'Forget checking me out,' he said. 'I don't know anybody important there. That's why I get lousy jobs like bringing you in.'

There was no sign of the Princess. From behind the cash register I took the handful of cash slips that were marked 'Charles'. I added fifteen per cent and signed. 'No need to hold the room,' I said. 'They are not expecting a tour-bus.'

He looked around the bar. There was enough daylight to expose the sleazy fly-blown wallpaper and the cracked lino. He smiled, and I smiled back, and then we went up to get my baggage.

Once inside my room, he became more confidential. 'You must be someone important,' he told me, 'judging by all the teleprint messages and what I hear about the cabinet du préfet complaining to London.'

'Why are you telling me?' I asked.

79

'Cops should stick together,' he said. He opened the door of the battered wardrobe, and spent a moment or two looking at his brown-speckled reflection. 'Last year I followed a suspect to Aachen, in Germany. I grabbed him and brought him back across the border in my car. There was no end of fuss. But luckily the Aachen CID lied their heads off for me. Cops have to stick together; bureaucrats arrest only pieces of paper.'

He pulled my suit out of the wardrobe and folded it carefully while I packed my case. 'They'll take you up to Paris, I think. If you want to make a quick phone call, I won't hear you.'

'No, thanks,' I said. I went into the bathroom and threw my shaving gear into the zip bag. His voice was louder when he next spoke and I could tell he'd started a new throat lozenge. 'And if you have a gun, I'd get rid of it. It will just give them something to hold you for.'

'I don't carry a gun,' I called from the bathroom. I could hear him going all through the drawers of the wardrobe.

I closed the bathroom door. Then I released the plastic bath panels with my knife. I reached into the dust and dead spiders to get the plastic bag I'd hidden there. I didn't have to swing out the cylinder, I could see the 125 grain round-nosed bullets that I'd loaded into the ·38 Centennial Airweight. I stuffed the pistol into the waist-band of my trousers and quickly replaced the panel. Then I flushed the toilet and emerged from the bathroom. It had taken me no more than ten seconds.

Fabre said, 'Because if they find a pistol anywhere in the room here, they can hold you under the new emergency laws – one month it is.' He slammed the last drawer closed, as if to punctuate the warning.

'I don't carry a pistol. I don't even *own* a pistol. You know English policemen don't have guns.'

'I was forgetting,' he said. 'And you have *habeas corpus* and all that crap, too. Hell, what a life for a cop. Are you sure you don't want to make a phone call? Call London if you want, but make it snappy.'

'Are you in traffic?'

'Renseignements Généraux,' he said. 'I told you I was from RG. Why?'

'Because you come on like a courtesy cop,' I said.

He smiled. 'I'm one of the graduate entries,' he said. He gave a self-conscious smile. 'I don't believe in rough stuff, unless it's absolutely necessary.'

'Have you got a car here?'

'And a driver. We must stop in Nice, at the Palais de Justice. I must sign the forms and go through the formalities. You don't need gloves: it's not that cold.'

'I've got a circulation problem,' I said.

It was a black Citroën. The driver was a mournful Negro of about fifty. He took my case and locked it in the boot. His skin was bluish black and his eyes heavy-lidded. He wore a shabby raincoat and battered hat. He hardly looked at us as we got into the car. The young one continued talking. 'The other day someone said that we were the Jews of Western Europe. Palais de Justice, Ahmed.'

'Who?' I said.

'Cops. The Jews of Western Europe; we're blamed for everything, aren't we? Everything, from traffic jams to strike-breaking – it's convenient to have someone to blame.'

I grunted.

'Park in the usual space, Ahmed,' he told the driver, as we turned into the Place du Palais. To me he said, 'I'll be as quick as I can. You wait with Ahmed.'

I nodded.

'What's wrong with you?' he said. 'A pain in the guts? Indigestion?'

'Could you get me something? It's an acid stomach. There's a chemist at the end of the street.'

Fabre looked at me for what seemed like a long time. Then he reached into a pocket of his fur coat and found a plastic box. 'You need two of these,' he said. 'I carry all that kind of junk; I'm a hypochondriac.'

'Thanks,' I said. He tipped two small multi-coloured capsules into the palm of my gloved hand.

'They melt at different times,' he explained, 'so you get this continuous anti-acid together with minute doses of regular aspirin and buffer – you must have seen the adverts . . .'

I put them into my mouth with my left hand and tried to look like a man who was holding on to his belly-ache with the other hand, rather than one who had been a little too premature in checking the butt of a ·38 Centennial Airweight.

'Shellfish,' I said. 'That always does it. I'm a fool, really.'

Fabre nodded his agreement, slammed the car door, and walked off across the square to the police offices. The driver was still looking at me. I smiled at him. He touched the evil-eye beads that dangled from the driving mirror, and then gave his whole attention to the horse-racing section of his paper.

Whatever Fabre did inside that imposing building took no more than five minutes. The driver had the engine running by the time Fabre got back in. 'We'll take the autoroute, Ahmed,' Fabre told the Negro. 'You'll see the Grasse exit marked.'

We followed the Mediterranean coast as far as Cannes, and then turned north, into the land of truffles, baccarat and fast cars that stretches from Mougins to Vence. No one spoke. I looked out of the window.

'This is Grasse,' said the driver. He turned to look back over his shoulder, and gave me a sad smile.

Palm Springs on a French hill-top. Daubed on a wall there was a slogan: 'Arabs Keep Out of Grasse.' It was raining in Grasse. We didn't stop.

'We'll be there by lunchtime,' said Fabre.

I tried to wet my lips and smile back, but my tongue was dry. These boys were all soft lights and sweet music, but I had the feeling that it was going to go dark and quiet at some chosen place on the highway north. And they weren't planning to leave long-stemmed roses to mark the spot.

'I'm sorry,' he said.

The driver kept to a steady speed and showed impeccable road manners. To them, it might have seemed convincingly like police procedure, but to me it looked as though they were extremely careful not to be booked on a traffic offence at a time when they had another crime in operation.

'Sorry about what?' I croaked.

'Mentioning food – when you have a *crise de foie*,' he said.

'Is that what I have?'

'I think so,' he said.

Instinct said use the gun and get out of here, but training said find out who, what and where.

The driver chose the N85, the *route Napoléon*. As we climbed away from the sheltered Riviera coast, a hell's kitchen of boiling storm-clouds came into view. The mountain peaks were white, like burned soufflés that some chef had hidden under too much powdered sugar. The sky became darker and darker, and the cars coming south had their headlights on. The rain turned to hail that beat a tattoo on the roof of the car, and at the La Faye pass the mountains echoed with the sound of thunder. Great lightning flashes froze an endless line of toy motor-cars that were crawling up the far side of the gorge. The wiper blades stropped the glass, and the engine's note changed to a whine that provided an undertone of hysteria.

'We'll be late,' the driver warned. It was the hard consonantal French of the Arab.

'It will be clear beyond Barrême.'

'Barrême is a long way,' said the driver. 'We'll be late.' He paddled the brake and swung the steering wheel as the tyres slid on a patch of ice. He lost enough speed to have to change down. There was the scream of a power-horn, and a small Renault sped past us on the wrong side of the road. There was a thud as his slush hit the door, and a fanfare of horns as the Renault prised open the traffic to avoid an oncoming bus. 'Bloody idiot,' said the driver. 'He won't get to Castellane, except in a hearse.'

The equinoctial storms that lash the great limestone plateau of Provence provide Nice with a rainfall higher than even London. But as we hurried north the black clouds sped over us, tearing themselves to shreds to reveal their sulphur-yellow interiors and, eventually, the sun. The inland roads were dry, and as the traffic thinned out we increased speed. I watched the fields, and the huge flocks of birds that circled like dust-storms, but my mind calculated every possible way in which the threat of death might come.

At first they pretended that it would be faster to take to the minor roads, but by the time we were as far as the military exercise zone they had grown tired of their game, or had decided that it was no longer necessary.

Fabre, in the back seat with me, was watching the road with unusual attention. 'You missed the turn-off,' he told

84

the driver. He tugged at his finger joints one by one, as if he was field-stripping his hand to clear a blockage.

The driver made no sign that he'd heard, until finally he said, 'I didn't miss *anything*. There's that tumbledown shrine and the wire, *then* comes the turn-off.'

'Perhaps you are right,' said Fabre. His face was even whiter than white, and he chewed down on one of his tablets in a rare display of emotion. He became conscious of my stare and turned to me. 'We must get the right road or we'll be lost – it's one of those short-cuts.'

'Oh, one of *those* short-cuts,' I said. I nodded.

He rubbed his hands together and smiled. Perhaps he'd realized that there had been undertones in that last exchange which denied any last chance that they were policemen.

Fabre spotted a wayside shrine with a few miserable wild flowers in a tin at the foot of a tormented Christ. 'You're right,' he told the driver. We turned on to the narrow side road.

'Take it easy,' Fabre said to the driver, his face tightening as the suspension thumped the rutted track. He was nervous now, as the time came closer. They were both nervous. The driver had stiffened at the wheel, and he seemed to shrink even as I watched him.

'Not the right-hand fork,' Fabre warned the driver. And then I suddenly recognized the landscape. A few stunted trees on rolling hills: I'd not seen this place since the war. We were taking the high road to the west side of the Tix quarry: Champion's quarry, as it now was. The old open-cast workings had been abandoned since the late 'fifties, and the mine had proved so expensive that it had closed a few years later. The quarry: it would be an ideal place.

As we came up the slope to the brink of the quarry I saw the same dilapidated wooden huts that had been there ever since I could remember. Fabre squirmed. He thought he was a hell of a hard kid, pulses racing and eyes narrowed. I saw him as a grotesque caricature of myself when young. Well, perhaps I was the same 'yesterday's spy' that Champion was, but my heart wasn't pounding. Shakespeare got me all wrong: no stiffening of the sinews, no summoning of the blood, not even 'hard favour'd rage'. There was only a cold sad ache in the gut – no longer any need to simulate it. And – such was the monumental ego a job like mine needs – I was already consoling myself for the distress that killing them would inevitably cause me.

I was concentrating on the pros and cons of striking while the driver had his hands full of car, and Fabre had his attention distracted. But because they were watching the road ahead, they took in the scene some five seconds before I did – and five seconds in this job is a long weekend elsewhere – ten seconds is for ever!

'*Merde!*' said Fabre softly. 'She's escaped.' Then I saw all: the woman in the short fur coat, identical to the one that Fabre was wearing, and the man on his knees, almost hidden in the thorns and long grass. The man kicked frantically to free himself. There were two loud bangs. The man in the grass convulsed at each gunshot and fell flat and out of sight. Then there came the thump of the wooden door, as the fur-coated woman disappeared into the hut.

Fabre had the car door open by that time. The car slewed to a stop in thick mud, almost sliding into a ditch. Even before he was out of the car Fabre had his Browning Model Ten automatic in his hand. Well, that was the right pistol! I knew plenty of French cops with those: smooth finish, three safeties and only twenty ounces in your pocket. A pro gun, and this one had long since lost its blueing. It was scratched, worn shiny at the edges, and

86

I didn't like it. Fabre stood behind the open car door, ballooning his body gently, so as never to be a static target. He was squinting into the dark shadows under the trees. Only men who have been in gunfire do that instinctively as this man was doing it.

The clouds parted to let the sun through. I glimpsed the face at the hut window. I remember thinking that it must be Madame Baroni, the mother of Caty and Pina, but she had died in Ravensbrück in 1944. Two more shots: one of them banged into the car body, and made the metal sing. Not Pina's mother but Pina herself, Caty's sister, her face drawn tight in fear. There was a flash of reflected light as the sun caught the nickel-finish revolver that she levelled through the broken window.

She depressed the gun and fired again at the man in the undergrowth. I remembered the German courier she'd killed, when we were together at the farmhouse. She'd shot him six times.

'You cow!' Fabre's face contorted, and he brought his Browning up in a two-hand clasp, bending his knees slightly, FBI target-shooting style. He'd need only one shot at this range. His knuckles were white before I made my decision.

I pulled the trigger of my revolver. The noise inside the car was deafening. At a range of less than two yards, the first bullet lifted him under the arm like a bouncer's grip. He was four yards away, and tilted at forty-five degrees, as the second shot collapsed him like a deckchair and threw him into the ditch. My ears rang with the noise. There was the smell of scorched cloth, and two holes in my coat.

Ahmed jumped out of the car at the same moment I did. With the car between us, he was able to cover a lot of ground before I was able to shoot. The bullet howled into the sky, miles away from him. I cursed, and moved back to the place where Fabre had fallen. I was cautious, but I needn't have been. He was dead. The Browning was still gripped tight in his hands. He was a real gunny. His mouth was open, teeth clenched, and his eyes askew. I knew it was another nightmare. I steeled myself to see that face again in many dreams, and I was not to be wrong about it.

Cautiously I moved up the track towards the wooden shack, keeping low and behind the scrub. I was on the very brink of the quarry before the door opened. Pina emerged, tight-lipped, dishevelled, her fur coat ripped so that its lining hung below the hem. The man she'd shot was dead: a dark-skinned youth in leather jacket and woollen hat, his tweed trousers still entangled in the thorns.

'Charlie! Charlie! Oh, Charlie!' Pina pushed the revolver into her pocket and then washed her dry hands, in some curious rite of abnegation. 'They were going to kill me, Charlie. They were going to kill me. They said so.'

'Are you all right, Pina?'

'We must get away from here, Charlie.'

There was a flash of lightning and a prolonged rumble of thunder.

Pina mumbled a prayer into my shirt-front. I held her tight, but I didn't relax. From here I could see right down to the puddles in the bottom of the quarry. It was a spooky place for me, its vast space brimful of memories and fears. In the war I'd hidden here, listening to the barking of the search dogs, and the whistles of the Feldgendarmerie as they came, shoulder to shoulder, across these very fields. Pina clutched my hand, and she felt there the anxious sweat that my memories provoked.

'But where?' she said. 'Where can we go?' Again, lightning lit up the underside of the dark clouds, and a perfect disc of its blue light flashed from the bracken a few yards in front of me. Violently I pushed Pina to the ground, and threw myself down into firing position. With one hand I pushed my spectacles against my face and capped one eye. With the other hand I put the pistol's foresight near the place where I'd seen the glint of reflected light. I pulled the trigger three times.

The sound of the gunfire was reflected off the sloping ground: three loud bangs, and the echo of them came rolling back from the far side of the quarry. Pina crawled nearer. 'Keep down,' I said.

'This grass! I'm soaked,' she complained.

'It's a sniperscope, a perfect disc of light. It must have been sighted on us.'

I rolled over enough to get some bullets from my pocket and push them into the chamber. Then I picked up the empty cases and wrapped them in my handkerchief. There was no point in trying to be clever about powder traces – the bullet holes in my pocket would be enough.

'They will try to get to the car,' said Pina. 'If you could get to that bracken you'd shoot anyone who tried to get down to the track where the car is.'

'You're riding the wrong sideshow,' I growled. 'I'm selling tickets for the tunnel of love.'

'You're going to let them take the car?'

'I'll check their oil, and polish the windscreen for them.'

Pina gave that sort of whistle that well-bred French ladies resort to when they want to swear. It was then that the Negro driver broke cover and went racing off down the slope towards the main road. If there was more than one man, this had to be the moment to rush them. I jumped up and ran as fast as I could to where I'd seen the glint of light. Pina followed me.

'I don't understand,' she said.

I said nothing; I didn't understand, either. There was no sniperscope, no high-powered rifle, no lethal weapons at all. The lightning had reflected from the front element of a zoom-lens fitted to a Beaulieu 16 mm movie camera. I fidgeted with the magazine until I got it open and then I pulled the grey film out into the daylight. A considerable footage had passed through the film-gate but the bulk of it was in the top magazine. Whatever it was intended to film had not yet happened.

I unlatched the camera from its pan and tilt head, and lifted it on to my shoulder. Then, in some irrational fit of destructive anger, I pitched the valuable movie camera over the side of the quarry. It hit an outcrop and bounced high into the air, spilling lenses and sprockets and trailing a long tail of film. It bounced a second time and then fell out of sight before landing with a thud.

Pina gave me the big pistol she had used. 'It's his,' she said, indicating the body of the dark-skinned man, 'I got it away from him.' After wiping it carefully, I threw it into the wooden hut. There was a new plastic-topped table there and two kitchen chairs. Cigarette ends, pieces of loaf and the remains of hard-boiled egg littered the table top, and a length of rope was on the floor. 'I tricked him,' said Pina. 'They had me tied up at first.'

'Go and wait in the car, Pina,' I said.

She shuffled off like a sleepwalker. Half-heartedly, I pressed my ·38 into the dead Arab's hand and threw my cotton gloves down alongside the body, to account for its powder-free hands. But I didn't fool myself that I was achieving anything more than a couple of hours at double-time for some junior assistants in the local forensic lab.

I started the Citroën. There was a full minute of wheel-spinning before the old brute crawled out of the mire and waddled off down the track, spewing mud in every direction. We left everything the way it was, the fur-coated gunny head-down in the ditch, the camera-operator – for so I had decided was the man Pina had killed – stiff in the long grass.

'What did it all mean?' Pina asked me, as we reached the main road.

I looked at her and then back down the road. 'You know what it means, Pina,' I said. 'And, by God, I'm going to wring it out of you, so just start getting used to the idea of telling me.'

We were both silent for a long time. I suppose we were both thinking about the Negro driver, and what he might do. Pina finally said, 'He'll not tell the police anything, unless they squeeze it out of him. They were there to kill you, Charlie. They grabbed me this morning on my way to the hairdresser's.'

'Why you, Pina?'

She didn't answer. My thoughts moved on to more urgent matters.

'Is there a plane service to Paris from Grenoble?' I asked her.

'Air Alpes fly Marseille–Grenoble–Metz, and connect with an Air France Düsseldorf flight. I did that last year.'

'No good,' I said, thinking better of it. 'Passports, credit cards and cheques – a trail of paper.'

'I've got a lot of cash,' she said.

'Give me a minute to think.'

'You'd better think fast, petit, or we'll be in Valence. And that's on the autoroute. It will be thick with cops.'

'I wish I knew whether this was a stolen car.'

'Don't be silly, Charlie. You saw those men. They don't work with stolen cars: they are assassins – cent-mille francs a time men – they don't use stolen cars.'

'Who are they, Pina?'

She picked at the dried mud that was plastered on her

fur coat. 'It's no good shouting at me as if I was a juvenile delinquent,' she said.

'You killed that man, Pina,' I said.

She didn't answer. I found it difficult to be patient with her, and yet I knew there was no other way. I said, 'The Tix quarry . . . Pina, and not far away, the mine, and the house where Champion lives. What the hell are you doing there?'

A police car came speeding towards us, with siren and light going. I watched it in the mirror until it disappeared over the hill. 'And the camera,' I said. 'I think you took it up there to spy on Champion. Is that it?'

She turned her head to see me more clearly.

'You and Champion are in it together,' she said, as if the idea had just occurred to her.

'In what?' I demanded.

She shook her head. Then she looked at her gold wristwatch and fidgeted with it, so that it jangled against the bracelets on her arm.

'You tell *me*,' she mumbled.

The rain mottled the windscreen and I switched on the wipers and the heater. She loosened her coat. 'OK,' I said, 'I'll tell you. You've always blamed Champion for the death of Marius. But your brother was arrested hours before Champion, and you know it because you saw it happen. And I saw it, too.' I waited for her to admit it, but she didn't.

She forced herself to smile. 'I was mad about Champion,' she protested. 'I loved him, you know I did.'

'And that's all part of the vendetta,' I said. 'You never forgave him for marrying your sister.'

She gave a little hoot of laughter. 'Jealousy!' she said. 'What a joker you are!' She took out a tiny handkerchief and wiped her nose. Only after she had taken a quick look at herself, run a fingertip over her eyebrows and clicked her handbag closed, did she speak again. 'It's the way he's *treated* Caterina that I resent so much. Have you seen her lately?'

'A week or so ago.'

'He's made her life hell, and it shows on her face.'

'No, Pina,' I said. 'She's just getting old, that's all.'

'You're pitiless, Charlie, do you know that?' It was a pleasant conversational voice she used. 'You don't have flesh and blood, you have clockwork. You don't live, you tick.' She wiped her nose again. 'Tell me, Charlie: do you ever love, or hate, or weep? Tell me!'

'No,' I said, 'I just blow a fuse.'

'And each time you do it, someone comes along and fits you with a bigger fuse, and finally you can tick-tock your life away, Charlie, without any problems of conscience, or morals, or thought of tomorrow.'

'It's a funny thing, Pina,' I said. 'Every time someone puts a bomb in a supermarket or machineguns a few airline passengers, it turns out that they are doing it on account of their conscience, or their morals, or some goddamned twisted idea of a new Jerusalem.'

I'd said it simply out of anger, but the reference to Jerusalem caused her to react.

'Me?'

Her eyes opened wide and her mouth slackened with amazement and indignation. 'You think I'm working with the Palestinian terrorists?'

'Then who are you working for?'

'The autoroute will be best,' she said. 'The car's not stolen, I'm sure of it. We'd best make for Paris.'

'Who?' I said again. 'Who are you working for, then?'

Pina had said too much and she knew it, and now she hunched forward in her seat and began to worry. The moment had passed.

For a few minutes she was very still. Then she turned her head to see the road behind us.

'I'll watch the road, Pina. You try and rest for a few minutes.'

'I'm frightened, Charlie.'

'It will be all right,' I said. 'Try to get some sleep.'

'Sleep,' she said. 'It's ten years since I was able to sleep without my pills.'

'Well, don't take any of those. We might need to be wide awake.'

A helicopter came over the road and then made off towards the autoroute. Pina leaned close to the window to watch it fly over.

'Traffic police,' I said.

She nodded and leaned back in her seat, her head resting against the window. I glanced at her. Her hair was knotted and her lipstick smudged. In her lap, her hands were clasped too tight, the knuckles criss-crossed with the marks of her nails. When she spoke it was in a different sort of voice, and I glanced across her to see that she had not opened her eyes. 'I must have a drink, Charlie. I must.'

'In Lyon.'

'You don't understand!' She rummaged through the rubbish and dog-eared papers in the car, as if hoping to find a bottle or a hip-flask.

'We'll find somewhere,' I said.

'Soon, Charlie.'

Her hands were shaking, in spite of the strength she used to clench them together. And I saw the way that her face was stiff as if with pain.

'The first place we see,' I promised.

'Oh, yes, petit.'

It was an elegant and yet a forbidding place. A pox of tourist-club badges studded the portals, and the flags of the world's richest nations flew from the battlements. The gravel was freshly raked and the grass clipped short.

'Let's go,' I said. I had already given her my lecture on being inconspicuous – don't over-tip, thank anyone or converse too long with the waiter – and we'd stopped a moment or two while she combed her hair and used tissues to clean her face. After that, we'd gone a couple of miles up the road, in order to enter the drive from the north, and so be remembered as a southbound car.

She left her muddied coat in the car. We came, huffing and puffing from the cold, into the warmed and scented air of the lobby. The tiles were polished and the carpets brushed. Behind the desk a middle-aged man looked up and reached for his jacket. He put it on before greeting us. 'Yes?' he said, as if he could think of no possible reason why people should break their journey there.

'Can we get a drink?' I said.

'I'll see,' he said, and disappeared through a door marked 'Private'.

There was a smell of disaster in the air, along with the scent of tile polish and coffee. About thirty tables had been set with cloths and cutlery but only one table had been used. On it there were two used cups, a coffee-pot and a newspaper folded so that the classified columns could be read.

A second man appeared from the service doors. Behind him there was the sudden sound of water going into a pot and a clatter of plates.

'A table for two?' He gave us a dignified smile. He was about sixty, a balding man with pale face and red hands: the legacy of a lifetime of steamy kitchens and hot water.

'Yes,' I said.

He raised a hand, turned on his heel and led us through the empty dining-room to a table near the window, as if we'd have had little chance of finding an empty seat without his assistance.

'*Omelette fines herbes*,' he suggested. His collar was twisted, as if the coat had been put on hurriedly.

'Give me a brandy,' said Pina, 'a *fine*. We just want a drink.' She sighed, and dumped her handbag on the table with a thud that knocked the cutlery askew. Then she opened the bag and began to search for cigarettes.

The waiter was patient. He handed me a menu.

'Two omelettes,' I said. 'And I'd like a glass of red wine.'

'Fleurie,' he suggested.

'And a green salad.'

'Perfect,' said the old man.

Pina found her cigarettes and lit one. She watched the old man stride away with his order. 'You just gave him his big moment of the week,' she said.

'The way you say it, it sounds like I gave him leprosy.'

She touched my hand on the table-top. 'You were being nice. And I'm being . . .' She shook her head, unable to think of a word, and inhaled on the cigarette again. She propped her hand under her chin, and did not turn her eyes away from the kitchen door, shivering so violently that, for a moment, her whole body trembled.

'Relax, Pina, relax,' I said. But she did not relax until the old man emerged with the drinks. When he placed the brandy before her, she reached out to touch the stem of the glass, and as she did so – just with the possession of the drink – I saw the tension die within her. As if exercising masterful restraint she raised the glass slowly and met my eyes before taking a sip of it.

'It's a good brandy,' she said.

'Drink it down, Pina, you need a drink.'

But she didn't gulp it. She pushed her gold cigarette case towards me, to offer me one.

'No thanks,' I said. 'I'm trying to give it up.'

She smiled, as if at some secret joke, and placed the jacket of the black Dior suit over the back of her chair, carefully enough for the label to be on display. 'Have a cigarette.' She touched her hair as if it was herself that she was offering.

'I'm trying to give it up,' I said again, but I opened the case and took one, in just the same way that I'd ordered the omelette: to be obliging.

The afternoon sun came through the window and lit up her hair. And it lit up the strange grey eyes. 'And what else are you trying to give up?' she said, and waved away her cigarette smoke and my answer with it. 'No, don't tell me, darling, let me find out.'

It would have been difficult to guess Pina's age. She needed no girdle, nor skin treatments. Neither the tiny wrinkles around her eyes, nor the freckles on her cheeks, were disguised under make-up. And when she'd combed through her hair, and tidied up in the car mirror, she'd done so without the narcissistic alarm that you see in the eyes of so many women over thirty. In Pina I could still see quite a lot of the foul-mouthed tomboy who had so alarmed me when I was a teenage subaltern.

'Go and wash your face,' she commanded. 'When I look at the mess you're in, I'm surprised they didn't ask us to pay for the meal in advance.'

I looked at my watch.

'They'll be ages yet,' she added caustically. 'They'll have to go and buy some eggs.'

Unlike the French restaurants that persist in modernizing dining-rooms while retaining medieval toilets, this place had reversed that configuration. The antique wood carvings, dark panelling and worn flagstones of the dining-room ill prepared me for the brilliantly lit stainless-steel sinks, the tinted mirrors and scented air of a washroom designed to look like a space-station.

I used the silver-backed hairbrush provided by the management, and stared at my reflection as I went over the events for the thousandth time. I'd put on my gloves before being brought out of the hotel and I had not taken them off until the shooting was done. Therefore no dabs on the car or at the scene of the crime. My Centennial Airweight had been bought new – in 1968 from a man in Rue Paradis, Marseille. He was well known, and well paid, for his skill at removing numbers from metal, and going deep enough to remove the impacted metal under the numbers. The gun had lived in a rented cash-box deep under a bank in suburban Lyon, until I collected it a week before using it. The gun was all right. They'd discover nothing from that. I stopped brushing my hair to finger the blackened holes in my coat pocket. All that would go for nothing, if the police lab got a sniff at my clothes. Oh, well.

Behind me, the toilet door creaked softly. In the mirror I saw it open just enough for someone to see inside. I turned. Perhaps I would have been fast enough, and even heavy enough, to handle one such man, but there were three of them. They were motor-cycle cops: giants in boots, breeches, black leather coats and shiny crash helmets. I thrashed about, until a butt in the face with a helmet, and a nicely timed kick behind the knee, tumbled me to the floor. As they pulled me to my feet they had me pinioned so tight I could hardly breathe.

There were two other men behind the cops. They were small, white-faced men, with tight-fitting overcoats and expensive gloves. One of them bent down to pick up my spectacles. He examined them to be sure they were not cracked and then placed them on my face.

The other civilian advanced upon me, clutching a handful of paperwork, as a priest might brandish a crucifix at a malevolent Lucifer.

I protested as much as a man can protest when he has a blue uniformed arm choking the life out of him, and the hard corner of a sink prising his vertebrae apart.

And they were still crowding into the place: autoroute police, motor-cyclists, civilians and helicopter pilots. 'Is this the one?' a voice asked, and they shuffled about until the person questioned could get a look at me.

He must have nodded, for another voice said, 'You know that under French law you can be held for questioning for up to forty-eight hours without charges being preferred against you.'

I was gasping for air. I got my arm free, and tried to loosen the arm round my throat. My captor mistook this for an attempt to escape. He gave me a kidney punch, nicely calculated to be less than lethal.

Now I was bent almost double. I could no longer see any of the men. 'This is a murder charge,' said another voice. 'Mrs Helen Bishop, alias Melodie Page, murdered in flat seven, twenty-three Victoria Terrace Gardens, London South-West. It's all here . . . French magistrate's signature, préfecture, as well as the extradition . . . You just cool it. We're taking you to Lyon airport, and then to London. You just cool it, or I'll beat you unconscious personally. Got it?'

It was the voice of Colonel Schlegel. The grip on my throat was loosened so that I could answer.

'OK, OK,' I croaked.

'Get the cuffs on the bastard,' said Schlegel. 'And if he looks like he's even *thinking* of escaping, beat him senseless.'

They let me straighten. There was a ghoulish smile on

Schlegel's face. If he was trying to convince these French policemen that this wasn't a way of getting a colleague out of trouble, he was overdoing it.

I took a few deep breaths. Over Schlegel's shoulder I could see through the open door into the dining-room beyond. Pina had gone.

11

'All you do is complain,' Schlegel told me.

Dawlish was pouring tea and cutting into a fruit cake.

'He's simply trying to irritate you, my dear Schlegel. He knows that that was the only way to do it.' Dawlish turned to me and smiled, challenging me to tell him a better way of getting away from the quarry, and the corpses, and the problems arising therefrom.

I couldn't. I took the slice of cake Dawlish offered.

'You moved quickly,' I said. Schlegel bit into his piece of fruit cake and smiled to show his appreciation of my grudging praise.

He said, 'Your friend – the Princess – came through with a description of the two men, the make and year of the car and the registration number. I'm telling you, she had me high-tailing down that highway in the police chopper before I was fully awake.'

My mouth was hardly open before Dawlish answered my question. 'Colonel Schlegel had the foresight to leave a contact number with her,' he said.

I scowled. Colonel Schlegel was too bloody fond of leaving contact numbers, and what he described as cutting through British red tape and deviousness. It was bloody dangerous.

'She *was* worried about you,' said Dawlish. 'I think the Princess is straight.'

'A pity she wasn't with Schlegel and that French heavy-glove squad when they found me.'

'We didn't know about the quarry and the shooting at

that time,' Schlegel explained. 'We thought we were picking up the hoods who were snatching you.'

'Well, when the cops find the bodies, Colonel Schlegel is going to have a lot of explaining to do,' I told them.

'Not so,' said Dawlish. 'We had one of our people go up to the quarry last night – no corpses, no guns; nothing.'

'Champion has cleaned up the garbage,' said Schlegel. 'No more will be heard.'

They had it all worked out. There was no arguing with them. And anyway, I had nothing to add. I walked across to the window. I rubbed the condensation away with my fingertip, and looked out. This was really gracious living. From the window I could see a few hundred acres of Wiltshire and Sir Dudley's new Bentley parked at the east wing entrance. Did the family know what we used the west wing for? Did the gardener, who watched them bury the Telex cables and the scrambler phone lines under his five-hundred-year-old lawn, know? Did he think we needed the eight Yagi aerials for TV, and the double-glazing to keep us warm?

I turned round to look at them. 'But why would Pina Baroni take a movie camera up there?' I said. 'That's what I still fail to understand.'

'Pin your ears back,' said Schlegel, waving a piece of fruit cake at me. 'Pina Baroni took nothing up there. She was snatched, the same way you were.' He bit into the fruit cake and chewed it for a long time before swallowing.

'Are you sure?' I said.

'Sure, we're sure,' said Schlegel, and Dawlish nodded.

Schlegel said, 'This Pina Baroni was wearing the identical fur coat to one that your guy was wearing. Right?'

'Identical,' I agreed.

'Not just a coincidence,' said Schlegel. 'She was going to get killed in that coat. Killed by you.' He pointed at me in case I needed a little help in following the conversation.

102

'Killed by you when you mistook her for the gunny in the same coat.'

'No,' I said calmly.

'Don't give me no,' said Schlegel. 'The movie camera was there to film it happen.'

'Why?'

Schlegel said, 'We know Champion killed Melodie Page . . . Oh, sure, he gave you all that crap about us conspiring to frame him – but he did it. So he dreams up the counterploy – and it has just that kind of poetic touch that a psycho like Champion likes – he was going to have you kill Pina Baroni, and with enough evidence to make it stick.'

'Why?' I said again.

Dawlish interrupted Schlegel's act. 'He'd threaten us. He'd offer a deal: we forget about the Page murder, and he lets you off the hook.'

Well, it did have the kind of crazy effrontery that had once been Champion's hallmark. 'It's the film camera gimmick that I find so difficult,' I said. 'The kind of blurred image you'd get on 16 mm film on a winter's day doesn't compare with eyewitnesses, or telephoto stills, that a court of law would want.'

'Court of law!' said Schlegel. 'Don't be so dumb. Champion knows it would never get that far. He wanted something that would capture the imagination. He'd be threatening to give it to one of the US networks or a TV agency. He was more interested in grabbing attention than getting a conviction.'

'It would have given us a headache,' said Dawlish, as if regretful that the department had lost such an employee.

'But why Pina Baroni?' I said. I was still not convinced. 'Why murder his sister-in-law? Why not a movie of me killing just anybody?'

'We thought about that,' said Schlegel, tapping the

103

papers on the desk. 'Sure why Pina Baroni, his sister-in-law? Finally we figured it this way. The girl hates Champion – really hates him. She's convinced that after Champion was arrested he talked. She thinks he betrayed her brother Marius to the Gestapo – you know all about that, I guess.'

'I know all about it,' I said. 'She's crazy. I saw Champion arrested at Nice station. And that was hours *after* Marius was picked up.' I thought about it. 'Yes, *hours* after.'

'It's water under the bridge now,' said Schlegel. 'She hates Champion's guts, and Champion divorcing her sister didn't help.'

'*Marrying* her sister didn't help,' I corrected him. 'There was a time when Pina Baroni was crazy about Champion.'

'Hell hath no fury like a woman scorned,' said Schlegel.

'You should write that down, Colonel,' I said. 'It has a fine ring to it.'

Schlegel was never slowed by sarcasm. He said, 'And the Baroni girl killed men in the war, she got a medal for it. So she's not the kind of doll who is going to sit at home, sticking pins into clay figures. I mean, this babe is going to do it!'

'OK,' I said, 'you've told me why she might kill Champion, but I'm still waiting to hear why Champion would want to kill her. This is someone we were both with in the war. Why her? Why not a stranger?'

Dawlish said, 'Any news agency would drag out all that stuff about you and Pina Baroni in the war. First they find out she was in the resistance, and then they find out you were with her. Then they start asking what work you are doing nowadays . . . It would cause us maximum embarrassment. It was just another perfect Champion touch.'

'But not quite enough,' I protested. 'Not quite enough.'

'Don't baby him along,' Schlegel told Dawlish. Turning to me he added, 'If you'd killed some broad you'd never met, you'd clam up and put your mind in neutral. You're a pro, and your training would make you proof against any kind of working-over the press, the TV or the law could give you. But if you'd killed this Baroni woman – especially in error – you're going to be full of guilt and remorse. With you in that kind of mood, a prosecutor presses the right buttons, and any guy will sing.'

He was right, and I didn't need to tell him so. In that moment any last doubt I'd had about Champion killing the Page girl disappeared completely. Champion was a dangerous bastard. As devious as ever and not too fussy about who got hurt, as long as it wasn't him.

'It all fits,' I admitted.

'Good,' said Schlegel. There was an indefinable change of atmosphere in the room. I felt as though I'd passed some sort of examination. I looked at Dawlish soon enough to see the tiny nod of his head. Schlegel looked down at the piece of fruit cake he was eating. 'Hell!' he said angrily. 'I don't eat fruit cake.' He stubbed it into the ashtray like an old cigar butt. 'You *know* I don't eat fruit cake,' he complained to Dawlish.

'I'm afraid we're all a little on edge today,' said Dawlish. He bent to pick up cake crumbs and put them into the ashtray.

Schlegel grunted a sort of apology and picked up a couple of crumbs.

I sat down in the red leather chair that is usually reserved for visitors. I closed my eyes for a moment. Schlegel mistook my weariness for anguish.

He said, 'You don't need to lose any sleep about the guy you knocked off. A real expensive hit-man out of Zürich. "The Corsican", a rub-out artist, who probably cooled more guys than you've had hot dinners. For my money, you'd get a medal for that job you did. A medal; not a murder rap.'

'Well, I didn't know I was getting either,' I said.

'Keep your voices down,' said Dawlish primly. 'These wretched guns. If you'd obeyed your orders about guns we'd not have to be sending chaps up to the quarry at dead of night, and faking up a lot of extradition paperwork for Paris.'

'If I'd obeyed orders about guns, I'd be D.E.D.,' I said.

'If they trace that handgun back to you, I'll make you wish you were,' said Dawlish.

'Just tell me your problem,' I said wearily. 'You want this in my file? Give me a sheet of paper, I'll be pleased to oblige you. Anything else you want – crimes you need a confession for? Typewriters missing from the inventory? Petty-cash slips without counterfoils? I'll make it all right in one bumper-size confession.'

I sank back in the chair and shook my shoes off. 'I'm very tired,' I said. 'Perhaps it would be easier on all of us if you told me what you had in mind, instead of straining to pretend that you're being hit by a succession of brilliant ideas.'

The brevity of the glance they exchanged in no way lessened its conspiratorial quality. 'There's a chance to stick a transistor radio up Champion's arse,' explained Schlegel.

I knew enough about Schlegel's allegorical syntax to guess that I was cast as the radio. 'If it's all the same to you,' I said, 'I'll stay with the murder charge.'

'We haven't got time for comic backchat,' said Dawlish.

'Don't look at me,' I told him. 'I'm the straight man.'

Dawlish said, 'Of course, Major Champion will guess

106

that charging you with the girl's murder was just a device . . .'

'. . . but he might believe that gunning down Fabre was too rich for the department's blood,' said Schlegel. 'Got me?'

'No,' I said.

There was a long silence. Finally, it was Schlegel who spoke. They were going to save Dawlish for the replay.

'Right now, you're charged with the murder of Melodie Page. OK, it's very phoney, but we think we could exploit it. We could leak that to Champion, and make it sound convincing. Right?'

'Carry on,' I said. I opened the VIP cigar box and lit one of Dawlish's Monte Cristos. Employees were not permitted access to the hospitality, but this wasn't the right time to remind me.

'Suppose we let the charge ride,' said Schlegel.

I pretended to search my pockets for matches. Dawlish sighed and lit it for me. I smiled up at him.

'Suppose?' said Schlegel, to be sure I was paying attention.

'Yes, suppose,' I said. He need not have worried; I hadn't paid such close attention to the spoken word since the day I got married.

Dawlish said, 'You're here, accused of the murder of the Page girl . . .'

Schlegel said, 'You break bail. You go to France, and ask Champion for a job with his organization. What do you think?'

'You know there's no bail on a murder charge,' I said. 'What are you two setting me up for?'

'No, well, break out of custody, then,' amended Schlegel.

'He's been seeing too many Bogart movies,' I told Dawlish.

'Well?' said Schlegel.

'It would have to make better sense to Champion,' I said. 'If a murder charge was brought against me, and then dismissed on some technicality – he'd see the hand of the department in that. *Then* if the department puts me out to grass . . . That might sound right to him.'

'Well, that fits in with what we know,' said Dawlish, and I realized too late that the two of them had deliberately led me into the planning of their crackpot idea. Dawlish hurried on. 'Champion has a contact with a contact with a contact – you know what I mean. He'd know what was happening to you if you were in Wormwood Scrubs sometime in the next two months.'

Obviously that meant a remand prisoner. 'Just don't ask me to plead guilty,' I said.

'No, no, no,' said Dawlish. The history of the department was littered with the corpses of men who had been persuaded to plead guilty, with the promise of a quiet trial and a release on 'unsound mind' clauses. 'No, no. You'll plead not guilty.'

'And none of those dumb little creeps from the legal department,' I said. 'You manufacture the flaw in the charge but I'll find some crooked lawyer who will discover it and think it was him.'

'Agreed,' said Schlegel.

'I'll go through the motions,' I said. 'But don't rely on it. Champion is a shrewdie: he'll compromise. He'll find me some bloody job with his potato farm in Morocco, and sit back and laugh his head off.'

'We don't think so,' said Dawlish. 'We've been through the reports he sent to London, in the war. He had a high opinion of your judgement then, and he probably still has it. He could use someone like you right now. He's under pressure to increase the Intelligence flow back to Cairo, or so we think.'

Schlegel said, 'But you see why we're worried about the Baroni woman. If this was all a set-up . . . if she was working *with* Champion. If you read the entrails wrong – then . . .' He ran a forefinger across his throat. 'There will be some corner of a foreign field . . .'

'I didn't know you were interested in poetry, Colonel,' I said.

12

It was not the first time that I'd been in Wormwood
Scrubs prison. In 1939, at the outbreak of war, the
prisoners had been evacuated and the prison building
housed Military Intelligence personnel. A few coats of
paint and improvements to the plumbing had not changed
the place very much. There was still the faint odour of
urine that reached every cell and office. And there was
still the resonance that made every sound vibrate and
echo, so that at night I was kept awake by the coughing
of some prisoner on the upstairs floor. And there was still
the same strangled silence: a thousand throats waiting to
scream in unison.

'And no reason why you shouldn't have toiletries –
decent soap, after-shave and bath lotion – and your own
pyjamas and a dressing-gown . . .' He looked round my
cell as if he'd never seen inside one before.

'You're not defending some East-End ponce,' I said
quietly. 'You work on my defence. Let me worry about
the deodorants.'

'Just so, just so,' he said. Michael Moncrieff, he called
himself, a name just as artificial as 'Michael the Mouth',
by which he was known to his gangland clients. Men like
him fight their way out of the gutters of every slum in
Europe. He was a tall man with broad muscular
shoulders, and a face pock-marked and scarred. And yet
time had softened those marks, and now his thick white
hair and wrinkled face could easily persuade you that he
was the genial country lawyer that perhaps he'd liked to
have been.

He reached into the waistcoat pocket of his expensive bird's-eye suit and found a gold pocket-watch. He looked at it for long enough to let me know that he was annoyed with me, but not so long that he might be deprived of the rest of the fee I'd promised him.

With some effort, he managed a smile. 'I've been going over the notes I've made. On both my last visits you said something that interested me very much.'

I yawned and nodded.

He said, 'It could just be that our friends have botched up their case even before it comes to trial.'

'Yes?'

'No promises, mind. Lots of legal work yet. I'll have to see a couple of people in Lincoln's Inn – and that will cost you a monkey . . .'

He waited until I nodded my assent to another five hundred pounds.

'I hope you don't think . . .' he said.

'Never mind the *amour propre*,' I said. 'You get your friends working on the legal double-talk. Right?'

'Not friends – *colleagues*. No fee-splitting, if that's what you're hinting at.'

'You get them working on it, and come back in the morning to tell me what they say.' I got up from the table and walked across to the bedside cabinet for my cigarettes.

'Probably take me two or three days to get a meeting – these chaps are the top people . . .'

'What am I?' I said. 'Bottom people?' I leaned over him to take his gold lighter. I used it, and tossed it back on to the table in front of him.

He didn't look round at me. He got out a red foulard handkerchief and made a lot of noise blowing his nose. He was still dabbing at it when he spoke again. 'You sit in here and get broody,' he accused me. 'You think I'm

111

sitting on my arse all day. You think I take your money and then don't give a damn.'

'Is it your legal training that makes you so perceptive?' I said. 'Or have you got second sight?'

'I work bloody hard,' he said. 'Worrying about people who if they had anything between the ears wouldn't be in here in the first place.' He sat down and fingered some papers on the table. 'Not you, I don't mean you, but some of them . . . Look, it will take me a few days to set up this meeting. Now, be patient, just trust me.'

I lit my cigarette. From behind him I leaned down and whispered softly, very close to his ear. 'Do you know what it's like in this lousy nick, waiting while some overfed mouthpiece spares time to earn the bread he's taken in advance?'

'I know, I know,' he said.

'I'm in here for topping this bird, Michael, old pal. I mean, I've got nothing to lose. You know what I mean: nothing to lose, except wonderful friendships.'

'Now, cut that out,' he said, but I'd shaken him. I saw his hands tremble as he put his typed notes back into the pigskin document case. 'I'll see them this afternoon, if I can. But it might not be possible.'

'I've got every confidence in you, Michael. You won't disappoint me.'

'I hope not,' he said, and again managed a smile.

Stupid bastard, I thought. Three QCs from the Public Prosecutor's department worked a holiday weekend to build mistakes into that paperwork. By now, any prison-visitor with *Everyman's Guide to the Law* could have sprung me in ten minutes, but this schnorrer needed ten days, and two consultants, and he was still only nibbling at the edges.

'I don't like the way they are treating you in here,' he said.

'Oh?'

'No association, no sport, no TV, no educationals, and your visits all closed. It's not right. I've complained about it.'

'I'm violent,' I told him.

'That's what they always say, but you're getting your forty-five minutes' exercise, aren't you? You're entitled to that.'

'I threatened a warder,' I told him. 'So they stopped it.'

He looked at me, and shook his head. 'You behave like you prefer it inside,' he said.

I smiled at him.

After he'd gone, I settled down with *Inside the Third Reich*, but it was not easy to concentrate. As a remand prisoner I'd been given a quiet landing, but there was always the clickety-clack of the peep-hole. As the screw passed, I'd hear his footsteps slow and then there was a moment or so as he watched me, to be sure I wasn't doing any of the forbidden things. It was the same when there was a visit. The peep-hole slammed shut and there was a jangle of keys and the clatter of the door-lock.

'Visitor! Stand up!'

It was Schlegel, complete with document case and a supply of cigarettes. I sat down again. Schlegel remained standing until we both heard the warder move away from the door.

'Stir-crazy yet?' Schlegel asked. 'They say the first ten years is the worst.'

I didn't answer. He went across to the wall cupboard, opened it, pushed my shaving brush and soap aside, and threw the cigarette packets well to the back of the second shelf. 'We'd better keep them out of sight,' he explained. He closed the cupboard door, and reached into his pocket to find his ivory cigarette holder. He blew through it noisily.

'And don't smoke,' I said. He nodded.

'Anything happened in here? Champion is in London, *that* we know! Anything happened here inside?' He smiled.

'Not a thing,' I told him.

'You got the butter, and the tea and stuff? Dawlish said it wouldn't be exactly what you had in mind, but we figured that a parcel from Harrods might be a bit too conspicuous.'

'Can't leave it alone, can you, Schlegel,' I said. 'Just couldn't resist coming in to take a look, eh?'

He said nothing. He put his cigarette holder back into his top pocket. A passing warder rattled his keys against the metal railings, making a sudden loud noise, like a football rattle. Schlegel was startled.

I whispered, 'Schlegel, come here.' He sat down opposite me and bent his head forward to hear better. I said, 'If you, or any of your minions, come here again, spy on me, pass me notes, send me parcels, ask for special privileges for me, ask me or even furrow your brow when my name is mentioned, I'll consider it a very, very unfriendly act. I not only will screw up your goddamned Champion project but I will wreak physical vengeance upon all concerned . . .'

'Now, wait just one minute . . .'

'You button up your Aquascutum raincoat, Colonel, and rap on that door. You get out of here in a hurry, before I cut you into pieces small enough to squeeze through the peep-hole. And you *stay* away – a long, long way from me, until I make a contact – and you make sure there are no misunderstandings, because I'm a very nervous man. Remember that, very nervous.'

Schlegel got to his feet and went to the door. He was

about to rap on the door to call the warder, but he stopped, his fist in mid-air. 'Did you hear the ruckus this morning?'

'No.'

'Twelve prisoners coming back from their meal. Staged a sit-down in the offices. Threw a scare into the clerks, threw a typewriter into the yard and tore the locks off the filing cabinets: all good clean fun.'

'And?'

'It was all over in an hour or two. No sweat. They threatened to stop their TV, or cut back on the smokes, or something.' He thumped the door. 'High spirits, I guess. Don't worry, we had all the exits covered, pal.'

If he was expecting some significant reaction from me, he was disappointed. I shrugged. Schlegel rapped on the door. Within a minute the door was unlocked. He tipped his hat to me, and left.

It was only after he'd gone that the penny dropped. Why a sit-in, and why would they break the locks off the filing cabinets, except that they wanted to read the files. There was a dossier for each of the prisoners in that office. It might simply be high spirits; or it might be an indication of how far someone was prepared to go to get a look at my prison documents.

I stayed in London after my release.

For the first few nights, I slept at Waterloo Station. The first night, I used the waiting-room, but the railway police come round asking to see rail tickets. Out on the concourse, it's cold. The regulars steal the unsold newspapers and line the slatted benches to stop the draughts, but you have to be tough, or very tired, to get much rest there.

By the third night I'd learned a thing or two. An old man they called 'the Bishop', who had arrived on foot

115

from Winchester, told me how to choose the trains. The heat comes from the front, so the residual warmth lasts longer at that end. The Bishop preferred dirty trains, because in those he'd be discovered by cleaners instead of by some railway cop who might turn him in. It was the Bishop who told me always to pretend to any inquisitive policeman that my wife had locked me out. His filthy raincoat tied with string, his broken boots and bundle of belongings, gave him no chance to try that story himself. But I used it three or four times and it worked like a charm. But now my shirt was dirty, and the sort of hasty shave I was able to have in the gents' toilet was stretching the errant-husband story thin.

It was the Bishop who found me a billet on Friday night. There were three of us. We got on to platform four, where the Guildford train was about to leave, and then slipped round behind the buffers to a darkened train that would not go until morning. It was the Bishop who had the square-sectioned key that opens the guard's-van doors. The Bishop settled into the narrow pew from which the periscope gives a view along the train top, while I kipped with Fuller, wedged behind some freight. Fuller was a hatchet-faced thirty-year-old. He wore a battered leather coat and a red-and-white woolly hat. He was a sociology graduate from Sussex University who 'weaseled' luggage for the boat-train passengers and was not above stealing the occasional camera or transistor radio. Such items went on sale in The Cut street-market, not thirty yards away, while the owner was still searching the taxi line to locate the 'well-spoken porter' and trying to remember when he last renewed the insurance.

'It's my back,' explained the Bishop. 'Sleeping on the floor plays merry hell with my back.'

'Spare us the details,' said Fuller. 'We know all about the state of your health.'

'You'll be old yourself someday,' said the Bishop.

'You need a bit of exercise,' said Fuller, 'that's what you need. You come and help me with that boat-train tomorrow. It'll be a good one, they say.'

'I wish I could, but I'd do myself an injury,' said the Bishop. He wriggled into the upholstered seat and searched inside his hat. He kept everything in there: paper money, cigarette stubs, string and matches. Finally he found the matches he wanted. Then he searched through his pockets until he found a tin. It was dented and all vestiges of advertising lettering had long since been polished away. Now it shone like silver, and from inside it he took a cigarette-rolling machine. 'Exercise is no good to anybody,' said the Bishop. 'Who lives to be a hundred? These fellers you see jogging down the road in a track suit at night, or those old cows with their poodles and their chauffeurs and their afternoon naps? You answer me that.'

'Trust you to rationalize it out,' said Fuller, but he found no easy answer to the old man's contention.

The Bishop smiled. He was like some down-at-heel Father Christmas, his beard stained with nicotine and his teeth long and yellow. And yet he did not smell: for a tramp, that was quite an achievement.

'Either of you two want a smoke?' he said. He rolled them carefully, thin tubes of white paper, marked with the Bishop's grey dabs, and spilling dried tobacco.

'Thanks, Bish,' I said. But Fuller did not smoke. Even before the Bishop had given me a light, Fuller was beginning to snore.

'First today,' said the Bishop proudly, holding the roll-up in the air.

'My first for six days,' I said.

'You want to give it up, son,' he said. As he inhaled, the burning cigarette lit up his arthritic knuckles and watery eyes. 'Money going up in smoke: my old mother said it, and she was right.'

'And what did your mother do with her bread?' I said. 'Play the stock exchange?'

'You've been in nick, haven't you, son?'

'I was working the North Sea oil rigs. I told you that.'

'Yeah, you told me that,' said the Bishop. 'But I'm saying you've been doing porridge!'

I pinched out the cigarette and pushed it into the top pocket of his tattered overcoat.

'Naw, no offence, son.'

'Get stuffed,' I said.

'No need to get nasty.'

'Think yourself lucky I didn't poke it down your throat,' I said.

'I'm old enough to be your father.'

'But not bright enough.' I turned over and closed my eyes.

I only dozed for a moment or two before I heard the old man's voice again. He was leaning out of the window. 'They're raking everybody out,' he said. 'Like they did last week. It must be another bloody bomb warning.'

We scattered before the police reached the front carriage. I evaded the half-asleep porters and ticket men, and shuffled off down the freight road that bisects the station layout.

'In here.' I was too tired to recognize the voice. For a moment I thought it was the Bishop, or Fuller.

'In here.' It was not any of the layabouts from the station. It was a short thickset man named Pierce, who was from the department, and behind him I saw Schlegel. They were crowded into a phone booth. I moved fast. I hit Schlegel first, and he reeled. There was a crunch as his elbow hit a metal panel. I saw the look of openmouthed bewilderment on Pierce's face, and then I slammed two body punches into him and hooked him as he doubled up. The two of them were jammed tight into the corner of the phone booth; neither stood much chance against me, for I had room to swing my elbows. I hit Schlegel again, and tapped blood from his nose. I gave him a moment to collect himself. 'Easy, easy,' he grunted. He was tucking his chin in and holding up his hands in a gesture that was neither defence nor surrender, but had a measure of both.

Pierce was huddled almost on the floor, and Schlegel was twisted into a corner, with the phone jammed into his backside. 'What did I tell you, that day in the Scrubs,' I said.

Schlegel stared at me. I not only looked different: I was different. The world had worn me shiny. Prodded awake by cops, cursed by screws, threatened by yobs who wanted your coat, or thought you might have cash. How did a man survive it, except by violence. The world was at your knees, or at your throat. Or so it seemed at the time. But the look in Schlegel's eyes made me realize how far I'd come down the long road.

'You got the passport and everything?' said Schlegel. 'You should be in France.'

'You stupid sod. You people never learn, do you? Champion is one of ours – or was once – he knows all that departmental crap. Our Swiss passports would never fool him for thirty seconds. It went into the furnace along with the letters of credit. Me and Champion set up that payment line back in 1941. It was his idea.' I straightened up, and pushed my fist into the small of my back, to ease the aches and pains of sleeping on the hard floor of the guard's van.

But I kept them both pinned tight into the booth, with Pierce on the floor. Schlegel tried to move, but I forced him back into the corner with my forearm, and he only retained his balance by treading on Pierce's leg. 'Champion is going to come and find *me*,' I told them. 'He won't buy it any other way. And I'm not sure he'll swallow it, even without you stupid bastards trying to hurry things along.' I stopped. I was so tired I could have lain down on the street and sobbed myself to sleep. But I rubbed my face, and blinked, and shook my brains from side to side until I heard a reassuring rattle. 'And if he *doesn't* buy it,' I said, 'I get dead. So forgive me, girls, if I'm a little bit sensitive. Because I've got a whole lot of dances on my programme, I don't need a hand up my skirt.'

'OK,' said Schlegel. 'You're right.' He found a handkerchief and dabbed his bloody nose.

'You'd just better believe it, Schlegel, because next time I won't be just tweaking your nose. You want to give me credentials for Champion? Great! I'll kill you, Schlegel. And I'll cool any of the boys you bring along, and not even Champion will think that was a set-up.'

'You don't talk to me like that,' growled Schlegel, and he coughed as he sniffed his own blood. I had him, and he knew it, and I leaned across and with the knuckle of my left fist I tapped his jaw, as one might when playing with a baby. And he didn't take his eyes off my right fist, that was all set to drive him into the wall.

'Give me some money,' I said.

He reached into his inside pocket and found three crumpled five-pound notes. I took them from him, and then I stepped backwards and I felt Pierce's feet sprawl out. I almost ran down the slope towards York Road.

It was a full moon. 'Hello, son,' said the Bishop, as I overtook him. He was hurrying down the traffic ramp, with his bundle of belongings slung over his back. 'A regular purge tonight, eh?' He chuckled.

'Looks like,' I said. 'But I can buy us a night's kip, and a plate of eggs and sausage.' I brandished the money.

'You shouldn't have done it,' said the Bishop. He was not looking at the notes in my hand, but at Schlegel's blood on my cuff and knuckles.

'We've been together all evening,' I said.

'Portsmouth train, platform eighteen,' said the Bishop.

'Near the front,' I agreed happily, 'in a non-smoker.'

The next day, I tried for job number eighteen on my list. It was a small private bank off Fetter Lane. It specialized in everything from sanction-breaking to fraud. I'd chosen my list of jobs with great care. A man with my qualifications, booted into the street, isn't going to apply for a trainee's job with ICI. These were all dodgy concerns, who knew how to double the five or six grand salary I was asking. But they put a hatchet-man with a big carnation alongside the drinks cabinet, and gave me two glasses of dry sherry and economic-recession talk. I was expecting it, because I had spent nearly five hours on the memo that ensured that each of these companies had a visit from a Special Branch officer at least a week before I arrived.

'Thank the Lord for Saturday,' said the Bishop late Friday night as we sat in our local, nursing one glass of warm beer, and taking simulated swigs at it whenever the landlord glared at us.

'What's the difference?' I said. As far as I was concerned, it simply meant that I couldn't approach the next on the list of prospective employers until the weekend was passed. I leaned back and watched the colour TV on the bar. It was tuned to a comedy show but the sound was turned off.

Fuller said, 'We go to the coast tomorrow.'

'Do you?' I said.

'The Bishop has this fiddle with the National Assistance . . .'

'I told you not to tell him,' said the Bishop. He found a half-smoked cigarette in his hat.

'Everybody knows, you old fool.' Fuller turned to me. 'There's a friendly clerk on the paying-out counter. He calls your name, pays you unemployment money, and then later you give him half of it back. He can't do it more than once a month, or they'd tumble to him.' Fuller produced his matches and gave just one of them to the old man to light his cigarette end. 'Bloody disgusting, isn't he?' said Fuller.

'The Phantom Army, they call it,' said the Bishop. He took a deep drag of the cigarette smoke, and then a swig of the bitter, to celebrate the next day's payment.

'We can row you in on that one,' Fuller offered. 'Can't we, Dad?'

'I suppose so,' said the old man grudgingly.

'You're on,' I said. 'How do you get to the coast? You don't pay the train fare, do you?'

'Couldn't make it pay then, could you?' said Fuller defensively. 'We fiddle the tickets from one of the booking clerks.'

'It's a complicated life,' I remarked.

'You don't *have* to come,' said the Bishop.

'I wasn't complaining,' I said.

'You went after a job today,' said the Bishop.

'That's it,' I admitted.

Fuller looked me up and down with interest. He paid special attention to my newly washed shirt and carefully brushed coat. 'You wouldn't catch me poncing off the capitalist system,' said Fuller finally.

'Same again?' I said. 'Pints of bitter?'

'I wouldn't say no,' said Fuller.

'Thanks, son,' said the Bishop.

Saturday morning. The Southampton train was not full. We caught it with only a few seconds to spare. Fuller led the way, through the buffet car and a luggage van. Even while the train was still stumbling over the points outside the station, I knew that this was the sort of way Champion would make contact.

'Go ahead,' said the Bishop. He indicated the door leading to the next coach and the first-class compartments.

I went forward.

In the corridor, outside his compartment, two men in lumpy raincoats took exceptional interest in the dilapidated back yards of Lambeth and did not give me a glance. Champion looked up from *The Financial Times* and smiled.

'Surprised?' said Champion.

'Not very.'

'No, of course not. Come and sit down. We've got a lot to talk about.' Beyond him the cramped slums became high-rise slums, and then semi-detached houses and sports fields.

In my hand I was holding one of the Bishop's roll-ups. I put it in my mouth as I searched my pockets for matches.

'Been having a rough time?' said Champion.

I nodded.

He leaned forward and snatched the cigarette out of my mouth. He clenched his fist to screw it up, and threw the mangled remains of it to the floor. 'Balls,' he said.

I looked at him without anger or surprise. He brought a handkerchief from his pocket and wiped his hands on it. 'Sleeping on railway stations: it's balls. I know you of old. You can't pass through a big town without dropping a few pounds here, and a gun there, and some beaver bonds in the next place. You of all people – sleeping on railway stations – crap, I say.' He looked out at the factories of Weybridge, and the streets crowded with weekend shoppers.

'You're losing your cool, Steve,' I said. He didn't answer or turn his head. I said, 'Certainly I've got a few quid stashed away, but I'm not leading the band of the Grenadier Guards there for a ceremonial opening.'

Champion looked at me for a moment, then he threw his packet of cigarettes. I caught them. I lit one and smoked for a minute or two. 'And I'm not even taking *you* there,' I added.

Champion said, 'I'm offering you a job.'

I let him wait for an answer. 'That might turn out to be a bad move,' I told him. 'A bad move for both of us.'

'You mean the department will be breathing down my neck because I've given you a job,' he nodded. 'Well, you let me worry about that, Charlie, old son.' He watched me with the care and calculation that a night-club comic gives a drunk.

'If you say so, Steve,' I said.

'You found out what those bastards are really like now, eh?' He nodded to himself. I believe he really thought they *had* framed him for the murder of Melodie Page. That was the sort of man Champion was, he could always convince himself that his cause was right and remember only the evidence he selected.

'Remember when you arrived – that night? Me, and young Pina, and little Caty and the bottle of champagne?'

'I remember,' I said.

'I told you that it would be up to you to keep me convinced you were loyal, not my job to prove you weren't. It's the same now, Charlie.'

I smiled.

'Don't think I'm joking, Charlie. It wouldn't need more

124

than a wave to a stranger, or an unexplained phone call, for you to lose your job . . . you know what I mean.'

'I can fill in the blank spaces, Steve.'

'Can you?'

'We're not going to be distributing food parcels to old-age pensioners.'

'*No one* distributes food parcels to old-age pensioners, and soon I'm going to be one, Charlie. I'm past retiring age: ex-Major, DSO, MC, and I'm cold and hungry, at least I was until a few years ago. I've done my bit of villainy for God, King and country. And now I'm doing a bit for my own benefit.'

'And where would I fit in?' I asked.

'I need an assistant,' he said. 'And you'd be perfect. Nothing to trouble your conscience; nothing to ruin your health.'

'It sounds a bit boring, Steve.'

'I have a lot of Arabs working for me. They do the tricky jobs. They are good workers, and I pay enough to take the pick of the workforce, from botanists to butlers. But there are jobs that they can't do for me.'

'For instance?'

'I've got to get a school for Billy. I can't send an Arab to take tea with a prospective headmaster. I need someone who can take a suitcase full of money somewhere, talk his way out of trouble, and forget all about it afterwards. I talk Arabic as fluently as any Arab, but I don't *think* like one, Charlie. I need someone I can relax with.'

'Sounds like you need a wife,' I said, 'not an assistant.'

He sighed, and held up his gloved hand in a defensive gesture. 'Anything but that, Charlie.' He let the hand fall. 'You need a job, Charlie; come and work for me. I need someone from our world.'

'Thanks,' I said. 'I appreciate it.'

'There's a Latin tag – "Render a service to a friend . . . to bind him closer", is that how it goes?'

'Yes,' I said, '"and render a service to an enemy, to make a friend of him". You wrote that on the report to London, and told the pilot to make sure the old man got it personally. And we got that reprimand with the next night's radio messages. You remember!'

He shook his head to show that he didn't remember, and was annoyed to be reminded. It was difficult for Champion to appreciate how impressionable I had been in those early days. For him I'd just been another expendable subaltern. But, like many such eager kids, I'd studied my battle-scarred commander with uncritical intensity, as an infant studies its mother.

'Well, you didn't sign up for a course in elementary philosophy, did you?'

'No,' I said, 'for one million dollars. When can I start?'

'Right now.' He pointed to a canvas two-suiter on the floor. 'That's for you. Use the battery shaver in the outside pocket, and change into the suit and shirt and stuff.'

'All without leaving your sight?'

'You catch on quick,' said Champion. The train gave a throaty roar as we rushed into the darkness of a tunnel and out again into blinding rain.

'And at Southampton: a false passport, a false beard and a boat?'

'Could be,' he admitted. 'There's no going back, Charlie. No farewell kisses. No notes cancelling the milk. No forwarding address.'

'Not even a chance to get a newspaper,' I said, reminding him of a device we'd used at Nice railway station one night in 1941, when Pina passed back through a police cordon to warn us.

'Especially not a chance to get a newspaper,' he said. I

126

sorted through the clothes he'd provided. They'd fit me. If Schlegel had a tail on me, in spite of my protests, they'd need a sharp-eyed man at Southampton to recognize me as I left the train. I was about to vanish through the floor, like the demon king in a pantomime. Well, it was about what I expected. I was changed within five minutes.

I settled back into the corner of my soft first-class seat, and used the electric shaver. Between gusts of rain I glimpsed rolling green oceans of grassland. Winchester flashed past, like a trawler fleet making too much smoke. After Southampton there would certainly be no going back.

'Have you started again?'

Champion was offering his cigars. 'Yes, I have,' I said.

Champion lit both cigars. 'The bearded one – the Bishop – was one of my people,' he said.

'I thought he might be.'

'Why?' said Champion, as if he did not believe me.

'Too fragrant for a tramp.'

'He told me,' said Champion. 'Bathed every day – every day!'

'No one's perfect,' I said.

Champion gave a stony smile and punched my arm.

13

'When a senior officer, like Champion, confesses to being outwitted – that's the time to run for your life.' The quote originated from a German: a Sicherheitsdienst officer giving evidence to one of our departmental inquiries in 1945. Champion – like all other British SIS agents captured by the Nazi security service – faced a board after the war, and heard his ex-captors describe his interrogations. Not many came out of such investigations unscathed, and very few such men were ever employed in the field again. Champion was an exception.

'I think it's yours,' said Champion. He picked up the red king and waved it at me. 'Unless you can think of something I can do.'

'No, it's checkmate,' I said. I am a poor player, and yet I had won two games out of three. Champion swept the pieces off the small magnetic board, and folded it. 'Anyway, we must be nearly there.'

'Nice airport have just given us permission to land,' said the second pilot. I looked out of the window. The land below was dark except for a glittering scimitar that was the coast. We continued southwards, for even a small executive jet must obey the traffic pattern designed to leave jet-noise over the sea. Champion looked at his wristwatch. There would be a chauffeur-driven limousine at Nice airport, just as there had been at the quayside in Le Havre. There was no fuel crisis for Champion.

'You must have questions,' said Champion. 'You never were the trusting type.'

'Yes,' I said. 'Why did you bring your queen forward?'

Twice you did that. You must have seen what would happen.'

The limousine was there. It was parked in the no-waiting area. The cop had moved a sign to make room for it. The dark-skinned chauffeur was holding a boy in his arms when we saw him. The chauffeur's gigantic size made the child seem no larger than a baby. But he was a big boy, dressed in a denim bib and brace, with a red wool workshirt: all tailored with the sort of care that only the French expend on children's clothes.

'Has he been a good boy?' said Champion.

The chauffeur stroked the child's hair gently. 'Have you, Billy?'

The boy just nuzzled closer into the shoulder of the dark wool uniform.

It was a starry night. The air was warm, and the white-shirted airport workers moved with a spurious grace. What had these men of the south in common with the stamping feet and placid anxiety of the bundled-up dock workers we'd seen sheltering from the driving rainstorms of northern Europe?

I sniffed the air. I could smell the flower market across the road, the ocean, the olives, the sun-oil and the money.

'Bloody odd world,' said Champion, 'when a man has to kidnap his own child.'

'And his friends,' I said.

Champion took his son from the chauffeur. He put him on the back seat of the car. Billy woke for a moment, smiled at both of us, and then closed his eyes to nuzzle into the leatherwork. Gently Champion pushed his son along the seat to make room for us. He gave no instructions to the driver, but the car started and moved off into the traffic of the busy coast road. A roar of engines became deafening, and modulated into a scream as a jet came low across the road and turned seaward.

'You said you'd bring Mummy,' said the boy. His voice was drowsy and muffled by the seat. Champion didn't answer. The boy said it again: 'You said you'd bring her.'

'Now, that's not true, Billy,' said Champion. 'It will be a long time. I told you that.'

The boy was silent for a long time. When finally he mumbled, 'You promised,' it seemed as though he preferred the dispute to continue, rather than be silent and alone. 'You promised,' he said again.

I thought for one moment that Champion was going to strike the child, but the arm he stretched out went round him, and pulled him close. 'Dammit, Billy,' said Champion softly. 'I need you to help your Dad, not fight with him.'

By the time we got to Cannes, the child's slow breathing indicated that he'd gone back to sleep.

You won't find the Tix mansion in any of those coffee-table books about the houses and gardens of the rich families of France. But the Tix fortune was once a notable one, and the house had been built without regard to cost. The quarry, two miles from it, had been the basis of the Tix empire, and even now in the summer, when there had been no rain for a couple of weeks, the yellow quarry-dust could be seen on the marble steps, the carved oak door and on the half-timbered gables.

A century earlier, the wealth from the quarry had built this great house, and created the village that had housed the men who worked there. But the riches of the quarry had diminished to seams that had to be mined. Eventually even the honeycomb of the mine's diggings yielded so little that it was closed. The village languished, and finally became a training ground where French infantry learned house-to-house fighting. But the mansion survived, its paintings and furnishings as intact as three great wars permitted.

The builder had made it face the entrance to the drive, a track nearly a mile long. It was a gloomy house, for the dramatic siting of this solitary building on the desolate limestone plateau condemned it to dim northern light.

The electricity was provided by a generator which made a steady hum, audible throughout the house. The hall lights dimmed as we entered, for the power it provided was fitful and uncertain. The entrance hall was panelled in oak, and a wide staircase went to a gallery that completely surrounded the hall. I looked to the balcony but could see no one there, and yet I never entered the house without feeling that I was being observed.

'Make yourself at home,' said Champion, not without some undertones of self-mockery.

The tiled floor reflected the hall table, where the day's papers were arrayed, undisturbed by human hand. The roses were perfect, too, no discoloured leaf disfigured them, nor shed petal marred their arrangement. It was as homely as a wax museum, its life measured by the pendulum of the longcase clock that ticked softly, and tried not to chime.

A servant appeared from a room that I later learned was Champion's study. This was Mebarki, Champion's Algerian secretary. He was about fifty years old, his eyes narrow, skin pigmented, and his white hair cropped close to the skull. He pulled the door closed behind him and stood in the recessed doorway like a sentry.

Champion carried his son, sound asleep, in his arms. A man in a green baize apron helped the chauffeur with Champion's cases. But my attention was held by a girl. She was in her early twenties. The dark woollen dress and flat heels were perhaps calculated to be restrained, as befits the station of a domestic servant who does not

131

wear uniform. But in fact the button-through knitted dress clung to her hips and breasts, and revealed enough of her tanned body to interest any man who knew how to undo a button.

'Anything?' said Champion to the white-haired man.

'Two Telex messages; the bank and the confirmation.'

'In gold?'

'Yes.'

'Good. It's a pity they have to learn the hard way. In that case tell the warehouse, and let them collect them as soon as they like.'

'And I confirmed lunch tomorrow.' Mebarki turned his cold eyes to me. There was no welcome there.

'Good, good, good,' said Champion, as his mind turned to other matters. Still holding his son, he started up the stairs. 'I'll put Billy to bed, Nanny,' he said. 'Come along, Charles. I'll show you your room.'

The servants dispersed, and Champion took me along the dark upstairs corridors of the house to my room.

'There's a phone in your room: dial two for my room, one for my study, and ten for the kitchen. They'll get you coffee and a sandwich, if you ask.'

'It's a plush life, Steve.'

'Goodnight, Charlie. Sleep well.'

My 'room' was a suite: a double-bedroom, ante-room and sitting-room, with a fully stocked cocktail cabinet and a balcony that overlooked a thousand acres of scrub. There were books too: carefully chosen ones. I was flattered by the care shown in choosing them, and affronted by the assurance that I'd arrive.

I picked up the phone and asked for tea and ham sandwiches. 'Tea with milk,' I said again. It was the nanny who answered. She replied in English. It was English English. 'Have cold chicken,' she suggested. 'They don't eat ham here – they're Arabs.'

'I'll come down to the kitchen,' I said.

'No, I'll bring it up,' she said hurriedly. 'Cheese or chicken?'

'Chicken.'

'Stay there. I'll bring it up.'

I walked out on to my balcony. There was still a light burning somewhere in the lower part of the house, and there were the mixed smells of capsicums being scorched in the style of Arab cooking, and the sweet smell of incense.

I was still on the balcony when the girl arrived with the tray. I watched her as she put it down on the bedside table. She'd unpinned her hair. It was corn-coloured and fell on her shoulders in an attractive disarray. She was tall and slim, with high cheekbones, a generous mouth and blue eyes. She seemed to sense that she was being watched, and she looked up suddenly and smiled, as if reading my carnal thoughts.

'You're English, aren't you?' The voice was home counties, but it had been a long time away from home.

I nodded.

'First Englishman I've seen in an age,' she said.

'No shortage in Nice.'

'These people won't let me borrow a car,' she said. 'Just because I dented their lousy old Fiat. And you change twice on the bus – I tried it once, and once was enough, I'll tell you!' She turned down the cover on the bed and tucked it in, with the quick nervous movements of a trained nurse. 'The maid should have done that before dinner,' she explained. 'No, I'm trapped here.' She smoothed her skirt over her hips as she straightened her body, and looked at me. 'I used to go for walks but I twisted my ankle, and there are mine-shafts out there with no fencing or warning notices or anything – just like the French – you could fall right down them and no one would even know about it.'

'And no cabs?'

'On my salary – you must be joking.' She gave me a knowing smile. It was the sort of smile that only beautiful young girls know about: a provocative smile from moist open lips, as sweet as fresh cream. And as ready to turn sour at the first sign of thunder.

I smiled. She walked across to the balcony where I stood. 'It's fantastic weather for this time of year,' she said. The sky was purple, and from somewhere over the hill there was a glow of red neon, like an electronic sunset switched on all night.

Even before she put her arm round me, I felt the warmth of her body and smelled the cologne. 'I think I'm going to like you,' she whispered. She reached around to clasp her hands in front of me. Then she pressed her body against my back. 'I'm going to like you very much.'

'Why?' I said.

She laughed. 'You're a cool bastard.' She blew on the back of my neck and then gently bit the lobe of my ear. 'I'm lonely,' she said finally, when she grew tired of the game.

'Not tonight,' I said. 'I've got a headache.'

She chuckled, and gripped me more tightly.

'Why don't you drink your tea?' she asked. 'It might start your blood circulating.'

'Good thinking,' I said. I took her wrists and gently broke free from her tight grasp.

I went across to the bedside table where she'd put the tray. It was an impressive spread. There were hand-embroidered napkins, solid silver cutlery and some spring flowers in a vase. The tray was set for two. I sat down on the edge of the bed and poured two cups of tea, and added milk. I heard a rustle of silk; by the time I turned round, with the cup and saucer in my hand, she was stark naked, except for a string of pearls and a heavy gold bangle that denoted her blood group.

'Damn!' she said mildly. 'I wanted to surprise you.' She flipped back the counterpane and climbed into my bed, stretching her legs down into the crisp starched sheets with a sound like tearing tissue paper. 'Oooh! The sheets are cold!'

'You want a chicken sandwich?'

She shook her head. She seemed little more than a child, and, like a child, was suddenly sad. 'You are angry?' she asked. 'Have I shocked you?'

'No,' I said.

'Be nice to me,' she pleaded. 'If you want me to go, I'll go. But be nice to me.' She was tanned, except for the places that would be covered by a small two-piece.

I gave her the cup and saucer. 'You want sugar?'

'You're very English,' she said. 'You don't want it yourself, but you can't bear to turn it away. No, no sugar.'

'Was this Mr Champion's idea?' I said. I turned to watch her as she answered.

She sat up in bed to drink her tea. 'You're his best friend, he said.' A drip of tea had dribbled down her breast. When she rescued it with her spoon she looked at me and giggled. She raised the spoon to my lips, and when I accepted it, giggled again.

'Was it his *idea*?' I persisted.

'Yes, but I told him I'd have to see you first.' She stretched her long tanned arm out, to run a fingertip down my back. 'My name is Topaz,' she said. 'It means yellow sapphire.' She was in her early twenties, with educated speech and calm confident eyes. Forty years ago, girls like this had converged upon Hollywood; now they can be found wherever there are yachts or skis or racing cars, and men to pay for them.

'So he's going to pay you?'

'No, darling, I do it for love.' She chuckled as if that was the greatest joke in the world. Then she drank her tea greedily and put her tea-cup down on the table at her side of the bed. 'Put your arms round me for a minute.'

I did so.

'I get frightened here,' she said in a whisper. 'I'm serious now, I really am.'

'Why should you be frightened?'

'These bloody Arabs arrive by the dozen and then literally disappear!'

'Now, come on, Topaz.'

'I'm not kidding. They arrive in cars in the night, and then next morning there's no sign of them.'

'Oh, yes.'

'I'm serious!' she said angrily. 'Footmarks on the hall carpet, and funny noises in the night. Sometimes I wonder if it's worth the money.'

'Why are you telling me all this?' I said.

'I don't know,' she admitted. 'Because you're English, I suppose.'

'But Mr Champion is English too, isn't he?'

She screwed up her face in deep thought. She was either the greatest actress I'd ever seen in action, or she was speaking right from the heart. I looked at her heart with more than casual interest. 'Not really English,' she said finally. 'They laugh and joke together in Arabic. I don't call that being English, do you?'

'You're quite right,' I said.

Her arms reached out again. 'Do you wear an under-vest?' she said. It was a rhetorical question. 'It's a long time since I met a man who wears undervests.'

'I can always take it off,' I said.

'Yes, take it off.' She had probably been telling me the truth, but I knew enough about Champion not to dismiss the idea that she might be the greatest actress in the world.

I looked at her. What was she: a housekeeper, a cast-off girlfriend of Champion, a nurse brought here just to look after Billy, or a spy planted to check out what I might say in my sleep. Or did she play some other unsuspected role in this strange household where no pork was eaten, and where the night air smelled of burning incense.

I said, 'It's just that I've stopped believing in Santa Claus, reincarnation and love at first sight.'

'And which of those am I supposed to be?' she asked. 'You want me to go? If you want me to go, say so.'

'A man can suss out Santa,' I said, 'without stuffing his presents back up the chimney.'

14

The N562 road from Grasse deteriorates after Drag-
uignan. From its sharp hairpins you can see the Mediterranean on a fine day, or at least the shiny new autoroute
that swings inland at Cannes and goes past Aix and
Avignon. That – if you have the right sort of car, and
keep your foot on the floor – will take you to Paris within
five hours.

But to the north of that '*route sinueuse*' is a barren
region of scrub and rock that the French Army have
possessed since the early years of this century. There are
no autoroutes there. In fact, the local people will tell
you that there are no roads there at all, although they
themselves drive north. The raincoated policemen and
armed soldiers who huddle around the *zone militaire*
barriers wave the grey corrugated vans of the grocer, the
butcher and the baker through the cordon, except when
the gunnery ranges are in use.

Champion's black Mercedes was well known to the
sentries. Champion had a local resident's pass, for the
Tix mansion and the quarry were close to the military
zone, and the most direct route was through the barriers.

The chauffeur showed the pass to the sergeant of
gendarmerie. The sergeant leaned into the car and stared
at all three of us before handing the papers back. There
was a buzz as the window was raised, and the car rolled
forward into the military exercise zone. With a rattle of
gravel we passed over the junction of the communications
roads. Soon we reached the reinforced surface that the
army built to withstand the weight of the AMX 50s,

brought up here to 'the Atelier' for testing under battle conditions.

Even in fine weather it is a grim place. Like all such military establishments, it is an example of decades of neglect interspersed with panic spending. The buildings at the north-western tip were built by the Germans during the war. It is a walled compound, with guard towers and ditches. The emplacement area, which the US Army built in 1946, included a cinema and swimming-pool that are still in use, but a more important legacy from the Americans is the line-up of artillery stands, where the big guns are anchored during the firing trials.

The heart of the Atelier is to the south of the plateau. It is called the Valmy complex. It was built in 1890, and the name of the great victory for French artillery is carved in stone above the main entrance. It's a curious-looking place: probably designed by some architect who had waited all his life for a chance to use poured concrete, for almost every wall is curved. It stands amid the stone barracks and the metal tank-hangars like a set for some old Hollywood musical, and it's not difficult to imagine lines of dancers kicking their way along the curved balconies, tap-dancing on the prow, or poking their smiling faces out of the circular windows.

'Stop a moment,' Champion told the driver.

'They'll move us on,' he replied.

'Go and look at the plugs or something,' said Champion. He turned to me. 'Quite a place, isn't it,' he said. 'That's the research block.'

I pushed the button to lower the window. The clouds were scudding low over the superstructure of the block, tangling in the aerials to make it look more than ever like a ship at full steam.

'Real research?'

139

'Missiles, atomic artillery . . . some interesting heat-seeking ideas, and one of the best electronic counter-measures research teams in the West.'

'And what are you interested in?'

'What are *we* interested in, you mean.'

'That's it.'

Champion had his gloved hands locked together. I noticed him pinching his fingers to find the place from which the tips were missing. I wondered if it gave him pain. 'I wouldn't pass anything to the bloody Russians, Charlie.'

I didn't answer.

He looked at me to see how I'd reacted to his promise about not working for the Russians, but I didn't react in any way. Champion wiped the back of his glove across his mouth as a child might after an indiscretion. 'The Arabs will pay for the best anti-aircraft defence that can be bought . . . defensive weapons, Charlie . . . you've been good not to ask before, but you deserve an explanation of what you are doing.'

'I've never had one in the past.'

Champion smiled grimly. 'No, I suppose not.'

'Fuses? Working drawings? One of the research team, is it?'

'They've taught you to think wholesale,' said Champion. 'Is that the way the department would do it?' He didn't expect an answer. He looked through the rain-specked windscreen to watch the driver prodding the engine. The bonnet closed, and Champion spoke hurriedly to provide an answer before the driver came back inside the car. 'You know what I'm trying to say, Charlie. If you've got any doubts about what I'm doing, for God's sake tell me.'

'OK.'

'Not just OK, Charles. Promise me!'

I smiled. It was not like the Champion I used to know. 'Scout's honour, you mean? Will it make you feel more secure if I say I won't betray you?' I asked him.

'Funnily enough,' said Champion irritably, 'it will.'

'I'll give you a contract,' I offered. 'And then if I shop you, you can sue me.'

Then even Champion saw how ridiculous it was to seek assurances from men who were professional betrayers. 'You killed the men at the quarry,' he said. 'Admit it!'

The driver opened the door and got in. I nodded.

The car turned away from the Valmy complex, and took the main road west. There is a large hotel only ten miles down the road. Crowded into the smoke-filled bar there were civilians from the administration and from the laboratories. In the restaurant sat a few off-duty artillery officers in uniform eating lunch. Three of them had wives and children with them.

Champion pushed his way through the noisy men at the bar and ordered drinks. He had dressed to be inconspicuous here – a short brown leather jacket and a stained hat. He made some joke to the bartender and the man smiled. We took our drinks to a battered wooden table under the window, and an old woman put a checked tablecloth on it and set the cutlery for four. She gave a nod of recognition to Champion. We had come a long way round by road, but as the crow flies Champion was almost a neighbour.

'One of the lab workers will be here,' said Champion. 'An old-time Communist, he thinks I make regular trips to Moscow. Don't disillusion him.'

'I'll try not to.'

'The test firings begin next week. He'll let you have whatever he can get hold of, but we might have to lean on him.'

The waitress brought three beers, and the menu. Champion tapped the plastic menu on the edge of the table and said to me, 'Remember what I told you, Charlie. I'm trusting you.'

I reached for my beer and drank some. It seemed unlikely that Champion trusted me, for he'd told me countless times that a spy should trust no one.

Champion stared at the menu. '*Choucroute!* It's a long time since I last had *choucroute garni*,' he said. He pursed his lips as if he was already tasting it. But he didn't order sauerkraut, he had fillet steak and imported asparagus.

15

It was my idea that Gus – Champion's contact in the Valmy depot – should get a local contractor's pass for me. He had doubts about it, but the application went through within seven days and they gave me the pass the following Monday. With it I was able to crisscross the whole military zone. Providing Gus came down to the door of the administration block, I was also permitted to enter the buildings there.

From the top floor I saw the flash of the guns far away on the other side of the range, and I could look down to the bottom of the old fault on the edge of which Valmy was built. On the firing days, yellow helicopters scoured the range for warheads and the striped dummy atomic shells. They clattered across the rift to deliver the target-graphs to the administration block's front lawn – that is to say, the wind-scoured piece of scrubland where stood two ancient field guns, an old missile ramp, and a sign saying 'No Admittance'.

'The French are being very co-operative,' said Schlegel.

'Too bloody co-operative,' I said. 'When that pass came through within seven days, this fellow Gus couldn't talk about anything else.'

Schlegel stopped pacing up and down and looked at me. He recognized other unspoken criticisms in my voice.

'We've got to keep in contact,' said Schlegel defensively. 'And this was the only place.'

I didn't pursue the argument. Schlegel was right. He looked at his watch. 'Mustn't keep you too long, or our friend Champion might wonder where you are.' He put the papers that Gus had given me into my document case and clicked the locks closed. 'Worthless,' he pronounced. 'If Champion can sell that to the Arabs, he deserves every penny he gets!'

'A dummy-run perhaps. Just to see if I'm going to blow the works.'

'What for?' said Schlegel. 'Who needs you, one way or the other? Why try to convince you that he trusts you – where's the percentage?'

'That's right,' I agreed.

'Now don't go all hurt on me. Champion doesn't need you, or any other cut-out. He's met Gus – Gus knows his face – Jesus! It doesn't make sense, does it?'

I blew my nose. Then I walked over to the window and looked down at the other buildings. I was suffering the first symptoms of influenza, and the weather promised nothing but thunder and lightning and endless torrents of rain. I put my hands on the radiator and shivered.

'Come away from that window, bird-brain,' said Schlegel. 'You want your pal Gus to see you?'

'It *could* make sense,' I said, moving away from the window. 'It would make sense, if there was something very big coming up. Something that the French don't want to talk about.'

Schlegel pulled a horrified face and waved his flattened hands at me to warn me to stop.

'I know, I know, I know!' I said. I looked round at the soft furnishings, the hand-tinted portraits of nineteenth-century generals and the faded plastic flowers. Such a reception room – in such a place – was sure to have electronic plumbing, but I continued anyway. 'If they are putting something really important through the Atelier in the near future, Champion will get his hands on it.'

Schlegel shrugged at what most people in the department would have considered a major breach of security.

144

'Not if our pal Gus goes into the cooler. That's the way they'd reason.'

'And perhaps that's the way Champion hopes they will reason.'

Schlegel sucked his teeth in a gesture that was as near as he ever came to admiration. 'You have your lucid moments, fella. For a Brit, I mean.' He nodded. 'You mean he might have *two* contacts here.'

'Champion was brought up on second network techniques.'

'Well, you should know. You were with him, weren't you.' He walked over to the plastic flowers, took one and snapped its petals off one by one, tossing them into an ashtray. 'There are still some questions, though.' He looked down at the broken pieces of plastic that remained in his hand and dropped them as if they were red hot. 'I'm trying to give up smoking,' he said. 'It's tough!'

'Yes,' I said.

Schlegel pulled a face, trying not to sneeze; sneezed, and then wiped his nose carefully. He went over to the radiator to see if the heat was on. It wasn't. 'You want to give me one of those aspirins? I think maybe I'm getting your virus.'

I gave him two tablets. He swallowed them.

He said, 'Champion has been made a colonel in the Egyptian Army.'

I stared at him in disbelief.

'It's true,' he said. 'It's not promulgated, or even distributed, but it's official all right. You know how these army chiefs like to get their claws into promising sources.'

I nodded. The army would want to get the allegiance of a man like Champion, rather than let his reports go back to the politicians. Giving him a colonelcy was a simple way of doing it.

'A colonel of the propaganda division, with effect from

January the tenth.' Schlegel folded his handkerchief into a ball and pummelled his nose with it, as if trying to suppress another sneeze. 'Propaganda division! You think that could be on the level? You think this could all be a propaganda exercise?'

'Propaganda? A sell so soft that it's secret, you mean?' I asked sarcastically.

'He's not through yet,' said Schlegel, with some foreboding.

'That's true,' I said.

'You'd better move,' said Schlegel. 'I know Champion likes you back there in time to dress for dinner.'

'You're a sarcastic bastard, Colonel.'

'Well, I'm too old to change my ways now,' he said.

There was a tiny mark on Schlegel's face, where I had punched him in the fracas at Waterloo Station. 'That other business . . .' I said.

'My Waterloo,' said Schlegel. He smiled his lopsided smile, and explained, 'That was Dawlish's joke.'

'It wasn't like me,' I said apologetically.

'Funny you should say that,' said Schlegel. 'Dawlish said it was *exactly* like you.'

16

'So this is the south of France?' I said, as the servant took my coat. Champion leaned forward in his big wing armchair, and reached for a log. He placed it upon the fire before looking up at me. The logs were perfect cylinders cut from young trees, a degree of calculation that extended to everything in the house. The three matching antique corner cupboards, with their japanned decoration, fitted exactly to the space outside the carpet, and the colours harmonized with the painting over the fireplace and with the envelope card table. It was the sort of home you got from giving an interior decorator a blank cheque. After a lifetime of bedsitters and chaotic flats I found the calculated effect disconcerting. Champion had the whisky decanter within arm's reach. That morning it had been full. Now it was almost empty.

Billy was full-length on the floor, drawing monsters in his animal book. He got to his feet and advanced upon me with an accusing finger.

'The fishes can't *hear* when you call them.'

'Can't they?' I said.

'No, because they have no ears. I spent hours and hours today, calling to the fishes, but Nanny says they can't hear.'

'So why do they follow me?'

'My nurse says you must have thrown bread into the pond.'

'I hope you didn't tell her I did, because she gets angry if I don't eat all my bread.'

147

'Yes, I know,' said Billy wistfully. 'I won't tell her, you needn't worry.'

Champion was watching the exchange. He said, 'You'll give him a complex.'

'What's a complex?' Billy said.

'Never mind what it is,' said Champion. 'You go with Nurse now, and I'll come up and say goodnight.'

Billy looked at me, and then at his father, and back to me again. 'I'd like a complex,' he said.

'Don't worry, Billy,' I said. 'I know a man who can get them wholesale.'

There was a discreet tap at the door. Topaz entered. She wore a white apron. Her face had no make-up, and her blonde hair was drawn tight into a chignon high on the back of her head. I knew it was what she always wore when giving Billy his bath but it made her look like some impossibly beautiful nurse from one of those hospital films.

She nodded deferentially to Champion, and smiled at me. It was the same warm friendly smile that she gave me whenever we saw each other about the house, but she had not visited my room since that first night together.

Love has been defined as 'a desire to be desired'. Well, I'd been in love enough times to think it unlikely that I was falling in love with Topaz. And yet I knew that curious mixture of passion and pity that is the essence of love. And, in spite of myself, I was jealous of some unknown man who might deprive her of this exasperating composure.

I looked at Champion and then I looked back to her, always watchful for a hint of their relationship. But the secret smile she gave me was more like the *rapport* two sober people share in the presence of a drunken friend.

'Come along, Billy,' she said. But Billy did not go to

her; he came to me and put his arms round me and buried his head.

I crouched down to bring our faces level. Billy whispered, 'Don't worry, Uncle Charlie, I won't tell her about the bread.'

When Billy had finally said goodnight and departed, Champion walked round to the table beside the sofa. He opened the document case I'd brought from Valmy, and flicked his way through it with superficial interest. 'Crap,' he said. 'The same old crap. I'll look at it later. No need to lock it away upstairs.'

'Does Gus know that it's crap?' I said.

'It makes him feel he's part of the class struggle,' said Champion.

'He won't feel like that if he gets ten years for stealing secrets.'

'Then you don't *know* him,' said Champion. 'I fancy that's his most cherished dream.'

'What's for dinner?'

'She's doing that bloody *tripes à la mode* again.'

'I like that.'

'Well, I don't,' said Champion. 'Don't you ever think about anything but food? How about a drink?'

'You do that journey up the road to Valmy three times a week, in that little Fiat, and maybe you'll start thinking about it, too.' I waved away the decanter he offered.

'All right. You think it's a waste of time seeing Gus. But we'll need Gus soon – really need him – and I don't want him getting a sudden crisis of conscience then.'

'This is just to implicate him?'

'No, no, no. But I don't want him picking and choosing. I want a regular channel out of that place. I'll sort it out when it gets here.'

'Dangerous way of buying crap,' I said.

'For you, you mean?'

'Who else?'

'Don't worry your pretty little head. If they are going to clamp down, I'll hear about it. I'll hear about it before the commandant.' He gave me a big self-congratulatory smile. I'd never seen him really drunk before, or perhaps until now I'd not known what to look out for.

'Well, that's wonderful,' I said, but the sarcasm didn't register upon him.

He said, 'You should have seen Billy this afternoon. Ever seen those toy trains the Germans do? They sent a man from the factory to set it up: goods wagons, diesels, restaurant cars and locomotives – it goes right around the room. Locomotives no bigger than your hand, but the detail is fantastic. We kept it a secret – you should have seen Billy's face.'

'He wants his mother, Steve. And he needs her! Servants and tailored clothes and model trains – he doesn't give a damn about any of that.'

Steve furrowed his brow. 'I'm only doing it for the boy,' he said. 'You know that.'

'Doing what?'

He drained his Scotch. 'He wants his mother,' he repeated disgustedly. 'Whose damn side are you on?'

'Billy's,' I said.

He got to his feet with only the slightest hint of unsteadiness, but when he pointed at me his hand shook. 'You keep your lousy opinions to yourself.' To moderate the rebuke, Champion smiled. But it wasn't much of a smile. 'For God's sake, Charlie. She gets me down. Another letter from her lawyers today . . . they accuse me of kidnapping Billy.'

'But isn't that what you did?'

'Damn right! And she's got two ways of getting Billy back – lawyers or physical force. Well, she'll find out that I can afford more lawyers than she can, and as for physical force, she'd have to fight her way through my army to get here.' He smiled a bigger smile.

'He wants his mother, Steve. How can you be so blind?'

'Just do as you're told and keep your nose clean.'

'*Tripes à la mode*, eh,' I said. 'I like the way she does that. She puts calves' stomach and ox-foot in it, that's what makes the gravy so thick.'

'Do you want to make me sick!' said Champion. 'I think I shall have a mushroom omelette.' He walked round the sofa and opened the document case. He shuffled through the Xerox copies that Gus had made at considerable risk. This second look at them confirmed his opinion. He tossed them back into the case with a contemptuous Gallic 'Pooof!' and poured the last of the Scotch into his glass.

I was surprised to find how much his contempt annoyed me. Whatever Champion felt about my fears, and Gus's motives, we deserved more for our pains than that.

'Yes,' I said. 'She puts those garlic croutons into the omelettes. Perhaps I'll have one of those as a starter.'

17

Thursday was a free day for me. I spent it in Nice. That morning I walked slowly through the market, smelling the vegetables, fruit and flowers. I ate an early peach, and put a blue cornflower in my buttonhole. From the market it was only a stone's throw to Serge Frankel's apartment. He was not surprised to see me.

'We'll have coffee,' he said. He ushered me into the study. It was in the usual state of chaos. Valuable stamps were scattered across his desk, and there were piles of the old envelopes that I had learned to call 'covers'. Catalogues, their pages tagged with coloured slips of paper, were piled high on a chair, and some were placed open, one upon the other, alongside the notebooks on his desk.

'I'm disturbing you.'

'Not at all, my boy. I'm glad of a break from work.'

I looked round the room, carefully and systematically. I tried to be discreet about it but there could be no doubt that Serge Frankel knew what I was doing. He waited for me to speak. I said, 'Aren't you frightened of burglars, Serge? This stuff must be worth a fortune.'

He picked up some creased stamps that he'd lined up under the big magnifier. Using tweezers, he put them into a clear paper packet and placed a small weight upon them. 'This is only a small percentage of what I have. A dealer has to keep his stock circulating to prospective customers.' He plugged the coffee-pot into a wall socket. 'I can give you cream today. It will make up for last time.'

'Is Steve Champion still buying?' I said.

The telephone rang before Frankel could answer my question. He answered the call, 'Serge Frankel,' and then before the caller could get launched into a long conversation, he said, 'I have someone with me at present, and we are talking business.' He watched the coffee-pot and interjected a few laconic and noncommittal words and a farewell. The coffee-pot was bubbling by the time he rang off. 'A stamp dealer faces a thousand problems,' he said. 'One or two of them are philatelic but at least nine hundred and ninety are simply human nature.'

'Is that so?'

'This woman, for instance,' he made fastidious movements with his fingers to indicate the telephone. 'Her husband died last month . . . a decent sort: a printer . . . well, you can hardly respond to his death by asking her if she wants to sell her husband's stamp collection.'

I nodded.

'And now,' said Frankel, 'she's phoning to explain that a Paris dealer called in to see them, was shocked to hear that her husband had died, offered to advise her on the sale, and wound up buying the whole eighteen albums for five thousand francs.' He ran his hand through his hair. 'About one quarter of what I would have given her for it. She thinks she's got a wonderful deal because her husband would never admit how much he was spending on stamps each month . . . guilty feelings, you see.'

'You get a lot of that?'

'Usually the other way about: the husband with a mistress and an apartment in the Victor Hugo to pay for. Such men tell their wives that they are spending the money on stamps. When that sort die, they leave me with the unenviable task of explaining to the widow that the stamp collection that she thought was going to pay off the mortgage, give her a world cruise and put their sons

153

through college, is just a lot of "labels" that I don't even want to buy.'

'Those collections you *are* offered.'

'Yes, dealers from Paris don't just happen by when there's a death in that sort of family. Worse, the widows so often suspect that I've been through the albums and stolen all the really valuable items.'

'A stamp dealer's life is tough,' I said.

'It's like being Cassius Clay,' he said. 'I thump this desk and proclaim that I'll take on all comers. You could walk through that door, and for all I know you might be the greatest authority on Ballons-Montes or the stamps of the Second Empire or – worse still – telegraph stamps or tax stamps. Everyone wants an instant valuation and payment in cash. I've got to be able to buy and sell from experts like that, and make a profit. It's not easy, I'll tell you.'

'Do you ever sell to Champion?' I asked.

'Last year I did. I had three very rare French covers. It was mail sent by a catapulted aeroplane from the liner *Ile de France* in 1928. It was the first such experiment. They ran out of stamps so that they overprinted the surcharge on other stamps. On these the surcharge was inverted . . . It's all nonsense, isn't it?' He smiled.

'Evidently not to Champion. What did he pay?'

'I forget now. Twenty thousand francs or more.'

'A lot of money, Serge.'

'Champion has one of the top ten airmail collections in Europe: Zeppelins, French airships, balloon mail and pioneer flights. He likes the drama of it. He doesn't have the right sort of scholarship for the classic stamps. And anyway, he's a crook. He likes to have the sort of collection he can run with, and unload quickly. A man like Champion always has a bag packed and a blank airline ticket in his pocket. He was always a crook, you know that!'

I didn't follow Serge Frankel's reasoning. It would seem to my non-philatelic mind that a mobile crook would prefer classic stamps of enormous price. And then he'd never need to pack his bag. He could carry his fortune in his wallet everywhere he went. 'You didn't tell him he was a crook in the old days,' I pointed out.

'Didn't say that when he ambushed the prison van and set me free, you mean. Well, I didn't know him in those days.' He drank the rest of his cup of coffee. 'I just thought I did.'

He brought the pot and poured more for both of us. He spooned some whipped cream on to the top of his strong coffee and then rapped the spoon against the edge of the cream jug to shake the remains off. The force of the gesture revealed his feelings. 'Yes, well, perhaps you're right,' he admitted. 'I must give the devil his due. He saved my life. I would never have lasted the war in a concentration camp, and that's where the rest of them ended up.'

'What's he up to, Serge?'

'You're out there in the big house with him, aren't you?'

'But I don't know what he's up to, just the same.'

'This oil business,' said Serge. 'It will change the lives of all of us.' He picked up the jug, and in a different voice said, 'Have some cream in your coffee?'

I shook my head. I would not provide him with another chance to move away from the matter in hand.

'I'm not a Communist any more,' he said. 'You realize that, I suppose.'

'I'd detected some disenchantment,' I said.

'Did the czars ever dream of such imperialism? Did the Jew-baiters dream of such support? The Russians have us

155

all on the run, Charles, my boy. They urge the Arabs to deny us oil, they pass guns and bombs and rocket launchers to any group of madmen who will burn and maim and blow up the airports and hijack the planes. They brief the trade unionists to lock up the docks, halt the trains and silence the factories.'

I reached for my coffee and drank some.

'Makes your throat dry, does it?' he said. 'And well it might. Do you realize what's happening? In effect we'll see a movement of wealth to the Arab countries comparable to the movement of wealth from India to Britain in the eighteenth century. And *that* generated the Industrial Revolution! The USSR has now become the biggest exporter of armaments in the world. Algeria, Sudan, Morocco, Egypt, Libya – I won't bother you with the list of non-Arab customers – are buying Soviet arms as fast as they can spend. You're asking me if I help the Israelis! Helping the Israelis might be the West's only chance to survive.'

'And where does Champion fit into this picture?'

'A good question. Where indeed! Why should the Arabs bother with a cheap tout like Champion, when all the world's salesmen are falling over each other to sell them anything their hearts desire?'

'Don't keep me in suspense.'

'Your sarcasm is out of place, my boy.'

'Then tell me.'

'Champion has promised to sell them the only thing their money cannot buy.'

'Eternal happiness?'

'A nuclear device. A French nuclear device.'

There was a silence broken only by my heavy breathing. 'How can you know that, Serge?'

Serge stared at me, but did not answer.

'And if he delivers?'

'Two hundred million pounds was mentioned.'

I smiled. 'You are taking a chance on me . . . suppose I went back to the house and told Champion . . .'

'Then either he would give up the plan – which would delight me – or he'd continue with it.' He shrugged.

'He might *change* the plan,' I said.

'I wouldn't imagine that alternative plans spring readily to mind for such a venture.'

'No,' I said. 'I suppose you are right.' I reached into my pocket, found my cigarettes and matches and took my time about lighting a cigarette. I offered them to Serge.

He waved them away. 'You haven't told me your reaction,' he said.

'I'm trying to decide whether to laugh or cry,' I told him.

'What do you mean?'

'You've been overworking, Serge. Your worries about the Arab–Israeli war, the oil crisis, your business, perhaps . . . you think that they form a pattern. You have invented a nightmare, and cast Champion as the arch-fiend.'

'And I'm right,' said Serge, but as soon as he said it, he realized that it would confirm my diagnosis. He was a lonely old man, without wife, child or very close friends. I felt sorry for him. I wanted to calm his fears. 'If Champion can steal an atomic bomb he deserves whatever it was you said he'd get.'

'Two hundred million pounds was mentioned,' said Serge, repeating the exact words he'd used before as if it was a few frames of a film loop that never stopped running through his mind.

'Why a *French* atomic bomb?' I said. 'Why not an American or a British or a Russian atomic bomb?'

I wished I'd not asked him, for he'd obviously worked out the answer to that one long ago. 'A French nuclear *device*,' he corrected me. 'The technology is simpler. The French made their bomb unaided, it's a far simpler device, and probably less well guarded.' Serge Frankel got to his feet with all the care and concentration of the arthritic. He steadied himself by touching the windowsill where there was a brass inkstand and a carriage clock that always stood at four minutes past one o'clock. I wondered if the hands had become entangled. But Serge was looking not at the cluttered sill but through the window, and down into the street below.

The word 'probably' left me an opening. 'Now, you don't really believe that the French leave their goodies less well guarded than anyone else in the world. Now, do you, Serge?'

'I take back the less well guarded,' he said over his shoulder. From his window there was a view of the market in Cours Saleya. I went over to where he was standing, to see what he was staring at. He said, 'Any one of them could be working for Champion.'

I realized he was talking about the dark-skinned North Africans, so evident among both the sellers and the customers.

'That's right.'

'Don't humour me,' he said. 'Champion's bringing Arab cut-throats into the country by the dozen. Algerians don't even need immigration papers. It was all part of de Gaulle's sell-out to them.'

'I'd better get going,' I said.

He didn't answer. When I left he was still staring down through the window, seeing God knows what terrible scene of carnage.

As I started to descend the stone steps, I heard someone hurrying behind me from the floor above. The metal-tipped shoes echoed against the bare walls and I moved aside cautiously as he came closer.

158

'Vos papiers!' It was the age-old demand of every French policeman. I turned to see his face, and that was my undoing. He struck my shoulder, from behind. There was enough force in it to topple me and I lost my balance on the last few steps of the flight.

I didn't fall on to the landing. Two men caught me and had me pinioned against the landing window, with no breath left in my body.

'Let's have a look at him.' He gave me a sudden push to flatten me against the wall.

'Wait a minute,' said the second voice, and they searched me with the sort of precision cops achieve in towns where the favourite weapon is a small folding-knife.

'Let him go! I know who it is,' said a third voice. I recognized it as that of Claude *l'avocat*. They turned me round very slowly, as a vet might handle a fierce animal. There were four of them: three coloured men and Claude, all in plain clothes.

'It was you who phoned Frankel, was it?' I said.

'Was it so obvious?'

'Serge went into a long explanation about stamp collectors' widows.'

Claude raised his arms and let them slap against his legs. 'Serge!' he said. 'Someone must look after him, eh?'

'Is that what you're doing?'

'He has acquired a lot of enemies, Charles.'

'Or thinks he has.'

Claude looked at the French plainclothes men. 'Thank you. We'll be all right now.' He looked at me. 'We will, won't we?'

'You assaulted *me*! Remember? What are you waiting for, an apology?'

'You're right,' said Charles. He held up his hand in a gesture of appeasement. Then he indicated the way

159

through the lobby to the street. The Nice cops had given him one of their stickers and now his white BMW was askew on the pavement under a 'No Parking' sign. 'I'll give you a lift somewhere.'

'No thanks.'

'We should talk, I think.'

'Another time.'

'Why put me to all the trouble of making it official?'

I said nothing, but I got into the passenger seat of his car. The anger, despair and humiliation of Claude's wartime betrayals boiled up inside me again.

We sat in the car for a moment in silence. Claude fussed around to find his cheroots and put on his spectacles, and dabbed at his natty gent's suiting. I wondered whether he'd spoken with any of the others and whether they'd told him that I wasn't likely to congratulate him about earning his medal and his pension.

He smiled. Claude smiled too often, I'd always thought so.

'We said you'd never last,' said Claude. 'When you first appeared on the scene, we had bets that you wouldn't last out.'

'In the war?'

'Of course, in the war. You had us fooled, Charles.'

'That makes two of us.'

'*Touché.*' He smiled again. 'We thought you were too headstrong then, too direct, *trop simple.*'

'And now?'

'We soon learned that you are anything but direct, my friend. It's unusual to find a man so ready to let the world think him a clumsy unschooled peasant, while all the time his mind is processing every possible permutation for every possible situation. Headstrong! How could we have ever thought that.'

'It's your story,' I said.

160

'But in one respect our first impressions were correct,' said Claude. 'You are a worrier. *After* the event, you worry. If it wasn't for that you would have been the greatest of the great.'

'The Muhammed Ali of espionage,' I said. 'It's an attractive idea. Serge just told me he feels like the Muhammed Ali of stamps, except that he called him Cassius Clay.'

'I know you're here for your government. I'm here for the German government. We're both after Champion. We might as well co-operate.'

He looked at me, but I said nothing. He looked away from me, to where the figs, apricots and new potatoes from Morocco were on sale alongside the oranges from Jaffa. A man stole a bean and walked on chewing it. Claude looked round at me to see if I'd noticed the larceny. His reaction was too studied. It was all too studied. I doubted whether Claude had been told anything about me – he just wanted to see me at close quarters. Perhaps he reasoned that if I was still in government service, I'd have to deny it hotly, while if I now worked for Champion, I'd want Claude to think I was still official.

What he decided about me I don't know. I opened the car door, and began to get out. I said, 'I've no inclination for all this play-acting, late-night TV spy stuff. If you, and that old man up there want to re-live the great days of your youth, very well, but leave me out of it.'

'Your youth, too,' said Claude.

'My childhood,' I said. 'And that's why I don't want to repeat it.'

'Close the door,' said Claude. 'Get back in, and close the door!'

I did so. I wanted to know what Claude was going to say next, because if he really had been tipped off by his office in Bonn, this would be the time to throw the details in my face and watch it dribble down my chin.

I had to know, because if Claude knew . . . it was only a matter of time before Champion found out.

But Claude was silent.

It was lunchtime. We both watched the stall-holders folding up their stands and stacking away the unsold fruit. As each space was cleared, the motor-cars – which had been circling the Cours for the last half-hour – dashed in to park. More than once there was a bitter argument between drivers. It was a famous local amusement. Claude's strong-arm men were still standing on the far side of the market. They had bought slices of hot pizza, and were eating them while watching both Claude's car and Frankel's window.

'Are they really cops?' I asked him.

'Yes, they are cops all right. Harkis – auxiliaries who worked for the French in Algeria. They can't go home and the French don't like them.'

'You realize that Frankel is terrified of the Arabs. If you have these jokers hanging around to protect him, you are probably giving him his nightmares.'

'They keep out of sight. And are you sure Frankel is terrified of the Arabs?'

'You don't know much if you don't know that,' I said. 'Frankel, the onetime exponent of Marxism and the brotherhood of man, now comes on like . . . Goebbels.'

'A Fascist, you mean, comes on like a Fascist. Don't worry about hurting my feelings. Yes, we're all fighting a new war: the battle-lines have been drawn afresh. Frankel is a racist, I've become a champion of parliamentary government, you are working to defeat the Communists you once fought alongside, and Champion has become an active anti-Semite.'

'Has he?'

'You don't do your homework very thoroughly, Charles. He's working for the Egyptians. Are you getting too old for this business?' He smiled, and touched the hair that was carefully arranged over his almost-bald head. 'You are a strange race, you English,' he said. He searched my face, as if he might find some answer there. 'I work in security in Bonn. We turned out our files, to keep London fully informed of what we are doing. We sent the usual notification to French security before I came down here to take a closer look at Champion. The French have been very good. I have an office with the police here in town. They keep me informed, and they've let me have those Harkis to help me. But you English are so arrogant! You'll never be a part of Europe. You don't reply to our correspondence. Your people come here without proper clearance with the French. And now, when I put my cards on the table and suggest some co-operation, you adopt the superiority of manner that we've learned to expect from the English.'

'You've got it all wrong, Claude,' I told him. 'I don't work for British security. I don't work for any kind of security. I'm not concerned in your problems with London. And I'm not interested in your simplistic generalizations about the British character.'

'Champion has bribed German government officials and senior officers of the Bundeswehr, and he threatened a police officer. He has conspired to import arms into the Federal Republic, and forged official documents. Within a week or ten days he'll be arrested, and there will be no point in his running away because, with the charges we're bringing, we'll extradite him from any country of Western Europe or the USA.' A car took the corner a little too widely. The driver hooted angrily before he saw Claude's police sticker and steered away. 'Have I made myself clear?' Claude asked me.

'You've made yourself clear, all right,' I said. 'You mean you want Champion to run, or else you'll have to start putting some real evidence together. If that happens, some of those bribed officials might get angry while they're still in a position to fight back. And, in that case, you and some of your colleagues will be out of a job.'

'You're protecting Champion!' he said.

'He doesn't need any protection, Claude. You found that out in the war, when you took him down to the Rock and removed the tips of his fingers without getting a squeak out of him.'

For a moment Claude looked as if he was going to argue, but he swallowed his anger. He said, 'Champion still has that same charm, doesn't he? He had us all eating out of his hand in the war, and now he's still got you in his pocket.'

'There's something you should know, Claude,' I said sarcastically. 'I work for Champion. He pays me every month; and I work for him. Have you got that? Now write it down in your notebook and send a carbon to your office in Bonn, so they can file it in their secret archives. And make sure you put your address on it, in case they want to send you another Iron Cross.'

I fiddled with the door catch, which was designed to baffle foolhardy children. This time I opened the door and got out.

'Frankel will make an attempt on Champion's life,' said Claude. 'You tell your boss that.'

I rested one hand on the roof of the car, and leaned down to talk to Claude. He wound the window down hurriedly. 'Do you believe everything that Frankel tells you?' I asked. 'Or do you just pick out the bits you like?'

'I'm looking after the old man,' said Claude.

'Just where does your concern end, and where does house-arrest start?' I said. 'You have men outside his

164

door – dark-skinned men who terrify him – you tap his phone, and you rough-up his visitors.' I waited for Claude to deny it; but he didn't deny it.

Claude didn't want to discuss Frankel; he was interested only in Champion. He said, 'Champion is an Arab terrorist, and no matter how many times you tell me which side he fought on during the war, he'll be treated like an Arab terrorist. And he can't even claim to be some perverted form of idealist – he's in it just for the money.'

'We're all in whatever we're in for the money, Claude. I forget the last time I met an unpaid volunteer.'

I'd got as far as this without realizing that Claude had the same bitter contempt for me that I had for him. But now, as he bit his lip, I could see that Claude had not escaped the war unscathed. His wounds had come after the surrender, as he co-operated with his conquerors and learned the apartheid of crime that all German policemen had to learn during the Allied occupation, but his wounds were none the less crippling for that. 'At first I'm a Fascist, and now I'm a mercenary. And I've got to smile, and take it all the time, have I?' He brought a clenched fist down upon the car's steering wheel with enough force to break it, except that German cars were so well made and safe to drive in. 'Well, I was never a Nazi – *never*! I hated those people. But I am a German, and I did my duty then as I do it now.'

'And if you'd been living just a few miles farther east, you'd be doing your duty on behalf of the Communists, I suppose.'

Claude smiled. 'I can remember a few nights during the war when you were telling us all how much you favoured theoretical Communism.'

'Yes,' I said. 'Well, almost everyone's in favour of *theoretical* Communism. Maybe even those bastards in the Kremlin.'

18

An atlas might show Marseille and Nice as two identical dots on the map. But Marseille is a sprawling Sodom-on-Sea, complete with bidonville and race riots, a city of medieval confusion, where the only thing properly organized is crime.

Nice, on the other hand, is prim and neat, its size regulated by the niche in the hills into which it nestles. Its cops nod politely to the local madams, and Queen Victoria shakes a stone fist at the sea.

Friday's sky was blue, and the first foolhardy yachtsmen were beating their way up the coast against a chilly wind.

I went through the usual contact procedure. I phoned the sleazy little office near Nice railway station, but I would have been surprised to find Schlegel there. In his present role, I knew he'd stay well away from a small place like Nice. And well before the secretary told me that Schlegel wanted to see me urgently, I guessed he was staying with Ercole out at the restaurant – *'vue panoramique, tranquillité, et cuisine mémorable'* – because it was the one place I did not want to go.

Old Ercole would greet me with a bear-hug, and a kiss on both cheeks, and he'd talk about the old days, and look up to the wall behind the bar where his citation hung. And where a silver-framed Ercole was frozen in an endless handshake with a stern-faced General de Gaulle.

There was nothing perspicacious about that guess. It was a natural place for Schlegel to hole-up. There'd be no resident guests there at this time of year, apart from the occasional use of a private room, booked with a wink and paid for with a leer. Ercole still had top security clearance with the department, and it was not only secluded but it was as luxurious a place as Schlegel would find anywhere along this coast. Had I been a computer, I would have put Schlegel there. But I'm not a computer, and try as I may, I could never get to like old Ercole, and never get to trust him either.

It all went as I knew it would. Even the fast drive along the high Corniche – that dramatic mountain road you see behind the titles of TV documentaries about the French Miracle, just before they cut to an economist standing in front of the frozen food cabinet – even that was the same.

All of these hill villages depress me. Either they have been taken over by souvenir shops and tarted-up restaurants with the menu in German, or, like this village, they are dying a slow lingering death.

The wind had dropped. Out at sea, the sailing boats, like neatly folded pocket handkerchiefs, hardly moved. I parked alongside the defunct fountain, and walked up the village's only street. The houses were shuttered, and the paintwork was peeling and faded except for the bright red façade of the Communist Party's converted shop.

It was damned hot and the air was heavy. The cobblestones burned my feet, and the rough stone walls were hot to the touch. An Air Tunis jet passed over, obeying the control pattern of Nice. From up here, I seemed almost close enough to touch the faces of passengers peering from its windows. It turned away over the sea, and its sound was gone. In the quiet, my footsteps echoed between the walls.

A newly painted sign pointed the way to Ercole's restaurant. It was tacked to the wall of a roofless slum. From its open door a lean dog came running, followed by a missile and an old man's curse that ended in a bronchial cough. I hurried on.

Built with the stone of the mountainside, the village was as colourless as the barren hill upon which it perched. But at the summit, there was Ercole's restaurant. Its whitewashed walls could be seen through a jungle of shrubs and flowers.

From somewhere out of sight came the grunts, puffs and smacks of a tennis game. I recognized the voices of Schlegel and Ercole's grandson. There were kitchen noises, too. Through an open window came steam, and I heard Ercole telling someone that a meal was a conversation between diner and chef. I went in. He stopped suddenly as he caught sight of me. His greeting, his embrace and his welcome were as overwhelming as I feared they would be.

'I had this *feeling* . . . all *day* I had it . . . that *you* would come here.' He laughed and put his arm round my shoulder and clasped me tight. 'I *hate* this man!' he proclaimed to the world in a loud voice. 'I hate him! That he comes here, and does not come to Ercole straight away . . . what have I *done*? This is your home, Charles. You know this is your home.'

'Jesus, Ercole. What's this goddamned mouthfest?' It was Schlegel. 'Oh, there you are, kid. They said you'd phoned. All OK?'

I didn't tell him whether or not everything was OK.

'Staying to supper?'

'I'm not sure I should,' I said. 'I said I'd be back in the late afternoon.' But Ercole was going into an encore, and I decided not to get too neurotic about Champion, lest I stir up the very suspicions I was trying to avoid.

'Give us a drink, Ercole. Splice the mainbrace! Right?'

'Right,' I said, with the sort of enthusiasm I was

expected to show for Schlegel's studied forays into English idiom.

'Sure, sure, sure,' said Ercole.

I looked round the empty dining-room. Soon it would be crowded. Ercole was making money, there was little doubt about that. He'd torn down most of the old buildings and built anew, spending additional money to make it all look old again.

On the far side of the room, two young waiters were setting a table for a party of fifteen diners. The glasses were getting an extra polish, and special flowers and handwritten *table d'hôte* cards were positioned on the starched cloth.

Ercole watched them until they'd finished. 'A drink, a drink, a drink,' he said suddenly. 'Apéritif? Whisky? What is the smart thing in London now?'

'I don't know what's the smart thing in London now,' I said. And if I did know, I'd make a special point of not drinking it. 'But a *kir* would suit me very well.'

'Two *kirs*, and an Underberg and soda for the colonel,' Ercole ordered.

'Bring ours down to the pool,' said Schlegel. He stabbed me with a finger. 'And you come and swim.'

'No trunks,' I said.

'The fellow mending the filter will show you,' said Ercole. 'There are all sizes, and plenty of towels.'

I still hesitated.

'It's a heated pool,' said Schlegel. I realized that he'd chosen the pool as a suitable place for us to talk.

The drinks arrived. Schlegel changed into nylon swimming trunks patterned like leopard's fur. He timed his activities so that his running-somersault dive off the board coincided with my emergence from the changing-room in a curious pink swimming costume about two sizes too big.

Schlegel devoted his entire attention to his swimming, just as he gave undivided attention to most of the other things I'd seen him do. For me, the pool merely provided a diversion for my arms and legs, while my mind grappled with Champion. Eventually even Schlegel grew tired, and climbed out of the water. I swam across to where he was sitting. I floated in the water as he sipped his drink.

'It's a long time since I did any swimming,' I said.

'Is that what it was?' said Schlegel. 'I thought you were perfecting a horizontal form of drowning.'

'Spare me the swimming lesson,' I said. I wasn't in the mood for Schlegel's Catskill comedy. 'What is it?'

Schlegel picked up the packet of cheroots that he'd placed ready at the side of the pool. He selected one and took his time lighting it. Then he tossed the dead match into the undergrowth.

Ercole had planted quick-growing bamboo, but it was not yet tall enough to hide the little village cemetery, with its decorated family tombs, faded photos and fallen flowers. There was a small child there, she was putting flowers into a tin can and singing to herself.

It was only the middle of the afternoon, but already the mist was piling up in the valleys so that the landscape became just flat washes of colour, with no dimensions at all, like a stage backdrop.

'Cu-nim. We'll have a whole week of this,' Schlegel predicted. He sniffed the air with an aviator's nose and looked respectfully at the clouds.

I waited.

Schlegel said, 'There's a Panamanian freighter coming in to Marseille from Alexandria tomorrow night. Dangerous cargo wharf. Five articulated trucks will be there to load. Those trucks belong to the Tix outfit – Champion's trucks, in other words . . .' He puffed on the cheroot. 'Know anything about that?'

'No,' I said. 'But if it worries you, get the dock police to turn it all over.'

He shook his head. 'Uh-uh-uh! Diplomatic cargo. Going to the embassy in Bonn. It will be sealed. Breaking into that baby and finding anything less than Hitler seated at the Wurlitzer is a sure-fire way to get yourself busted. That cargo has exactly the same protection as a diplomatic bag.'

I related my conversations with Serge Frankel and with Claude.

'And now you're going to start telling me that Champion is going to stash a nuclear bomb into those trucks,' said Schlegel.

'I'm just telling you what Frankel said,' I told him. 'Do we know the route the trucks will take?'

'Don't mastermind me, bubblebrain,' said Schlegel. 'We're checking out all likely targets along the routes. Including airfields where nukes are stored,' he added. 'But Champion is not after a nuke.'

'How can you be so sure?'

'Nah! If you'd ever seen a nuke, you'd know why. They bring those cookies in on freight cars, shielded with lead, and crawling with guys in protective clothing . . . and even if Champion got his hands on one, what does he do – take off down the road in an articulated truck?'

'Threatening to detonate it,' I offered.

'You've got a nasty overdose of Serge Frankel,' he said. 'For all we know, he's in this with Champion.'

'Frankel's a Jew,' I protested.

'Spare me the schmaltz, buddy: my violin is in my other pants. If your pal Champion was planning to hijack canned pork, I wouldn't eliminate the chief rabbi.'

'If Champion was planning to hijack tinned pork,' I said patiently, 'we wouldn't have to worry about the Arabs dropping it on Tel Aviv.'

171

'But how would they move a bomb?'

'Steal a loaded bomber?'

He stared at me. 'You are determined to lay this theory on me, aren't you?' He kicked the water, very hard, with his heel. It splashed all over me.

'It's the only theory I've got,' I said. I wiped the splashes from my face.

'Bombers loaded with atomic weapons are guarded like . . .' Unable to find a comparison, Schlegel shook his head. 'I'll do the necessary,' he promised. 'The people who guard nukes scare easily.'

'I know the feeling,' I said.

Schlegel nodded. 'Come into town Sunday morning, when Champion goes to Mass. I'll see you at the port – Ercole's cabin-cruiser: the *Guilietta*. Right?'

'I'll do my best.'

'Let's hope the smoke's clearing by then,' he said. He wrapped his sunglasses and cigars in his towel and gave them to me. 'You want to take my stuff round the pool while I swim back?' Schlegel gave orders in the American style, as if politely inquiring about certain aspects of obsessional behaviour. I didn't answer him and I didn't take his towel.

'There's something else you want?' said Schlegel.

'I want Melodie Page's reports, contacts and sheets – anything, in fact – for the month before she died. I want to look at it for myself.'

'Why? Of course you can have it, but why?'

'Murdering the girl was the only hurried and uncharacteristic move Champion has made so far. Something must have panicked him, and it might be something that the girl discovered.'

Schlegel nodded. 'Anything else?'

'See what you can find out about this Topaz kid.'

'OK,' said Schlegel. He pushed the towel into my hand

172

and dived into the water, leaving barely a ripple. He swam underwater, turning his head only enough to bite air. I envied him. Not only the ability to swim like a basking shark, but also for his jet-jockey readiness to press buttons, pull triggers and dive into the deep end of life, while people like me drown in indecision, imagined loyalties and fear. If Champion was yesterday's spy, Schlegel was tomorrow's. I can't say I looked forward to it.

By the time I started walking round the pool, Schlegel had taken a fresh towel from the rack and disappeared into a changing-room. I took my time. The sun was moving behind the hill-tops, so that the landscape was turning mauve. But high in the stratosphere, a jetliner caught the sun's rays and left a contrail of pure gold. In the cemetery the little girl was still singing.

'Did you enjoy the duck?' said Ercole proudly.

'One of these days,' said Schlegel, 'I'm going to fix you one of my special cheeseburgers. With all the trimmings!'

For a moment Ercole was taken aback. Then he roared, 'I hate you, I hate you,' and kissed Schlegel on the cheek.

'That'll learn you, Colonel,' I said softly.

Schlegel smiled bravely while Ercole placed a large piece of goat's cheese on a crust of bread, but stopped smiling when Ercole put an arm-lock on him and forced it into his mouth. 'It's not possible that a man won't eat a fine cheese like this,' shouted Ercole. 'I make it myself – with my own hands.'

It was in Schlegel's mouth by now, and he pulled a face as he tasted its sharp flavour.

Louis – Ercole's grandson – watched the cameo, disapproval showing clearly on his face. He was in his late teens, dressed in the dark well-cut suit that befitted the heir to a gastronomic mecca, but it was difficult to imagine him presiding over it with the sort of passion that his Falstaffian grandpa never failed to show.

Ercole leaned back in his chair and sipped a little of the vintage Burgundy. He turned to Schlegel. 'Good?' he asked Schlegel finally.

'Wonderful,' said Schlegel, without conviction.

Ercole nodded. It was enough.

We dined that night in Ercole's office. It was large enough to hold a table and half a dozen chairs, as well as the tiny desk at which he did his paperwork. The office was a glass-sided box situated between the dining-room and kitchen, and providing a clear view of both. Such a 'cash-control booth' was not unusual in large restaurants, but perhaps only Ercole's was walled with the mirrored-glass exterior that provided such privacy.

We could see the whole dining-room and kitchen, but the clients and staff saw only their own reflections. We watched a bearded boy walk from table to table, holding aloft carefully drawn landscape sketches. He said nothing, nor did his expression change. Few people for whom he displayed his work granted him more than a casual glance before continuing their meal and their conversation. He moved on. It was a sad society, in which all these property salesmen, plastics executives and car rental tycoons could not only humiliate this boy, but inure him to it.

I asked Louis to purchase a drawing for me. It cost no more than a bottle of Ercole's very cheapest wine.

'Have you gone off your trolley?' asked Schlegel, with no more than passing interest.

'It's a good drawing,' I said.

'At least you can tell which way up it's supposed to be,' said Schlegel. He took it from me and examined it, and then looked through the mirror-glass to see the artist. 'Well, now he'll be able to buy himself some soap,' he said.

174

'What's so special about soap?' I said. 'Why can't he buy himself some food and wine?'

Schlegel didn't answer, but Louis smiled approvingly and was emboldened to ask me a question. 'Is that Ferrari yours?' His voice was almost a whisper, but it was not so quiet that Ercole didn't hear. He'd moved his chair so that he could watch the restaurant. He answered without turning his head.

'Table twenty-one,' he said. 'The flashy fellow with the open-neck shirt. He arrived in the Ferrari. I wish now I'd made him put the tie on. They both had the hundred-franc menu. He owns a handbag factory near Turin – she's his secretary, I should think.' He took a long look at her, sniffed, and jerked a thumb at Louis. 'Cars and football: that's all this one thinks about.'

'But you said Louis prepared the duck,' I protested.

Ercole reached forward and ruffled his grandson's hair. 'He's not a bad boy, just a bit wild, that's all.'

We were all too polite to remark that the boy's conservatively tailored suit, and deferential whispers, made it difficult to believe. But already Ercole's attention was elsewhere. 'Table nineteen have been waiting hours for their coffee. Tell that fool Bernard to pull himself together.' As Louis slipped quietly away, Ercole said, 'Or you do it.' He didn't take his eyes from the restless people at table nineteen for more than a few seconds at a time but he was able to continue talking as if using some different part of his brain. 'You know what the theory of relativity is?'

'You tell me,' Schlegel invited.

'Bernard's let those two tables in the corner get to the fish course at the same time. They all want it off the bone. Now, for Bernard, the minutes fly like seconds. While for those people who asked for coffee three, perhaps four, minutes ago each minute seems like an hour.'

'So that's the theory of relativity?' said Schlegel.

'That's it,' said Ercole. 'It's a miracle that Einstein discovered it, when you remember that he wasn't even a restaurateur.'

Schlegel turned to follow Ercole's gaze. 'That guy's impatience is nothing to do with Einstein,' he argued. 'With a plug-ugly broad like that facing you, *every* minute seems like an hour.'

It was Louis who served the coffee to them. He did it well, but he didn't once look at the people he served.

'And the special hand-dipped chocolates,' remarked Ercole approvingly, after Louis had sat down with us again. 'She'll gobble her way through them, just watch. Did you notice her ask for a second portion of the *profiteroles*?'

'Are you going to the football match on Sunday morning?' Louis undid the lace of one shoe and rubbed his foot. He lacked the stamina of the professional waiter.

'He's staying out at Champion's house,' said Ercole.

'Yes, I know,' said the boy. I saw contempt in the glance he gave the old man.

'I think I might have a morning in bed,' I said.

'No Mass for these heathens,' said Ercole.

'It's just a friendly match for charity,' said the boy. 'Really not worth the journey. But next month it will be a good one.'

'Perhaps I'll come next month, then,' I said.

'I'll send you tickets,' said the boy, and seemed strangely pleased at my decision.

19

Compliant with Schlegel's prediction, the next few days brought perfect spring weather. When Sunday morning came, there was a clear blue sky and hot sun. I went into Nice with Champion, and Billy decided that he would come too. The chauffeur stopped outside St François de Paule. Billy asked why I wasn't going with them to Mass, and I hesitated, searching for a reply.

'Uncle has an important meeting,' said Champion.

'Can I go too?' said Billy.

'It's a private meeting,' Champion explained. He smiled at me.

'I'll leave my coat,' I said, anxious to change the subject. 'The sun is warm.'

'See you later,' said Champion.

'See you later,' said Billy, but his voice was almost lost in the pealing of church bells.

There was a rehearsal in progress at the opera house across the road. A few bars from Verdi's 'Requiem' were repeated over and over. The red carpet was laid for the 'Caisse', but in the shabby doorway marked 'Paradis', a policeman barred the way.

I cut through the market. It was crowded with shoppers, and with country people in their well-brushed black suits, black dresses and shawls, arguing over cages of rabbits and chickens and snails and brandishing brown eggs.

Out at sea, a yachtsman hopefully hauled upon an orange-striped spinnaker as he was passed by a ketch. The sea still had the milkiness of winter, but the surface was calm. The waves lapped the shingle with no more than a gentle slap, and disappeared with a deep sigh of despair.

There is always a blustery wind around the great hillock of rock under which the port of Nice shelters. There was everything there, from a sailing dinghy to tramp steamers moored close to the cranes. The quayside was piled high with pale-yellow timber, and on the far side of the water I saw the *Giulietta* tied up along with half a dozen yachts and cruisers. There was no sign of Schlegel on its deck.

The main port of Nice is not the sort of place where you see the fancy yachts double-parked, with film stars dining *al fresco* on the poop deck, and borrowing a cup of caviare from the tycoon next door. This is a strictly business-only mooring, the Club Nautique is another call. But for a Sunday morning, it was unusually crowded: a dozen men stood around a Peugeot van, and watched two frogmen having their equipment checked. The metal barriers that divide the car-parking area had now been rearranged to cordon off the quay, and a uniformed policeman guarded the only gap in it.

'Where are you going?'

'A little walk,' I said.

'Little walk somewhere else,' said the cop.

'What's happening?' I said.

'Did you hear me? Get going!'

I walked, but kept to the other side of the fence until I came to some other spectators. 'What's happening?' I asked.

'A body, I should think,' said a woman with a shopping bag. She didn't look round to see who'd asked, in case she missed something.

'A suicide?'

'Off one of the yachts,' said another man. He was dressed in an orange-and-yellow yachtsman's wind-cheater, with a heavy-duty zip in bright red.

'Some millionaire, or his fancy piece,' said the woman. 'On drugs, probably – an orgy, perhaps.'

'I'll bet they are Germans,' said the man in the wind-cheater, anxious lest the woman's fancies should be so elaborate as to eliminate his own prejudices. 'Germans can't hold their drink.'

The officious policeman came back to where we were standing. 'Move on,' he said.

'Move on yourself, you dirty pig,' said the woman.

'I'll put you into the van,' said the policeman.

'You ponce,' said the woman. 'What could you do with me in the back of the van?' She let out a cackle of dirty laughter and looked round at the rest of us. We all joined in, and the policeman went back to the barrier.

The unity of our gathering thus demonstrated, a hitherto silent member of the crowd was encouraged to speak. 'They think it's a tourist,' he said. 'Tangled in the anchor ropes of one of the boats – the *Giulietta* or the *Manxman* there – they think he went in during the night. The frogmen will soon get him.'

'It will take them an hour,' said the man in the yachting-jacket.

Yes, I thought, it will take them an hour. I moved away from the spectators, and walked slowly up the steep connecting street to the Boulevard de Stalingrad.

Everywhere seemed closed, except for the bakers across the street and a large café, its name, 'Longchamps', in white plastic letters on a hand-painted acid-green background. The floor was cleared, as if for dancing, or a bout of bare-fist fighting. There were a dozen or more customers, all men, and none of them dressed well enough for Mass. In a far corner, a man in a booth accepted bets, and all the while the customers were prodding the racing papers, writing out slips and drinking pastis.

I ordered a cognac, and drank it before the girl behind the bar replaced the cap on the bottle.

'That's an expensive way to satisfy a thirst,' she said. I nodded, and she poured a second one. This one I took more slowly. The radio music came to an end and a weather forecaster started a lot of double talk about areas of high pressure. The woman switched it off. I sipped my brandy.

A man came up, put a one-franc coin into the machine on the counter and got a handful of olives. 'Have one,' he offered. It was Schlegel.

I took one without comment but my eyes must have popped.

'Thought they were untangling me from an anchor chain, did you?'

'Something like that,' I said.

Schlegel was wearing native costume: stone-coloured golf-jacket, dark pants and canvas shoes. 'Well, you started celebrating too soon, blue-eyes.'

'Did you ever think of wearing a black beret with that outfit?' I asked.

We took our time before moving to the quietest corner of the café, alongside a broken juke-box.

'Here's what you asked for,' said Schlegel. 'The contacts that Melodie Page made with her "running officer" and the report dated six weeks before her death.'

I opened the brown envelope and looked inside.

'She stuck with Champion – very close,' said Schlegel. 'She went with him to stamp exhibitions in Zürich and Rome. The last three cards have special exhibition cancellations, you'll notice.'

I looked at the postcards that Melodie Page had sent to her cut-out. They were the sort of thing that several aerophilately firms sell: picture postcards of the *Graf*

180

Zeppelin airship anchored at some place in South America, the *Hindenburg* airship flying over New York and a grim one that showed the same airship exploding in flames in Lakehurst in 1937. The last card was a picture of an American airship, *Macon*, sent after her return to London.

'Nothing complicated about the code,' explained Schlegel. 'She met her contact five days after the postmark date. Seven days after if the postcard was coloured.'

I went through the cards again.

Schlegel said, 'Why did she suddenly become interested in aerophilately?'

I said, 'The cards were easy to obtain. Champion likes using them to send to his collector friends. And if she's at these stamp shows, what could be more natural?'

'This couldn't be a big stamp racket, could it?' said Schlegel.

'Champion might transfer money that way. A stamp is a bit like a bearer-bond but it's not much of an investment. After all, the value has got to go up at least thirty per cent before you've covered the dealer's mark-up.'

'What about forgeries or stolen stuff?'

'No,' I said.

'How can you be sure?'

'On the scale we're talking about, it would be impossible. The word gets around. A stamp crook has to nibble a mouthful at a time. Making a halfway decent forgery of a stamp is a long expensive business. And you can't recoup by suddenly putting a hundred forged rare stamps on the market, or prices would slump to nothing. Even with genuine stamps they would. And what kind of dough are we talking about? Even in the swish Bond Street auctions you won't find many single stamps fetching more than fifty pounds sterling. That kind of swindle isn't going to meet Champion's wine bill!'

He opened his case and brought out the five-page report that the London office had sent. It was an analysis of Champion's movements, and the spending and activities of his companies, during the previous six months. Or as much as London knew of them. 'Not to be taken away,' said Schlegel, as I opened it hurriedly. He went to the counter and brought two espresso coffees. By the time he'd returned, I'd scanned it.

'Nothing there, is there?' He tapped the coffee with his spoon. 'You'd better drink that. Two brandies under is no way to face that boy, even if he's half of what you say he is.'

I drank the hot coffee, folded up his sheets of typing, and handed them back to him.

'And the trucks in Marseille?'

'They are being loaded. The manifest says engine parts, chemicals and heavy-duty plastics and fabrics. It's a diplomatic load, just as we were warned it would be.'

'Did you find out anything about the Topaz girl?'

Schlegel studied me carefully before replying. 'She's twenty-five. British subject, born in London. Only child. Doting parents to whom she writes each week. Her father is a retired research chemist, living on a small pension in Portsmouth, England. She hasn't lived at home since she first went to college in London. She graduated with honours in thermo-chemistry but she's never had a proper job. She's worked as a waitress and gas-pump attendant . . . you know the kind of thing. Seems like she's hooked on kids. Her last three jobs have been as a children's nurse. She's not a qualified nurse, of course.'

'No,' I said. 'She's a qualified thermo-chemist.'

'Oh, Jesus!' said Schlegel. 'I knew this was going to start you shovelling that Serge Frankel shit all over me. Thermo-chemists don't manufacture nukes.'

182

'No,' I said patiently. 'Thermo-chemists don't manufacture nukes. But thermo-chemistry does relate to the explosion of nukes.' I opened the manila envelope he'd given me, and I found the photo postcard of the *Hindenburg* disaster. 'And the conversion of hydrogen into helium also relates to the explosion of nukes.' I stabbed my finger at the great boiling mass of flame erupting out of the airship.

Schlegel took it from me and bent close to look at the photo, as if he might discover more there. He was still looking at it when I left.

20

The cars of Nice are mostly white, so Champion's black Mercedes was easily spotted on the Place Massena. The driver was in the car, but Champion and his son were sitting outside a café-bar under the stone arcades. Champion was drinking an apéritif, and Billy was arranging sweet-wrappers on the circular metal table-top. Billy waved when he saw me. He'd saved me two cubes of chocolate, which by now were soft, misshapen and coated with pocket-fluff.

Champion got to his feet too. They'd clearly had long enough sitting there, and he didn't offer me a drink. The chauffeur had the door open as we reached the car, and there was a discussion about whether Billy was permitted to sit in front. Billy lost and was seated between us in the back.

Champion opened the window. The sun had heated the interior enough to explain why most cars were white.

'Now don't get chocolate all over the upholstery,' said Champion. He got a handkerchief from his top pocket.

'I'll be careful,' I said.

'Not you, stupid,' said Champion. He grinned, and wiped Billy's hands and mouth.

'You can't always be sure, these days,' I said.

'Don't say that, Charlie.' He seemed genuinely hurt. 'Have I changed so much?'

'You're a tough cookie, Steve,' I told him.

'Welcome to the club,' he said. He looked to Billy to see if he was listening to us.

Billy looked up at me. 'I'm a tough cookie, too,' he told me.

'That's what I said: Billy is a tough cookie, Steve!'

Billy looked to his father to check me out. Steve smiled. 'We don't want too many tough cookies in the family,' he said, and straightened Billy's tie.

By this time we'd reached the airport turn-off. The chauffeur was overtaking the Sunday drivers creeping along the promenade. An Air France Caravelle came down alongside us, to land on the runway that runs parallel to the road. There was a roar, and a scream of rubber as its jets reversed.

Billy watched the Caravelle until it disappeared from sight behind the airport buildings. 'When will we go in an aeroplane again, Daddy?'

'One of these days,' said Champion.

'Soon?'

'Perhaps.'

'For my birthday?'

'We'll see, Billy.'

'Will Uncle Charles come too?'

'I hope so, Billy. I'm counting on it.'

Billy smiled.

The car sped on over the Pont du Var and to the toll-gate of the autoroute. Like any good chauffeur, our driver had the coins ready, and so we joined the fast-moving lane for the *automatique*. A few cars ahead of us, the driver of a VW camper tossed his three francs into the plastic funnel. The barrier tilted upwards to let the VW through. Before it dropped back into position again, a lightweight motor-cycle slipped through behind it. The long lines of cars at the other gates kept the gate-men too busy to notice the infringement.

'Young bastards!' said Champion. 'Bikes are not even *allowed* on the autoroute.'

By that time we were through the barrier, too. The two youths on the motor-cycle had pulled into the slow lane and were weaving through the traffic. The pillion passenger had a golf-bag on the shoulder, and kept turning round to be sure there was no pursuit. They were a sinister pair, both in black one-piece suits, with shiny black bone-domes and dark visors.

'That's what I mean, Steve. There was a time when you would have laughed,' I said.

He'd been watching the motor-cycle riders through the rear window, but now he turned away. 'Perhaps you're right,' he said tonelessly.

The traffic thinned. The driver pulled out to the fast lane and put his foot hard down. The car leaped forward, passing everything on the road. Champion liked speed. He smiled, and glanced triumphantly at the cars that were left behind. The motor-cyclists were the only ones who chased us. We went faster and faster still, and they kept on our tail.

I put my hand out to steady Billy as we accelerated. As I did so, Champion's face tightened with rage. The light inside the car changed dramatically. The windows frosted, one by one, as if whitewash was being poured over us. Champion's hand hit my shoulder and knocked me aside. I toppled, falling upon Billy, who let out a loud yell of protest.

Champion seemed to be hammering upon my back with all his strength, and under both of us, Billy was squashed breathless. The Mercedes rocked with a succession of spine-jarring jolts, as if we were driving over railway sleepers. I knew that the tyres had torn, we were riding on the wheel-rims. As the car struck the verge, it tilted. The driver was screaming as he fought the steering-wheel, and behind his shrill voice I heard the steady hammering noise that can never be mistaken.

186

'Down, down, down,' Champion was shouting. The car began to roll over. There was a sickening thump, and a squeal of tortured metal. The horizon twisted, and we fell upwards in a crazy inverted world. The car continued to roll, tossing us around like wet clothes in a tumble-dryer. With wheels in the air, the engine screamed, and the driver disappeared through the windscreen in a shower of splintered glass that caught the sunlight as it burst over him like confetti. For a moment the car was the right way up, but it started to roll for a second time, and now fir-tree branches, clods of earth and chopped vegetation were coming in through the smashed windows. When upside down, the car slowed, tried to get on to its side, but with a groan settled on to its roof, wheels in the air, like a dead black beetle.

If I expected hordes of rescuing Samaritans, I was to be sadly disappointed. No one came. The trees made it dark inside the narrow confines of the bent car. With great effort I extricated myself from under Champion's bloody limbs. Billy began to cry. Still no one appeared. I heard the buzz of traffic speeding past on the autoroute, and realized that we were out of sight.

I struggled with the door catch, but the car had warped enough to jam the door. I rolled over on to my back and braced my hands behind my head. Then, both feet together, I kicked. There was a sound of breaking glass and the door loosened. I clambered out. Then I got Billy under the armpits and pulled him clear.

Any last doubt I'd had about the two motor-cyclists machinegunning us was dispelled by the bullet-riddled body of Champion's driver. He was dead, shiny with bright-red blood, upon which thousands of particles of safety glass stuck, like sequins on a party dress.

'Daddy's dead,' said Billy.

I fumbled around for my spectacles and then took

Champion's limp arm and dragged him from the car. It was now an almost unrecognizable shape. There was the stink of petrol, and the loud gurgle of it pouring from the inverted petrol tank.

'Go over there and lie down, Billy.'

Champion wasn't breathing. 'Steve,' I whispered. 'Don't kid around, Steve.'

The irrational thought that Champion might be shamming was all I had to comfort me. I pushed a finger into his mouth and found his dentures. They were halfway down his throat. I tipped him face-down, and thumped him in the small of the back. Billy was staring at me wide-eyed. Champion gurgled. I hit him again, and shook him. He vomited. I dropped him flat on his face and began to pump the small of his back, using a system of artificial respiration long since discarded from the first-aid manuals. Soon I felt him shudder, and I changed the pressure to coincide with his painful inhalations.

'Where's Billy?' His voice was cruelly distorted by the absence of his dentures.

'Billy is absolutely all right, Steve.'

'Get him away from the car.'

'He's fine, I tell you.'

Champion closed his eyes. I had to lean close to hear him. 'Don't send him to wave down a car,' he mumbled. 'These French drivers will run anyone down to avoid being late for lunch.'

'He's right here, Steve.'

His mouth moved again, and I bent close. 'I said it would be like old times, didn't I, Charlie?'

21

'Don't ask me for a medical reason,' said the doctor. He finished dressing a cut on my arm. 'Let's just say that it wasn't Monsieur Champion's time to go.'

'But how sick is he now?'

'Most people would need a couple of months' convalescence. But then most people would probably have died in the smash. Most people would need an intensive-care unit, instead of sitting up in bed asking for whisky. But the police can't talk to him until next week. I told them that.'

'I'm sure he stopped breathing,' I said. 'I thought he was dead.'

'Will-power,' said the doctor. 'You see a lot of it in my job. Had he been in a depressed state, he might have died. As it is, he's probably got all manner of plans that he simply won't give up.'

'You're probably right,' I said.

'You saved his life,' said the doctor. 'I told him that. It was lucky that you were only slightly hurt. You saved him. Those damned dentures would have choked him: he wouldn't have been the first, either. Airlines tell people to remove them if there's the danger of a forced landing.'

'We've known each other a long time,' I said.

'Don't talk to him tonight,' said the doctor. 'Well, let's hope he's around to do the same thing for you some time.'

'He already has,' I said.

The doctor nodded. 'There are tablets for the pain. He'll go to sleep now, I've given him a powerful dose of sedative – big frame and very restless – I'll keep him well sedated for the next few days. I don't think we'll have to move him into the clinic.'

'And the boy?'

'He needs a good night's sleep, that's all. Children have an extraordinary recuperative facility. I don't want to give him my knock-out drops. I suggest that you give him some warmed wine with plenty of sugar in it. Nature's remedy, the grape. Better than all the chemicals.'

'Thank you, doctor.'

'Don't thank me. I am pleased to be of service. I like them, you see. The child has inherited his father's charm, hasn't he?'

'Yes, he has.'

'He made me promise you'd say goodnight to him. I told him his father's asleep. I don't think he's anxious, but . . .'

'I'll go and see him now.'

I need not have tiptoed in.

'Did you see Henry? He was covered in blood.'

'You must go to sleep, Billy.'

'Where's Daddy?'

'He's got to have a good night's sleep, the doctor said so.'

'Is Henry dead?'

It was a trap to test my story about his father. 'Yes, Billy. Poor Henry is dead, but your father is just shaken up, and you and me are just fine. So we must count our blessings.'

Billy corrected me. 'We must thank God,' he said.

'That's what I meant,' I said.

'Can I see Daddy?'

'If you want to, you can. But I thought you'd take my word for it.'

'Yes, I do,' said Billy. 'I *do* take your word for it.' He

wriggled down into his bed and put his face into his pillow. I waited for him to peep out at me. When he did, I pulled a face at him. Usually he laughed, but this time he was very serious. 'Is Aunty Nini in prison?'

Pina had always been called Nini, ever since Billy had found her real name too difficult to pronounce. 'Why, Billy?'

'For shooting Henry.'

'Who says she shot Henry?'

'I *saw* her,' said Billy. 'She was driving the motor-cycle. I saw her and she saw me.'

'It looked like her, Billy. But Aunty Nini would not shoot us; we're friends, aren't we?'

Billy nodded, and swallowed. 'It looked like her, though,' he said.

'I'll bring you a glass of wine,' I said. 'Then we'll put out the light, so that you can sleep. In the morning we'll try talking to the fishes again.'

22

'Don't switch on the light, lover man.'

Topaz was waiting in my bedroom. She'd pulled the curtains open and stood near the balcony, so that the moonlight made her hair shine like polished silver.

I moved towards her. She threw herself into my arms. 'It gives me the creeps, this house.'

'Is everything all right?'

'All right? How could it be, in this dump? Those Arabs eating couscous and watching me all the time. And Mr Champion in some sort of coma.'

'He's only under sedation,' I said. 'And I like couscous.'

'Gives me the creeps,' she said. 'This whole house gives me the creeps. If it wasn't for poor little Billy, I would have packed my bags weeks ago.' As she put her arms round me, I could feel the thinness of the white cotton dress, and I could feel that she wore nothing under it. She kissed me.

'Don't undo my shirt,' I said.

'What are you, a poof or something?'

'Some other time, Topaz,' I said. 'Right now, I've got things to do.'

She hugged me tighter, confident that she could make me see reason.

'You know enough of those English words for "go away" without forcing me to use them,' I whispered.

'I am English,' she said.

'And that's another reason,' I said.

'What have I done?' she said. 'Am I using the wrong sort of toothpaste, or something?'

'You're a doll,' I told her, 'but for the next hour I'm going to be busy.'

'Oh, an hour.' She gave me her sexiest smile, and a sigh to match. 'I might be able to last out an hour.'

'Well, don't blow a gasket,' I said, 'the steam fogs up my glasses.'

There was enough light coming from the night sky for me to see her as she smiled, and kicked off her shoes. She plumped up the pillows and sat on the bed. She kept her handbag close to her and began to rummage through its contents.

Footsteps came hurrying along the corridor outside my room. An Arab voice called softly for Billy, but there was no answer. The footsteps moved away downstairs, and I heard the call repeated somewhere down in the hall.

'They are all leaving,' said Topaz.

'Sounds like it,' I said. Now they were calling for Billy from outside in the grounds.

'I'm not involved in any of this,' she said.

'I'll see you in an hour,' I said.

'No,' said Topaz.

There was enough light to see that she was holding a small pistol. 'I thought it might be like that,' I said.

'Sit down on that little chair.'

I sat down very quickly. She gave a mocking laugh. 'What are you?' she said. 'A man or a mouse?'

'Do I have a choice?'

She looked at me for what seemed like a long time. 'I'll bet you keep your small change in a little purse.' She waved the gun to show that she didn't like the way I was leaning towards the door. Her position on the bed gave her a clear field of fire should I go to either the balcony window or the door. There was enough moonlight coming through the window to make such a dash very dangerous.

'You shouldn't have got into this one, cream bun.'

'Stay here until morning, and you'll be safe, and I'll collect one hundred thousand francs,' she explained. 'Go downstairs, and you'll be knocked unconscious, and I'll lose my money.'

'Sweet talk!' I said. 'These people pay debts with bullets.'

'You let me worry about that,' she said.

I moved. The little gold-painted chair creaked. Such chairs are not designed for sitting on.

'It will be a long night,' she said. 'It's too bad you wouldn't do it the easy way.'

'I'll get my cigarettes,' I said. I reached into my jacket for them. Topaz smiled her agreement. She had already run her hands over every place I might have hidden a gun.

I smoked my cigarette, and gave her no cause for alarm. She held the pistol as if she knew how to use it, and she'd left the room in darkness, so that if I tried to get away I would be silhouetted against the light from the balcony window or the light from the hall when I opened the door. I wasn't sure how much of this was luck, and how much of it judgement, but neither was I in a hurry to learn.

Elsewhere in the house there were sounds of movement. Footsteps came up the stairs, past the door, and returned slowly and with enough deep breathing to make me sure that Champion was being carried downstairs.

'Light another cigarette,' said Topaz.

I did as I was told. At that range its glowing ember provided her with a target that she could not miss.

What was the plan, I wondered. If the girl was going to kill me, she could have done so already. If they were going to take me with them, there was no need for her to get me into bed for the night. If she was going to delay me until morning, how would she prevent me then from giving the alarm. Holding me at gun-point was one thing, locking me up, or knocking me unconscious was another.

I wondered how much of this was Champion's idea.

'If they kill Champion, you'll be an accessory,' I said. 'And they still have the death penalty in France.'

My eyes had become accustomed to the gloom. I could see her stretched out on the bed, her hands clasped loosely in front of her. In her hands, the gun. 'I'll have a hundred thousand francs,' she said. 'You don't think I'm going to hang around here, do you?'

'The Riviera,' I said. 'Why not?'

'I've had one winter in this lousy climate and I'm not planning another. To think that I believed all that travel-poster bilge about hot sun and swimming all the year. No, mister, my future is all planned.'

'Husband?' I asked. 'Or someone else's husband?'

'You should have been on the stage,' she said. 'I don't need anyone to help me spend. Especially I don't need *men* to help me.'

'Where in the sun?' I persisted.

'Close your eyes and go to sleep,' she said, as if angry with herself for revealing too much. 'Or I'll sing out and someone will put you to sleep.'

There was the sound of heavy diesels coming slowly up the road. Topaz slid off the bed and went to the window. 'Four huge trucks,' she said. 'No, five, I mean. Really huge. They've stopped down near the lodge.'

'Use your brains, Topaz,' I said. 'We've got to get out of here.'

'You're frightened,' she said.

'You're damned right,' I said.

'I'll look after you,' she said sarcastically. 'If they were going to hurt us, they wouldn't have let me have the gun, would they?'

'Have you tried it?'

'Funny man – just don't give me an excuse, that's all.' She went back to the bed.

'Champion's badly hurt,' I told her. 'The Arabs have taken control. They are not just going to leave us here.'

'Oh, shut up.'

I chain-smoked that night, my muscles so tense that I hardly inhaled the smoke, and I don't know how many cigarettes I used before there came a soft tapping on the door.

'Topaz!' The voice was no more than a whisper but I could see Mebarki, the Algerian secretary, as he came into the room. 'Are you both there?' Already some reflex action had turned my cigarette to conceal its light behind my palm.

'Yes,' said Topaz. The man stepped forward to the bed. There was a blaze of light. I might have mistaken it for a photo-flash, except that it was a rich yellow colour, rather than a thin blue. The flash of light printed Mebarki in full colour upon the black negative of the room. He stood leaning forward, like a man digging his garden. His eyes were half closed and his lips pursed in mental, moral and physical effort. The resounding bang of the gun he held seemed to come a long time afterwards. It was followed by the sound of gun-shot buzzing round the room like angry flies. Then he pulled the second trigger.

There was a clatter as the shotgun was dropped upon the floor, and a softer noise that I later discovered to be the leather gloves he'd thrown after them. From outside came the sound of the diesel engines. They revved and then moved away, until the sound of the last truck faded.

Topaz was past help. I could see that without even switching the light on. The point-blank shotgun blasts had torn her in two, and the bed was soaked with warm blood.

196

I owed my life to a semantic distinction: had Mebarki said 'Are you both in bed?' instead of 'Are you both there?', he would, no doubt, have devoted the second barrel to me.

I reached forward gingerly to retrieve her gun, and rinsed it under the tap in a process that was as much exorcism as it was forensic science.

Poor Topaz. Even traffic casualties who have played tag in the road deserve our tears, but I could find none. In Portsmouth two would grieve, each Sunday morning of their final years marred by long bus rides to a chilly cemetery.

Armed only with the little pop-gun that the Arabs had given Topaz, and equipped with a torch from beside my bed, I went through the house.

Billy's room was empty, but I threw some of his clothes into a canvas bag and hurried down to the back door and went outside. I moved quickly and spoke softly: 'Billy! Billy!' There was no response. I went round past the kitchen door until I got to the fish pond. 'Billy! It's Uncle Charlie.'

There was a long silence, and when an answer came it was no more than a whisper. 'Uncle Charlie.' Billy was behind the summerhouse from which we played our games of calling to the fish. 'Is that you, Uncle Charlie?'

'Were you banging the doors, Billy?'

'It was those men – did you see the big lorries? They made the doors bang twice.'

'That's all right, then,' I said. 'As long as it wasn't you.' I picked him up. He was dressed only in his thin pyjamas. I felt him shivering. 'We must hurry, Billy.'

'Are we going somewhere?'

'Perhaps Aunty Nini will take you to England. Take you to Mummy.'

'For always?'

'If you want.' Keeping off the gravel path, I carried Billy down to the copse where I'd left the Fiat under the trees.

'Promise?'

'You know I'll try.'

'Daddy says that when he means no.' Billy put both arms round my neck. 'Aunty Nini shot Henry,' he said.

'But only in the game,' I said.

'Was it?' he said, coming fully awake and staring at me.

'You and I always play jokes on Sunday,' I reminded him. 'There was the man trapped inside the fire extinguisher, and the toy rabbit who hid . . .'

'And the fishes you talked to.'

'There you are,' I said.

'Daddy will be awfully cross about the car,' said Billy.

'That's why he went to bed,' I explained. 'I've had to promise to mend it.'

'Oh dear,' said Billy with a deep sigh. 'But I'll help you, Uncle Charlie.'

I found the Fiat parked where I had left it. I unlocked the front door and put Billy inside. As I looked back towards the house I saw a light shine from one of the upstairs windows. I got into the car and closed the door without slamming it. Another light shone from the upstairs windows of the house. I was beginning to understand how they worked now: someone had come back to sweep up the remains.

I started the Fiat. 'Hold tight, Billy!' I said. 'This might be a rough ride!' The car careered over the rutted tracks.

'Yippee! Are you going to drive right across the back fields?' said Billy excitedly.

'Yes,' I said. 'It's so dull always going out through the front gate.'

23

There was a bright moon, but cloud was building up with every sign that the promised storms would arrive by morning. I kept up a good speed on the dry moonlit roads. I took my own route into Nice rather than follow the obvious one. I crossed the River Var high up, leaving behind the chic region where wealthy psychiatrists throw poolside parties for pop-groups.

East of the Var is another landscape. Routiers and quarrymen work extra time to buy a few hundred breeze blocks for raw little villas, that squat upon steep hillsides and at the weekends excrete small cars. In record time we were at St Pancrace. I raced through the empty streets of the northern suburbs and along the Boulevard de Cessole to the station. From there it was only two minutes to the Rue de la Buffa where Pina Baroni lived.

I found a parking place near the Anglican church. It was still only about one A.M., but as the sound of the Fiat's motor faded there was not a sound or a movement in any direction.

Pina lived on the fourth floor of a new apartment block, at the fashionable end of the Rue de la Buffa. Across the street was Pina's boutique. Its neighbours included two foreign banks, a poodle-clipper and the sort of athletic club that turns out to be a sun-lamp salon for fat executives.

In the moonlight the white marble entrance was as bright as day. The foyer was all tinted mirror, concealed lighting and locked glass doors, with a light behind the intercom and a thief-proof welcome-mat. 'It's Charlie,' I said. The door opened with a loud click, and a sign lighted to tell me to push the door closed behind me.

Pina was dressed as if ready to go out. 'Charlie – ' she began, but I shook my head, and at the sight of Billy she bent down to him. 'Darling Billy,' she said, and embraced him tightly enough to squeeze the breath from his body.

'Aunty Nini,' he said dutifully, and stared at her thoughtfully.

'He got his feet wet,' I told her. 'He went down to talk to the fishes in his pyjamas.'

'We'll give you a hot bath, Billy.'

'These are clean pyjamas and underclothes and things,' I said. I indicated the bag I'd brought.

'Your Uncle Charlie thinks of everything,' said Pina.

'But always a bit too late,' I said.

As if anxious to avoid talking to me, Pina took Billy into the bathroom. I heard the water running, and Pina came out and fussed about with clean sheets and pillow-cases for the spare bed.

'I want you to take him to England, Pina. Take him back to Caty.'

Pina looked at me without answering. 'Hot milk or cocoa?' she called loudly. 'Which would you like, Billy?'

'Cocoa, please, Aunty Nini.'

'I can't,' said Pina.

'It's all over, Pina,' I said. 'Even now I can't guarantee to keep you out of it.'

She pushed past me and went into the tiny kitchen. She poured milk into a saucepan, mixed cocoa into a jug and added sugar. She gave it all her attention. When she spoke it was without looking up. 'You know about the others?'

'Serge Frankel masterminding the whole thing, with you and old Ercole's grandson doing the commando stuff? Eventually I guessed.'

'Is Champion dead?'

'No,' I said. 'They took him away when the big trucks came. Where are they going, Pina?'

She bit her lip and then shook her head. 'It's a mess, Charlie.' The milk boiled and she poured it into the cups. She pushed one cup towards me and took another one to Billy.

I sank down into an armchair and resisted a great desire to go to sleep myself. I heard the water running, and the voices of Pina and the child. I looked round the room. Amongst the colour TV, indoor plants and the sort of steel-and-leather furniture that looks like office equipment, there were one or two items still remaining from the farmhouse where she'd lived with her parents during the war. There was a sword that some long-dead Baroni had carried in the Battle of Solferino, at a time when Nice and Savoy were speaking Italian. Alongside it hung a faded watercolour of a house near Turin, and a photo of Pina's parents on their wedding day. In the glass-fronted cabinet a place of honour had been found for a Staffordshire teapot with a broken spout. In the old days that had been the hiding place for the radio crystals.

'He's asleep,' she said. She looked at me as if still not believing I was real.

'I'm glad you kept the teapot, Pina.'

'I've come close to throwing it over the balcony,' she said tonelessly. She went over to the cabinet and looked at it. Then she picked up the photo of her late husband and sons and put it down again.

'I should have come here and talked to you,' I said. 'Every day I planned to, but each time I put it off. I don't know why.' But really I did know why: it was because I knew such a conversation would probably end with Pina going into custody.

'A husband and two fine boys,' she snapped her fingers.

'Gone like that!' She pouted her lips. 'And what of the kid who threw the bomb. Someone said he was no more than fifteen years old. Where is he now, living there, in Algiers, with a wife and two kids?'

'Don't torture yourself, Pina.'

She took Billy's coat and mine from a chair, and with the curious automatic movements that motherhood bestows she straightened them, buttoned them and hung them in a closet. Then she busied herself arranging the cups and saucers and the small plates and silver forks. I said nothing. When she had finally arranged the last coffee spoon, she looked up and smiled ruefully. 'The war,' she said. 'It makes me feel so old, Charlie.'

'Is that why?' I said.

'Is that why what?'

'Is that why you tried to kill Champion today, and damned near killed me and the kid as well?'

'We didn't even know Billy was in France.'

'So it was Champion's fault,' I said bitterly.

'Did you recognize me?' she asked.

'Billy did.'

'We came back,' she said. 'You were on your feet, and Billy was all right. So we didn't stop.'

'You and old Ercole's grandson,' I said. 'Bonnie and Clyde, eh?'

'Don't be bloody stupid, Charlie.'

'What, then?'

'Someone's got to stop Champion, Charlie.'

'But why you? And why Ercole's grandson?' But I didn't have to ask. I'd heard Ercole's stories about the war and the glorious part he'd played in the liberation of France. Who could miss the citation, and the photographs, so beautifully framed and well displayed near the lights ostensibly directed at the Renoir reproduction?

I put more sugar into the cocoa.

'I said you'd guess,' said Pina. 'He sounded you out about the football match, to make sure you wouldn't be in the car at the time. But I said you'd guess.'

'It will be a fifteen-year stretch,' I said. 'The driver's dead, do you know that?'

'We talked about it,' said Pina. She took her coffee and drank some. 'But finally we decided that we'd go ahead, even with you in the car, we'd go ahead.'

'So I noticed,' I said. I drank some cocoa and then I sniffed at it.

'It's only cocoa, Charlie,' she said.

I drank it. 'And did you decide to go ahead even if Billy was in the car?'

'Oh, my God, Charlie. What have we come to?' Her eyes filled with tears. 'Will you forgive me, Charlie? We didn't see Billy. You must believe me. You must!'

'I believe you, Pina.'

She reached out and clung tightly to me, but there was no passion, just that terrible wail of despair with which survivors lament being left alone.

'Take Billy to his mother, Pina.'

She nodded, but her face was contorted with grief and she soon began to cry again. I put my arms round her, and tried to steady her as the sobs racked her frail body. I felt the hot tears on my cheek and I caressed her back as a mother might calm a fractious child.

'I'll phone my people right now. I might be able to arrange a plane immediately. In any case, you mustn't stay here.'

She stopped crying, and looked at me. 'Serge Frankel said you were an important man.'

'Go to Caty, in Wales. Stay, until I tell you it's safe to return.'

She gripped my arm to tell me that she understood. I pulled myself away from her and stood up. She huddled in the corner of the sofa and sobbed into her hands. I remembered the tomboy who had never shed a tear, not even when the Germans took her mother away. Pina had a lot of crying to catch up with. Or perhaps she was crying for all of us.

24

I was too late. We were all too late. If you are trying to do a totalitarian job within the permitted limits of a free society, you are always too late. The vegetable market, that after dark is as deserted as anywhere in the city, had become a copper's carnival.

Where the vegetable stalls usually stood, there were the shiny black police cars of the Divisional Superintendent, the police doctor and the examining magistrate. Parked tight to the pavement there was an ambulance and the Criminal Records van.

The entrance to Serge Frankel's apartment block was rigged with lights, and guarded by two policemen, their pinched faces blue with cold.

'Everybody wants to get into the act!' It was Claude.

He nodded to the guards and I was permitted inside. 'It looks that way,' I said.

There was a cop on each landing, and the residents stood about in pyjamas and dressing-gowns as plainclothes men searched through every room. But when we got to Serge Frankel's study there was hardly room to move.

Frankel was spreadeagled across the threadbare carpet, one thin arm extended to the wing armchair in which I'd sat that day in 1940. There were enough valuable stamps and covers scattered around the room to make some casual observers believe that it had been robbery with violence. Claude did not look directly at Frankel. He found excuses to look at other things in the room, and to examine the stamps and covers on the desk, as the

205

policeman entered them into the evidence book. 'It was clean and quick,' said Claude.

I picked up the sheet. 'Through and through wound,' I read aloud. 'Grease collar on the entry side . . .'

'He was a big man in the 'thirties,' said Claude. 'He brought a lot of people out of Germany in 'thirty-three and 'thirty-four. He helped the Princess escape, did you know that?'

I looked at him. Claude was taking the old man's death very badly. Very badly for a professional, that is. I realized that my suspicions about Claude's intentions were unfounded: he simply liked the old man.

'He was never bitter,' said Claude. 'Never suspicious.'

'This time, he wasn't suspicious enough,' I said. 'No break-in. He must have opened the door for whoever did it.'

Claude nodded.

Dawn was breaking, chiselling the horizon open like a blue steel oyster knife. The first of the market-men were throwing boxes of vegetables about, with all the noisy glee of men who are early risers.

'Schlegel said that you would know what to do,' said Claude.

'Here?'

Claude looked towards the Divisional Super, who was near enough to be listening to what we said. The police-man nodded, and looked at me. 'Schlegel said you know more than any of us.'

'God help us, then,' I said.

A plainclothes officer was outlining the position of Frankel's body in white chalk upon the carpet. As he finished and stepped aside, a photographer did the necess-ary three-shot set. Then two men in white coats put Frankel on to a stretcher, tied a label to his wrist, and carried his body away.

'The end of an era,' said Claude.

'Only for us, Claude,' I said. 'For these boys it's just another night of overtime.'

'It's shaken you, too, hasn't it?' said Claude.

'No,' I said.

'They should never have sent us,' said Claude.

Well, perhaps Claude was right, but as soon as the ambulance men had removed Serge Frankel's body I took hold of the situation. 'Three of your men,' I told the Divisional Super. 'Get all the rest of them out of here. Three of your best detectives must go through all this stuff, piece by piece.'

'Looking for what?' said Claude. 'A piece of paper?'

'This man Frankel had some sort of inside line to the Champion household. By some kind of alchemy this arthritic old man sat up here in this apartment, plotting and planning everything from murder to geopolitics. Until yesterday I thought his contact was Champion's English nanny, but now I'm sure it wasn't her.' I turned to look at the amazing chaos of the study: thousands of books, thousands of covers, countless stamps and a muddle of bric-à-brac. 'Somewhere here something will tell us who, what, why and where Frankel's contact was.' I sighed. 'No, I don't know if it will be a piece of paper.'

A plainclothes officer stood behind Frankel's desk, putting keys and money and personal papers into separate plastic bags and labelling each one with the same number that was registered in the evidence book. 'Stop him doing that,' I said. 'We'll need those keys: I want to open these drawers and boxes and filing cabinets.'

The Divisional Superintendent gave the necessary orders, until the room was almost empty. His chosen detectives took a handful of keys and began to work methodically.

'What's the latest on the big trucks?' I asked Claude.

Claude straightened the shoulder strap of his impeccable white trenchcoat, coughed and said apologetically, 'We can hardly put out an all-stations alert, can we?'

'It might look that way now,' I said. 'But if it all fouls up, you'll have lots of little men in pin-stripe trousers explaining exactly why you could have.'

'Five trucks,' said Claude. 'Still all together, and following the expected route to Bonn. At first light, the traffic helicopters will take a look at them.'

I didn't answer.

Claude said, 'You're blown, Charlie. You're not going to get back into Champion's set-up again. The whole thing is blown wide open. Schlegel sent you across to investigate Frankel's death. It's absurd to go on pretending you are just a bystander.'

'You're right, Claude,' I said.

'Your request about the plane for Pina Baroni and the Champion child came to me,' explained Claude. 'I got permission to use the plane belonging to our ambassador in Paris. So I know all the details.'

'Schlegel talks too much,' I said.

'You're wrong,' said Claude. 'Colonel Schlegel is brighter than you. He knows that he can get more co-operation from people who know what is happening.'

One of the detectives had found the key to the big safe behind the door. It looked like a rusty old refrigerator and was about as invulnerable.

'You think this Algerian secretary has taken control?' said Claude.

'How do we know he is Algerian? He might be an Egyptian – a nuclear physicist, a general or an executioner. If I hadn't been in that shoot-up on the autoroute, I'd even be suspecting that that was another of Champion's tricks.'

'He's got us all like that,' said Claude. 'But perhaps Champion's ultimate trick is simply to pull no tricks.'

We both turned to see the two detectives hammering the handle of the gigantic safe. With one final heave they wrenched the door open.

Just for one moment, I thought he was still alive. He was sitting inside, cross-legged, on some dented cash-boxes, with box-files resting on his shoulders. Then, very slowly, Gus tilted forward, and crashed on to the carpet, in an avalanche of stamps and covers. He had not yet stiffened, and, under the weight of his body, his arms and legs reached out, so that he seemed to be trying to crawl out from under the debris.

'Gus!' I exclaimed loudly. 'The Spanish Civil War – the International Brigade. Why the devil didn't I think of those two getting together.'

'Someone murdered both,' said Claude. It was a guess, but it was obviously the right one.

One of the detectives leaned close to look at the body. 'Same wound as the old man,' he said.

'Damn, damn, damn,' I said. 'Every time they are a jump ahead of us.'

Claude's Teutonic reaction was a more practical one. 'Get the doctor and the photographers and the records people back,' he told one of the detectives. 'Now we start all over again.'

A uniformed policeman brought me a small green official envelope from the police station. His raincoat was shiny with rain and I had already heard the rumble of thunder. I tore open the envelope. Schlegel had sent a Telex from the CRS office at Nice airport. He wanted me there as quickly as possible.

'I've got to go,' I said.

'Schlegel is probably taking you up to talk to our Border Police in Aachen.'

'Where the hell is that?' I said. I knew where it was, but I was angry that Claude knew more than he told me. Perhaps that was what was wrong with all of us.

'Nordrhein-Westfalen,' said Claude. 'The German frontier with Belgium and Holland. It's a health resort.'

I waited, but Claude said nothing more. 'Well?' I said. 'He's not going up there to take a cure, is he?'

'There was a tip-off . . . a shipment of guns being smuggled. Schlegel felt it might have a bearing on the Champion business.' Claude's face was quite impassive. It was impossible to know whether he agreed with Schlegel.

'We have a car here,' said the uniformed policeman, in a polite attempt to hurry me.

'One more thing,' said Claude.

I bowed my head and pinched my nose waiting for it.

'It was Champion who betrayed the network. The rest of us all worked through cut-outs. Only Champion knew that Marius was collecting the radio messages from the Princess, and circulating them through the confessional.'

I looked at him for a long time before replying, wondering why he wanted to hurt me. 'I was there at Nice railway station when Champion was arrested,' I told him. 'You know that Marius and the others had already been arrested about five o'clock that morning – seven hours earlier!'

Claude shook his head. There was the sound of distant thunder, and dawn was making the windows red enough to see the dabs of rain hitting the glass. When Claude spoke, it was in the dull monotone of a speak-your-weight-machine. 'That was part of the deal. We arrested Champion the previous morning. It was part of the deal that we would let him come down on the train, so that you would see him being arrested.'

'The departmental inquiry after the war. Your people cleared him.'

'We all lied. We thought it would be clever to have a hold over a man like Champion. But it was never of any use.' He sighed as though his life had been filled with brilliant ideas for blackmail that he'd found no chance of using.

'Why tell me now?' I asked. 'After all this time. Why tell me now?' It was all happening as I knew it would if I came back here to find the remembered magic: I was stumbling over broken wires, bent pulleys and jammed trapdoors, left over from a bungled stage conjuring act.

'You've been assuming that Champion is some kind of entrepreneur. He might be the victim of blackmail.'

'I'll write it into the report,' I promised. 'Meanwhile, dig out something on that old bastard Santa Claus. Why do the poor kids get the paper-hats, and the rich kids get the ponies?'

'Have a good time in Germany,' said Claude. I heard the thunder again. Or was it some old man in the wings, shaking a sheet of tin?

25

Monday morning: Germany: the helicopter touched down on the rain-soaked earth, and lurched slightly as it settled into the mud. I opened the Plexiglas door, and jumped down, landing with a loud squelch. Schlegel jumped out too, and the mud spattered over my trouser-legs. 'So Champion was taken away by force?' asked Schlegel. He squinted through the driving rain to the far side of the clearing, where a group of foresters conferred beside a fallen fir tree.

I didn't answer. Schlegel asked me again. It was one of those examination questions; any square you tick loses you marks.

'Billy went into the garden and hid,' I said. 'I can't imagine Champion moving off, and leaving his boy there.'

'I'm glad to hear that some of it's not going according to plan,' said Schlegel, with uncharacteristic low spirits.

'I just can't decide whether the death of Gus, and Serge Frankel, was part of the plan – or a reckless way of dealing with an emergency,' I said. 'If we knew that, it might all fall into place.'

Schlegel sighed, wiped his face and nodded, all at the same time. Behind us I heard the helicopter blades chug to a halt. 'Come along,' he said. For a moment or two there was no sound except the squelch of our shoes, and the splash of rain running off the firs that made this path as green and gloomy as the ocean deeps. But then the first axe fell, and the chopping continued like the beating of a heart.

'We should have put a transponder into Champion's cars,' grumbled Schlegel.

'Yes, we should have,' I said. It was like wishing that Champion was sporting enough to leave a trail of paper.

We came off the pathway on to the road, stepping along a wooden duckboard to cross a drainage ditch. On the road three cars and a small van were parked askew to improvise a roadblock. The cars had the insignia of the state police, but the van belonged to the Border Police, a force with federal authority. There was no way of recognizing which men were which, for they were all wearing the same wet raincoats and sou'westers. They had adopted the relaxed and patient attitudes with which outdoor workers endure steady rain. One of the men detached himself from the group and hurried towards us.

He was an elderly man, and under the collar of his oilskin I saw the badges of a captain. He saluted gravely. 'We're holding them in the truck.' He spoke good English, with just a trace of an accent. 'They'll admit nothing.'

'While you get wet!' said Schlegel. 'Bring the little creeps out, and let them get rained on.'

'We'd have to handcuff them,' said the policeman. He handed Schlegel two detonators, and a map drawn upon a page torn from a school exercise book.

'So?' said Schlegel aggressively. 'So?' He looked down the road in the direction of Roetgen. It was several kilometres to the Belgian frontier. There are many such minor roads crossing the border. Some of them are little more than fire-breaks through the mighty wilderness of the Eifel. Even when the Ruhr disgorged its hunters, campers and holidaymakers, you could still get lost among these hilly forests that have to be cut by handsaw.

Here the US First Army faced Germans fighting on home-soil, for the first time. The Americans had been fed into the dense mine-strewn forest like coffee beans into a grinder. There was no room for a tank to pass between the trees, so the infantry had dug deep and listened to the artillery barrage. It chopped the limbs off the trees, and left a legacy of steel that even today tears the teeth out of power-saws.

'Grim bloody place,' said Schlegel. He brought out his cigars, but thought better of it and put them away again.

'Here they come,' I said.

There were two of them: wretched-looking hitch-hikers, bearded, tired and crumpled. It was surprising that they had strength enough to manage the gigantic rucksacks and bedding rolls that were on their backs. The policeman had not handcuffed them, having probably decided that the equipment and accessories were more than enough to hamper their escape. Now the policeman stepped back from them.

The police had found twelve detonators, two Sten guns and some maps – including one of the USAF–Luftwaffe air-base at Ramstein – buried in their camping gear. The taller of the pair looked back at the uniformed officer, and then at Schlegel. 'I want a lawyer! This is the twentieth time I've asked for a lawyer. I know my rights!' Even Professor Higgins would be hard-pressed to place such an accent: Birmingham, England, at first-hand, perhaps, Brooklyn, New York, at second-hand and a sprinkling of Hollywood, California.

'So you can count?' said Schlegel. He didn't look up. Schlegel seemed oblivious of the pouring rain that was fast reducing the maps in his hands to pulp.

Schlegel passed the maps to me. There were half a dozen of them: small practical Xerox copies of the suburbs of Bonn, the centre of Bonn – some of the more important buildings indicated in additional felt-pen notes – and a Michelin map of this area with the cross-border roads scribbled upon.

Without a word to me, Schlegel reached back for the maps and I gave them to him.

'Yeah, I can count, Yank!' said the boy. Schlegel still didn't look at him. The boy glanced up at the sky, as if looking for some reassuring patch of blue. But the only break in the dark clouds revealed a kingdom sulphurous and fiery.

The boy used both thumbs to ease the weight of his pack and equipment. 'And you'd just better know it, Yank. 'Cos you'll find out I can count real good.' They both wore red-star badges, pinned into the sort of beret that Che Guevara wears in posters.

Schlegel looked up at him and then at his silent companion, who was a few inches shorter, and carried notably less equipment. 'I haven't got a great deal of time,' Schlegel explained, as if the boy had invited him to take tea and cucumber sandwiches. 'So just tell me where you got the maps, the Sten gun and the detonators, and then I can get some lunch and go back to my office.'

'Drop dead, Yank.'

'This is no time to be cute, sonny. Tell him, Barrington. This is no time to be cute, is it?'

Schlegel often made up names on the spur of the moment. I recognized his use of Barrington as a sign of his impatience with my Island Race. 'It's not the time,' I said obediently.

The boy's lips moved as if he was salivating to spit but it was simply a show of anger. 'Get stuffed!' he said. His voice was pure Birmingham now.

Schlegel moved so fast that both boys were caught off balance, but it was only the silent boy that he hit. He walloped him twice, swinging his elbow back in a great show of force, so that the blows looked far harder than they were. But, for a boy with forty or fifty pounds strapped on his back, and metal studs in his shoes, it was

215

more than enough to send him reeling and sliding. A third jab tumbled him into the rain-filled ditch that gurgled under a jungle of thorns and weeds. The boy landed with a splash, and was trapped by the weight of his burden. He let out a scream that was strangled as the cold water took away his breath.

'You bastard,' said the Birmingham boy. It was a different sort of voice now: just as bitter, and even more angry, but there was an undertone of defeat there, too. 'Jerry's not strong,' he shouted. 'Leave him alone, you old bastard. It's not fair!'

Schlegel had not used his left hand, in which the map and detonators were still clasped. He spared no more than a glance at the boy who was struggling to climb out of the ditch. He stared at the talkative one. 'It's fairness we're talking about now, is it? I thought we were talking about dynamite. About blowing the bourgeoisie into hamburger.' He waved the detonators about. 'Not strong, your friend Jerry, eh? Strong enough to carry a machine-gun and two hundred shells, right? And strong enough to pull the trigger, providing both you punks think you'll get away unhurt.' By now Jerry had hauled himself up the side of the steep ditch. He was on his hands and knees, shaking the water from his head and whimpering to himself.

Schlegel was close to him. He looked down at him for what seemed like ages. Shivering and wet, the boy did not look up. Schlegel gently put his foot on the boy's shoulder and pushed. He grabbed Schlegel's ankle but could not hold on to it. There was a cry of despair as he tumbled back into the ditch.

'He'll get pneumonia!' shouted the boy from Birmingham.

'Are you a medical student?' said Schlegel, with polite interest.

'The boy swallowed. 'I'll talk,' he growled. 'I'll talk. You win, I'll talk.'

The rain lessened but the wind was cold. Schlegel buttoned his collar tight against his throat, and flicked the brim of his corduroy hat to get the rain off it.

From the clearing where our chopper had landed, there came the sudden clatter of a two-stroke motor, and then the terrible scream of a chain-saw biting into wood. I shivered.

'You heard me, Yank. I'll talk!'

Schlegel said, 'Go ahead, son. I'm listening.'

'Outside the American Express in Amsterdam – that place on the pavement, you know . . .' He looked at his friend sprawled in the ditch.

'I know,' said Schlegel.

'A guy named Frits – he bought hot dogs for us. The next day we went back to his pad and smoked. He had a friend . . . least, he said he had a friend. There was a thousand guilders for starters. Another fifteen hundred for delivery of the stuff to an address in the village of Schmidt. We thought it was pot, honest we did.'

'Sure. And the Sten guns you thought were pipes, to smoke it,' said Schlegel. 'Come out of there, you stinking little fairy.' He reached down and grabbed the rucksack straps of the boy in the ditch. With apparent ease, he hoisted him back on the road. 'OK,' said Schlegel. 'I'll believe you.'

'Can we go?'

'You sort that one out with the German cops,' said Schlegel. 'Come on, Barrington. Just standing downwind of these little creeps makes me throw up.'

'We could identify Frits, the man in Amsterdam. Do a deal . . . huh?' said the boy.

'A man for all seasons,' said Schlegel. 'I don't do deals with kids like you – I squeeze them; and they drip.' He

217

flicked the boy away, as he would some insect buzzing around his head.

'In Schmidt. We had to meet our contact in the Haus Rursee,' added the boy anxiously. The police officer took the boy's arm.

'Come on,' said Schlegel to me. He turned and I followed. The scream of the chain-saw grew louder. When we reached the clearing the tree was dismembered, the amputations marked by bright circular wounds, and pools of sawdust.

The police pilot sat at the controls of the helicopter waiting for the order to go. Schlegel did not give it immediately. We sat back on the seats, with rain forming puddles underfoot, and the world multiplied ten thousand times in the raindrops on the Plexiglas.

'It's Champion, no question of that,' said Schlegel. 'He wanted us here, but what the hell are we supposed to do?'

'They are just stupid kids,' I said.

'I know they are,' said Schlegel. 'But I had to know if they were more than that.'

'Could those trucks be across the border by now?' I asked.

'They were going like hell all last night,' said Schlegel. 'No reason why not.'

I looked at Schlegel.

He said, 'Why should he stage a diversion like this, while the trucks cross the border? They have diplomatic protection: borders make no difference in this case.'

'There has to be a reason,' I said. 'Something happened when those trucks went across the border. And that something would have told us what the plan was.'

'The drivers were all checked at the dock gates. All of them are French-born professional drivers, with at least eight years' experience. Already we have checked their fingerprints with London, Washington, Paris and Bonn. Not a whisper of a clue.'

'No, it must be the vehicles.'

'You think Champion is inside one of those trucks?'

I said, 'I only wish I had a theory.'

'What happens to trucks when they cross a frontier?' Schlegel asked the pilot of the police helicopter.

'They check the manifests and the personal papers. They make sure the load is firmly secured. Perhaps they check the brakes and the roadworthiness. It's according to how busy they are.'

'No,' I told Schlegel. 'It's not going to be something that the customs men would notice. It's something that would only seem strange to you or me, or to someone who knows the situation. Otherwise there would be no point in staging a diversion that would take our attention.'

Schlegel sat hunched forward in his seat, while the rain beat down upon our plastic bubble. 'They must be on the Autobahn to Cologne by now,' he said finally. He reached for the pilot's map and opened it on his knees. 'If they are going to Bonn, they will turn off the Autobahn at that big clover-leaf there – *Autobahnkreuz Köln West* – and follow the circular road as far as the next clover-leaf.' He stabbed the place on the map. 'From there, it's only a lousy twenty kilometres to Bonn.' He looked at me and then at the pilot. 'When those trucks get halfway between Cologne and Bonn – we stop them, and screw the diplomatic ruckus.'

'You want me to radio for permission?' the pilot asked.

Schlegel looked at him unenthusiastically. 'I'm giving the orders, Baron von Richthofen! You just pull the levers! Let's go!'

The pilot clipped his helmet chinstrap tight, and twisted the microphone wire so that it was close to his mouth. Schlegel, having made his decision, twisted his nose in his hand, and then pinched his own cheeks as a physician might help a patient recover from a coma.

I looked at the pilot's map. On both sides of the River Rhine, from Cologne to Bonn, the land is flat and, by the standards of the great industrial complex of the Ruhr, comparatively lightly inhabited. But there were towns there – Wesseling and Niederkassel – I wondered how they would like being expendable in favour of the great cities each side of them.

The starter banged and I watched the pilot's lips moving as he began his litany of radio signals. I guessed he would call the traffic police who had been tailing the convoy of trucks at a discreet distance.

The helicopter tilted forward and lifted away over its cushion of downdraught. It, too, belonged to the traffic police and the pilot was used to flying through this sort of weather. Even at tree-top height, black puffs of cloud scudded past us like Indian signals. I stared at the scenery. The forest stretched as far as I could see. To the south, yellow sky was reflected in the ruffled water of the Rursee, so that it looked like a fiery volcano just about to boil over.

26

By the time the River Rhine gets to Bonn, it is wide and grey and cold, smeared with fuel oil and flecked with detergent. And north of the capital it meanders through flat featureless land that continues all the way to Holland and the North Sea, and the wind makes the river choppy.

The police helicopter came low over the waterway, lifting enough to clear the masts of a liquid-gas tanker, and then of a big Dutchman, low in the water, with a deck-cargo of yellow bulldozers. Once over his cranes we crossed waterlogged fields and high-tension cables that sparkled in the rain, like a spider's web wet with dew. And then we saw them.

The helicopter reared, and turned abruptly as we came to the concrete of the rain-washed Autobahn. The five trucks were keeping to a steady fifty miles per hour and the pilot had timed our approach to coincide with a burst of speed by the two white Porsche cars that had been following them.

The flashing police-lights made long reflections on the road, and the trucks slowed and followed the police cars into the heavy vehicle park of a service area. Our helicopter put us down gently just before the huge diesel trucks cut their engines, one by one.

'Perfect,' said Schlegel. I'd never heard him use that word before.

The policemen got out of their Porsches, put on their white-topped caps and stretched their limbs. They had been providing us with a commentary for the last half hour. Now they saluted Schlegel and awaited instructions.

'Ask them for their driving licences,' said Schlegel derisively. 'Jesus Christ! Don't tell me a traffic cop can't find something wrong with everybody.'

They didn't smile, and neither did the men who climbed down from the cabs of the trucks.

'Check the manifests, check the customs seals, check the brakes,' said Schlegel. He tapped my arm. 'You and me are going to give them the once-over lightly, before we open them up.'

They were gigantic fifty-ton diesels: twelve forward speeds and two reverse. Cabs like glasshouses, ergonometrically designed seats, and behind them a rest bunk. There were racks for vacuum flasks of coffee, and cheap transistor radios were taped to the sunshields. A set of Michelin maps was duplicated for each of the five cabs, and there was a German phrase-book and a repair manual. They had been on the road for almost twenty-four hours. The cabs had become a smelly clutter of empty cigarette packets and butts, squashed paper cups and discarded newspapers.

'We would see it,' Schlegel reminded me. 'Champion was frightened that we would see it, smell it, or hear it. Otherwise there was no point in arranging that charade with those kooks.'

One of the traffic policemen brought the manifest to Schlegel. It was the same as the ones we'd got from the dock office in Marseille. It described the load as a general consignment of engine parts, construction materials, fabrics and chemicals. Schlegel handed it back. 'Frisk all of them,' he told the policeman. 'If you find as much as a pocket knife, it might be enough to hold them for inquiries. And I want the exterior of the trucks examined by someone who knows how many differentials a truck like this needs and where to find them.'

'Yes, sir,' said the policeman.

There was a steel towing-cable padlocked to the under-side of the chassis and, in special cradles behind the cabs, there were steel wheel-chocks. Schlegel rapped one of them. The metal was too heavy to get an echo out of it.

Schlegel looked at me and raised an eyebrow.

'Why?' I said. 'When you can put it inside so easily?'

'I suppose you are right,' said Schlegel. 'We're going to have to bust them open.' The vehicles were so large, and the wheels so big, that we were able to get right under the chassis without crouching very low. 'Look at the suspension,' said Schlegel. 'With one of these brutes you could schlepp Cologne cathedral away in the middle of the night, and still throw the opera house in the trunk.'

'And it could take plenty more, too,' I remarked. We looked at the massive leaf springs. The upper one was still curved, and the lower, supplementary spring not yet tensioned.

'That's got to be it!' said Schlegel, in great excitement. 'You've hit it.'

'The weight!'

'Exactly. These trucks must be almost empty. Look at that! We should have noticed that from the way they were sitting on the road.'

'And a customs man would have noticed. In fact they might have put them on a weighbridge while the manifest was stamped.'

'Why? Why? Why?' said Schlegel. He punched the great rubber tyre.

'So that we would be talking about fifty-ton diesel-truck suspension, somewhere on the banks of the lower Rhine, while Champion is earning a promotion from colonel of propaganda to general of god-knows-what.'

Schlegel grunted, and came out from under the truck. He waved to the policeman. 'Forget it,' he called. 'Let them go.'

'They say they are going right the way down the Autobahn to Munich,' said the policeman.

'Are the papers in order?'

'They say they are going to get new papers in Bonn.'

'Let them go,' said Schlegel. 'They can keep going all the way to Vladivostok for all I care.' He smiled. 'That's all, boys: go get yourselves some coffee.'

The policemen looked at Schlegel with that same inscrutable superiority with which they look up from your driving licence.

Schlegel turned back to me. 'Munich,' he said with disgust. 'And after that, Brindisi or Lisbon – it's a merry dance he's been leading us.'

'There's something else,' I said.

'Like what?'

'I don't know – but he didn't send five empty trucks from Marseille docks to Bonn just to grab our attention.'

'Why not?' said Schlegel. 'He did it! And while we chased them, he got to where he wanted to go.'

'You don't know Champion,' I said. 'That's not fancy enough for him.'

Littered with old food wrappings, smelling of spilled fuel and warm fat, these coffee shops on the Autobahns are the most desolate places in Europe. An endless succession of strangers gobble mass-produced food and hurry on. The staff are glassy eyed and melancholy, trapped in a river of traffic, which swirls past so that the fumes, noise and vibration never cease.

'And lousy coffee,' added Schlegel.

'Do you know how much it costs to hold a chopper on the ground while you dunk that doughnut?'

'You're a lot of fun to have around,' said Schlegel. 'Did I ever tell you that?' He opened his shirt and scratched himself.

'Not lately,' I admitted.

'Hit me with one of your dust-packets, will you.'

I gave him one of my French cigarettes.

'Why?' he said for the hundredth time. He lit the cigarette.

'There's only one explanation,' I said.

He inhaled and then waved the match violently to put the flame out. 'Give.'

'He brought something off that boat.'

'And unloaded it during the night,' finished Schlegel. 'On the other hand, they've been making such a good average speed.'

'It's all double-think,' I said.

'Let's get back to Nice,' said Schlegel. He scratched himself again, but this time there seemed to be an element of self-punishment in it.

27

When Champion broke from the department, we set up this small office in Nice. The modest entrance bore the trademark of a well-known British travel company, and three of our staff gave their full-time attention to legitimate travel business.

Schlegel had taken an office on the top floor. He was standing in the window when I entered, looking across the square to Nice railway station. When Cimiez, in the northern part of Nice, had been chic, this section had also been fashionable. But now it was dirty and run-down. The tourists arrived at the airport, and they wanted hotels near the sea. I walked over to the window.

The railway station had hardly changed since the day I waited for Champion to arrive, and watched him being arrested. The tiled floor was a little more chipped, the mural of the Alps a little dirtier, but what else had stayed so much the same? Certainly not me.

Schlegel could always find himself a clean shirt, but his suit was creased and baggy, and the oil-stain on his knee was the one he'd got from the wheel of the big truck. His eyes were red, and he rubbed them. 'They should tear this whole lousy district down. Put the bus depot and the railroad station in one complex, and stack twenty floors of office accommodation overhead.'

'Is that why you sent down for me?' I said.

'What are you doing downstairs?'

'Trying to catch up on my sleep. First time since I got up on Sunday.'

'You want to learn to cat-nap. No. I mean what are you working on down there?'

'I sent out for some maps. I'm waiting for them,' I told him.

'I know all about that,' said Schlegel. 'When people in this office send out for things, I get a copy of the requisition. Your goddamn maps have arrived. I've got them here.'

'I can see you have,' I said.

'That's the way I work.'

'Well, good luck, Colonel. I'll go back downstairs and try to get a little more sleep.' I got up and went to the door.

Schlegel suppressed a yawn. 'OK, OK, OK. We're both tired. Now come over here and show me what you want the maps for.'

I went around to the other side of his desk and sorted through the survey maps of the country round Champion's house, and copies of the land registration, and some data about drainage and changes of ownership. I tipped everything – except the map that showed the whole region – into Schlegel's wastepaper basket. 'That stuff was just to make it look like an ordinary lawyer's inquiry,' I said.

'You want to tell me what's on your mind?' demanded Schlegel.

'Those five empty trucks. Suppose they unloaded the contents at the Champion house.' I spread the map.

'No, no, no,' said Schlegel. 'I thought of that, but the gendarmerie patrol that area up there. They fixed a new lock on the back door. They go in there to look round.'

'Let's suppose,' I said patiently.

'That Champion is sitting in the dark up there, testing the spark plugs in some reconditioned dragster?'

'Engine parts,' I said. 'That might mean pumps, to get the old workings going again.'

227

'The mine.' He snatched the map and unrolled it across his desk. He used the phone, a paperweight and his desk-set to hold the corners. He sucked his teeth as he looked at the full extent of the mine workings: the shafts, seams and the long haulage roads. 'That was quite a layout.'

I rapped my knuckle against the telephone with enough effort to make the bell tinkle. 'And just about here, remember – the artillery depot, Valmy.'

'Jesus!' whispered Schlegel. 'They've got atomic shells in that store.' For the first time Schlegel took the idea seriously.

'Nuclear artillery shells – at Valmy! And you knew that all along?' I said.

'It was need-to-know,' said Schlegel defensively.

'And I didn't need to know?'

'Keep your voice down, mister. You were going to sit in Champion's pocket. Telling you that there were nukes in Champion's back yard would have been stupid.'

I didn't reply.

'It wasn't a matter of *trust*,' said Schlegel.

'You're a stupid bastard,' I said.

'And maybe you're right,' he admitted. He ran his thumb and index finger down his face, as if to wipe the wrinkles from his cheeks. It didn't work. 'So what do we do about this?' He smacked the map with his fingers so that he made a tiny tear in the brittle paper.

'We'd better tell Paris,' I said.

'If we're wrong, they'll hate us. If we're right, they'll hate us even more.'

'You'd better tell them,' I said.

'You don't know those people like I do,' said Schlegel. 'Champion was once one of ours – that's all they will need to blame us for everything.'

'We've had these maps from the municipal authority – and that's on record – you've been told about the atomic

228

shells – and that's on record, too. They will crucify us if we don't tell them immediately.'

Schlegel looked at his watch. 'They will have packed up by now. I don't want to spend an hour explaining things to the night-duty officer.' He looked up at me. 'And I know that you don't, either. Let's go out to the house and take another look at it. It might be just another false trail. If it's worth a damn, we'll tell Paris in the morning. What do you say?'

'I don't like it,' I said.

'Why not?'

'I don't like it,' I said, 'because when we get out there, you'll want to go inside. And then, you're going to want to find the entrance to the mine. And then you're going to want to go down there . . . and all the time, you're going to be holding me in front of you.'

'How can you say that! Did I ever do that to you before?'

Before I could answer, Schlegel picked up the phone to get a car.

28

It was dark. I fidgeted enough to send the blood back through my dead arm, and looked round to where Schlegel was hiding, in the scrubland just a few feet away. The western horizon was still pale. But there was not enough light to see the Tix house, except through the night-scope that we'd set up on the rise behind it.

There was precious little moon, just a well-honed sickle, cutting its way out of the clouds every few minutes. But it was during such a flicker of light that the 'scope showed a movement at the back door. I held my breath: it was a man, tall enough to be Champion. He had a gun slung over his shoulder, and was wearing a helmet and some sort of boots or gaiters. I released the trigger on the night-scope so that the intensifying tube could build up a fresh charge. I used it again as the man started to walk across the yard, picking his way past the mud, and then climbing the wooden stairs to a vantage point on the platform outside the hayloft. It made a good sentry post; too good – if he turned this way he'd need no night-scope to see us moving.

Schlegel moved closer. 'Champion's people,' he said. On the cold air his voice was dangerously loud. He rubbed his mouth, as if to punish it, and when he spoke again it was in a whisper. 'Not real policemen; I checked the patrol times before we left.'

The dew had soaked my clothes and there was enough of a breeze to make me shiver. I nodded, lest the tone of my voice revealed the state of my morale.

We'd already seen another such man, standing at the

place where the tracks divided for the house and the quarry. Equipped with a radio-phone it would be easy to warn of the approach of the gendarmes on their regular patrols.

Schlegel elbowed me aside, and took the eyepiece of the 'scope for a moment. There was a movement beyond the clump of half-dead olive trees that we were depending upon to screen us from the house. Lying full-length in the grass, I felt the vibrations of a man stamping his feet to keep warm. He was not more than forty metres away from us. Perhaps only the woollen scarf wrapped round his head, plus the numbness that comes from long spells of sentry duty, had prevented him from hearing Schlegel's voice.

When the second man stamped his feet, a third sentry moved. This one was up the slope to the rear of the house. I swung the night-scope to see him. He'd unbuttoned his overcoat and, after a considerable search of his clothing, he brought out cigarettes and matches and lit up.

'That lame-brain is asking for it,' whispered Schlegel.

It was true that he'd offered himself as an easy target to anyone within range. For a moment I was puzzled by his action.

Even an imbecilic sentry should know enough to step behind cover while he strikes a match, if only to keep it secret from his sergeant. And then I understood. 'They're not sentries,' I told Schlegel. Each one of them was facing the wrong way, which was probably why we'd got so close without being detected. 'They're *guards*.'

I crawled forward to get under the shelter of the low stone wall that separated the yard from the long meadow. Would they patrol, I wondered, and which side of the wall did our fellow keep to?

I waited while Schlegel moved up to me. 'Champion is in there,' I said. 'They are holding him.'

231

He didn't answer for a moment or two. Then he said, 'The imbecile would be our best chance.'

The kitchen door opened, making a bright-yellow smoke-filled prism. Out of the kitchen came a man. A smell of burning fat confirmed that he was the cook. To be that indifferent to the police patrols they must obviously be about to pull out.

'Champion is a prisoner in there,' I told Schlegel.

'I heard you the first time,' he said.

'I want a closer look.'

He thought about it for a moment or two. 'Give me that night-scope.'

'I'd better look inside the house,' I said. He didn't reply. I wondered if he'd heard my whisper.

He stretched forward to hand me a Walther P·38 and four magazines of bullets. I pushed it into the waistband of my trousers.

I waited until the nearest guard moved down to exchange a word with the man who was still coughing his heart out in the back yard. I vaulted over the low stone wall, lost my balance on the dew-wet stones, and slid down the incline, to land in a heap against a neatly stacked log-pile. I remained dead-still, hardly daring to breathe, but the lung-racking coughs were loud enough to prevent the clatter of my fall from reaching the men in the yard.

I looked back to where Schlegel lay hidden. The lens of his night-scope caught the light from the kitchen window, and flashed like a searchlight. Seen from this end, it was a dangerous toy, but I could do nothing to warn Schlegel now.

Beyond the stacked logs there was the door to the dairy. I crawled forward, and pressed gently against it. It was ajar and swung open with hardly a sound. There was a smell of cheese. A glimmer of light, from the kitchen at the other end of the hall, glinted on the big stone crocks that held the separated milk. I could hear the cook still coughing, and I could feel the draught of air that was clearing the kitchen of smoke.

If I was to get to Champion's study, I would have to get through the kitchen while it was still empty.

I peered into the smoke. The spilled fat was still burning with fierce flames on the coal-fired cooking stove. I held my breath but the acrid fumes made my eyes water, and took a layer off the back of my throat. I ran into the smoke.

I remembered the two steps down to the scullery, and the slippery mat that was at the bottom of the back stairs. When I reached the entrance hall, I planted myself in the recess under the stairs and listened. Someone was coming. I heard unhurried footsteps on the upstairs landing. The balcony creaked as someone put his weight on the rails, and looked down into the hall. There was a whirr of clockwork and then the longcase clock struck the half hour. The footsteps moved away.

Before I could move, the front door opened and one of the guards came into the hall. He was a huge man, an Algerian, in raincoat, helmet and gumboots. He wiped his feet on the doormat, plucked the chinstrap loose, took off the helmet carefully, and placed it on the hall table. Then he discarded the raincoat, too, leaving it in a heap in the hall, like the skin shed from some shiny black insect. Under the policeman's coat and helmet, he was dressed in blue overalls. He came past me close enough for me to smell the garlic on his breath, but he looked neither to right nor left. He stopped in front of Champion's study. He sorted through a bunch of keys, then opened the door and went inside. I waited. Soon there was a noise that I'd always associated with the generator that supplied electricity for the household. Now I had another theory.

I looked at my watch. Fifteen minutes had already passed. I stepped across the hall and to the door of the study. I put my ear to it. No sound came from inside and I leaned forward to look through a crack in the door. As far as I could see it was empty. I pushed the door and went in.

I walked through Champion's large study. I looked behind the curtains and behind the inlaid Sheraton bookcase. There was no sign of the Algerian sentry and there was only one other door. It was open, and I stepped into a small ante-room, in which Champion kept filing cabinets, typewriter and office materials of a sort which might make his elegant study unsightly. I stepped inside. The second of the filing cabinets was unlocked. I slid the drawer open and found inside, not documents, but a phone and a panel with buttons marked 'open doors', 'close doors', 'top floor' and 'lower level'. I pressed the last button. The sliding door closed. A motor mechanism whirred, and the lights dimmed. This was the sound that I'd mistaken for that of the generator. Very slowly at first, the whole room began moving. It was not a room at all: it was a lift.

It stopped at what I guessed was about fifty feet below ground level. I pushed against a heavy metal door, keeping flat against the cabinets, but when the door was fully open I saw only a short corridor, brightly lit by fluorescent lights. There was no one in sight. I pulled the gun out of my waistband and moved warily along the corridor until I reached a large office-like room. It too was empty. I breathed a sigh of relief, and tucked the gun away again.

It was a square room, with cheap wall-to-wall carpet, and a plastic sofa arranged to face an office desk, swivel chair and telephone switchboard. It could have been the reception office of any penny-pinching little company, except for the notice that said 'No Smoking' in both French and Arabic.

But now I knew what to look for, I had no difficulty noticing the tiny gap that ran down the mirror from floor to ceiling. And then – on the telephone switchboard – I found a switch around which the paint was exceptionally worn and dirtied. I pressed it. The mirrored doors slid apart.

This was another shaft, but quite different to the one behind me. This was a part of the original nineteenth-century workings. From up the shaft there came the draught that is the sign of an active mine. And the draught smelled sour, as the dust it carried hit my face.

The Tix mansion was built on a rise that brought its ground floor level with the old winding gear. The lift from Champion's study had brought me down to the level of the old fan drift. This was the upcast shaft, which had been built only for the filled tubs to come out.

This was not a lift – it was not a padded box with concealed lighting, Muzak and seats for the elderly – it was a cage. It was an open-fronted cage, with rusty chain-link sides, a wire-netting top, to catch falls of rock from the roughly hewn shaft, and an expanded-steel floor, through which I could see a glimmer of light a thousand feet below me. I stepped inside and the cage jiggled and clanged against the stay-wires. The sound echoed in the dark shaft, so loud that I expected some reaction from below, but I saw none. I locked the safety bar in place in front of me, and swung the crude lever mechanism to close the outer doors. For a moment I stood in the pitch darkness, listening to the whirr of engines and cables. Then, with a sickening lurch, the cage dropped, gathering speed as it went. The winding mechanism screeched loudly, the pitch of its cry growing more shrill as the speed increased.

The cage stopped suddenly, so that it bounced on the springing. I was at the bottom of the mine. It was dark. There was a steady beat of the pumps and the hum of fans. I reached forward, to touch the rocky face of the shaft, but a crack of light showed that I faced doors with a crush-bar opening device.

I could hear the pumps somewhere close at hand, and under my feet, in the bottom of the shaft, there was the sump and its running water. I opened the doors, and found the shaft-landing brightly lit with fluorescent light. This must have been one of the earliest shafts sunk. The landing was a large one, with concreted walls and lockers and safety notices, and a time-keeper's box that contained all the comforts of a ramshackle home. These 'No Smoking' notices were only in Arabic. From here stretched three galleries, forming a junction at the corner of the landing. One gallery was sealed. The other two had rails for the tub-trains. One gallery's tracks were rusted and dirty, but the other's were shiny bright and slightly oiled, like a guardsman's rifle.

Keeping close to the wall, I moved out of the light into the gallery that seemed still in use. Its walls were wet, and there was the steady drip of water, its sound magnified by the narrow confines of the tunnel. For illumination there was only the dim yellow glow of a few safety lights, recessed into wired and armour-glassed fittings. The line of bulbs showed me the inclines and curves of the workings, but there was not enough light to prevent me stumbling into pot-holes and falling over outcrops of rock. More than once, I went ankle-deep into the syrupy liquid that the dust and water made. Times without number I barked my shins and ankles upon the uneven sides of the gallery. There were rats everywhere: pairs of tiny green lights that stared at me, before disappearing with a scamper of feet that sometimes disturbed the litter of paper and tin cans.

I was a hundred and fifty yards along the gallery when I heard the train start. I looked around for somewhere to hide. The dim wall lights glinted on the sides of the gallery. I could see no recesses or cross-cuts ahead, and I'd certainly not passed anywhere that could conceal a man.

The sound of the train grew louder. I guessed that it was pulling a train of empty tubs, for there was a metallic rattling as the trolley wheels bounced on the poorly made track. It moved slowly, and as it turned the curve the diesel loco and its driver obscured the safety lights. I pressed myself flat against the wet rock-face.

The train was only fifty yards away by now, and its noise was almost deafening. I sank down on to my knees, and then went flat. It was a gamble, for if they did spot me, I'd have no chance to defend myself. I turned up my collar to hide the whiteness of my neck, and tucked my hands out of sight. The locomotive roared close to my ears, and its diesel exhaust scorched my arm. One of the tubs had been left in the inverted dump position. The edge of it struck my arm. I bit back an involuntary yell, and then the noise of the train overwhelmed my gasp of pain.

I remained still for several minutes after the train passed. When I got to my feet again, it was out of sight, although I could hear its rumble as it crossed the junction at the shaft landing. I heard voices, too, as the driver exchanged greetings with someone. The winding gear started again.

I moved forward, and this time I kept the gun in my hand. Now I heard other voices from the distant shaft landing. There were lots of men, and even my lousy

Arabic was enough to tell me that a new shift of workers was coming on duty.

I hurried forward. Behind me I could hear the voices of the men as they climbed aboard the train. There were curses, and cheers, and the unfunny jokes that men exchange at moments of tension. The men's voices were amplified by the narrow mine workings, and for a moment I panicked. I ran forward, hammering my fist against the rock, and desperately praying for any small niche in which to hide. My prayer was answered and I groped my way into a low tunnel that gave off the main gallery. It was wide, but there was so little head-room that I was almost bent double. I realized that it was not a gallery: it was a working face. I stumbled, banged my head and fell heavily. I felt the blood trickle down the side of my cheek and reached out to help myself to my feet. It was then that I touched the chilly surface of a steel rail. The tracks ran along this working, too. I went cold with fear. I realized that the train – filled with the workers – would not return along that same gallery down which I'd seen it go. The mine would be sure to work a one-way system, so that the unloaded trains could complete a circuit, to return the empty tubs to the work-face.

The train was coming up this road to meet me.

I turned and ran along the tunnel, now crouched even lower to avoid hitting my head. To my left there was the ancient conveyor and to my right what had once been the working face. The face was not flat, like a wall, it was an endless series of 'rooms' eaten out of the rock. Some of them were no more than a few feet wide, while others were just a black void. But that side of the workings was closed off with wire fencing. Several times I almost lost my balance as I tripped upon the loose uneven surface. I grazed my hand on the sharp edges of the conveyor-belt, with all its pulleys and rollers. Growing panicky, and ever more careless, I blundered into a wooden pit-prop and momentarily was knocked senseless. I doubled up over the conveyor, and heaved deep breaths that took the sharp dust deep into my lungs.

I looked back. The tunnel shone yellow. The driver was using the headlight on the locomotive. When it turned the corner this time, they surely must see me.

Desperately, I decided to crush myself into the space between the conveyor-belt and the bench over which it ran. I got my legs inside but only the great beam of yellow light, and the noise of the locomotive, persuaded me to cram myself into a space far too small.

I held my breath as the train approached with agonizing slowness. On it there were a dozen or more men. Most of them were dressed in the same dungarees that the others had been wearing, but four of the men were differently dressed. I blinked in amazement to see that they were wearing the leather helmets and goggles of old-time aviators. And, in case I was still in doubt, each of them was nursing on his lap the heavy canvas harness and unmistakable brown canvas pack of a parachute.

29

I watched the tub-train as it trundled away from my hiding place. There was enough light now to see that this track was entirely new. The air-doors at the end of them were also new. The train, with its strange subterranean aviators, thudded through the air-doors with a flash of lights and a shrill call of its whistle.

I waited a long time before extricating myself from my hiding place. When I was sure there was no one following them, I made my way along the track to the air-doors. I opened them and stepped through quickly.

The air-door shut behind me with a muffled bump, and cold night air hit me in the face like a custard pie. I was standing on a ledge, some twenty feet up one side of a vast underground cavern. It was about fifty yards across, and just as deep, but it must have been well over one hundred yards in length. Suddenly I realized that the roof was the sky, and I recognized it as the Tix quarry where I'd hidden for two nights and days of the war. But far more astonishing than the man-made hollow was the huge black metallic egg that completely filled it.

It was smooth and symmetrical, elegant and futuristic like those storage tanks that the oil companies depict on the covers of their annual reports, when shares have tumbled. On an airfield, perhaps I would have recognized it more quickly, but only when I saw its whole shape against the starry sky did I realize that the quarry was being used to house an airship.

An airship. Melodie Page had died after sending us the postcard photos of the *Graf Zeppelin* and the *Hindenburg*, and it had been too obvious to see. Not that this was a giant rigid, like those airships of the 'thirties. This was no more than a blimp, of the sort I'd seen drifting over the cities of Europe and America advertising drink and cigarettes. This, then, was the consignment of engine parts, heavy-duty fabrics and plastics, and hydrogen or the plant to manufacture it – hence all those 'No Smoking' notices in Arabic.

Lacking a proper mooring mast, its nose was tethered to the shovel of a rusty excavator, and dozens of ropes held the restless shape down, close upon the floor of the quarry. The Dacron envelope had been roughly covered with matt black paint, and the gondola had been modified for freight-carrying. The engine nacelles were fixed to each side of the gondola. One engine had a servicing platform still in position. Three mechanics were bending over it, clanking spanners. They stood upright and exchanged looks of satisfaction.

As I was looking down upon them, one of the mechanics signalled to someone at the pilot's controls, in the gondola. The engine started with a bang. It roared and came up to full revolutions, before being throttled back to a steady tick. They let it run for a couple of minutes, and then cut it. The quarry was silent, except for the generator that powered the lights and tools, and, from behind me, the faint hum of the fans in the mine.

I still had the P·38 in my hand, and my first impulse was to fire into the gas envelope, but there was little chance that such pin-pricks would do it any great damage. Also it would be dangerous. I was still thinking about it when a voice said, 'Put it down, Charlie!'

I looked round, but I could see no one, apart from the mechanics who were displaying the same sort of interest in the voice as I was. It was Champion's voice and it had come from a loudspeaker – or several loudspeakers. His voice echoed as the sound of it travelled back from the farthest loudspeaker and bounced off the gas-filled envelope and the quarry walls.

'Put it down, please!' A bird fluttered fearfully and flew across the airship. I still did not move.

'I have a marksman here. The gallery behind you is sealed, and there is no way out of the quarry, except up the cliff side.'

I looked at the sheer sides of the quarry from which his voice still reverberated, and I put my pistol back into my belt.

Champion took his time, crossing the bottom of the quarry and climbing the crude steps to the ledge where I'd emerged from the mine gallery. I suppose I would have been equally cautious, or perhaps I would have shot first and parleyed afterwards. But Champion climbed up the steps, smiling his tired old smile and smacking the quarry dust off the knees of the grey, multi-zippered flying-suit he was wearing.

'You cost me fifty francs,' he said. 'I bet you'd get Schlegel to come in.'

'You knew we were out there?'

'No, no, no. First thing we knew was that the cage was left at the bottom. We guessed then. Someone had got in. You and Schlegel, was it?'

'And a couple of battalions of CRS.'

'You wish!' said Champion. 'Well, we probably have Schlegel too, by now. You got through the road block but I brought them close in afterwards. They'll phone down to me.'

'I'm way ahead of you, Champ,' I said.

'Don't tell me you thought of the airship.'

'No, that was a surprise. But I knew that whatever it was it would be here.'

He walked to a door built into the cliff at one end of

242

the ledge. It was his control room. Inside, there were a couple of chairs, and the control console for launching the airship. There was a battery of telephones, an intercom, and six small TV screens that provided a view of the airship from each direction. Champion indicated a chair and sat down at the console. The little control room was glass-faced, and before sitting, he lifted an arm to the mechanics below us, to tell them that all was well.

'Why here?' he said.

I said, 'Remember that day we were caught by that German spot-check at St Tropez, and the German guard shot at the kid who stole the chickens?'

'I remember.'

'You told them we'd found the Renault on the road. And then, after we'd watched them taking the car away, you phoned the police station, and said there was a Renault with RAF escapers inside, going to a safe house in Nîmes.'

Champion smiled.

'I was pretty impressed, Steve,' I said. 'The cops followed those German soldiers in the Renault. They followed them all the way to Nîmes . . . stake-outs, checks . . . mobiles . . . all kinds of stuff . . .'

'And meanwhile we put Serge Frankel, and his junk, into the submarine at Villefranche,' said Champion. He frowned.

I said, 'Afterwards you said, "Make the deceit do the work". I remembered that last week.'

He nodded.

I said, 'You deliberately let us suspect the manifest. You let us think you'd go to all kinds of trouble to get some mystery cargo into position in Germany. While all the time the trucks *were* loading at Marseille docks – loading this airship, envelope folded and engines crated – and then you drove here and unloaded.'

243

'It worked,' said Champion.

'Like a conjurer – you told me that: make enough sly play with your left hand, and they won't even look at your right one. You made them look at your empty trucks and see loaded trucks, because that's what they wanted to see.'

'It worked,' repeated Champion.

'Almost,' I said.

'You didn't discover it,' said Champion, 'you *sensed* it. No plan is proof against a hunch.' He grinned. 'You told me there was no place for hunches any more. So perhaps we are both yesterday's spies.'

'It had crossed my mind,' I admitted.

'And . . . ?'

'You're going to have to kill me, Steve. And that's another hunch.'

He looked at me and wiped his moustache. 'We'll see, Charlie.'

'You don't teach an old dog new tricks, Steve. You know it, I know it. Let's not kid around, at least you owe me that. There are thoughts I might need to have, and things I might have to do.'

'Like . . . ?'

I shrugged. 'Like getting out of here!'

He looked at me and smiled wearily, like the governor of Devil's Island indenting for more shark food. 'It doesn't have to be like that,' he said. 'We'll work out something. How's the boy?'

'Billy's fine. We're going to build a plastic model of the *Cutty Sark* before he goes back to school.'

'You sent him back to Caty.'

'That's it,' I said.

'It will make no difference in the long run,' said Champion. 'The important fact is that he'll grow up with a bit of money in his pocket.'

244

'The money you'll get for this caper?'

Champion nodded. 'If my old dad had left me a bit of money, it might have worked out differently.' He reached inside his flying-suit and found the big gold pocket-watch I remembered from the old days. He held it up to show me that it was all his father had left him. Or perhaps it was just Champion's way of checking what the time was.

'Inconsiderate of your old man,' I said. 'Not to sell out.'

'Thirty-five years teaching in Egypt,' said Champion. 'Scrimping and saving to send me to school, and the only time he ever hit me was when I didn't stand up for "God Save the King".'

'What an incurable romantic he must have been, Steve. Old fools like that can never match the wits of realists like you.'

Champion stared at me. 'That's not cricket, old pal.'

'I thought we were all-in wrestling,' I said.

'You have to learn cricket *and* all-in wrestling, if you are the only boy at Sandhurst who plays cricket in second-hand togs.'

'And that kind of resentment spurred you on to get all the prizes.'

'Perhaps,' admitted Champion. 'But don't ask me to say thank you.' He wiped the back of his hand across his mouth, as if wiping away a bad taste. 'By God, Charlie, you're a working-class boy. You know what I mean.'

'I know what you mean,' I said, 'but I am not planning to deliver an atomic bomb to back up the demands of the Trades Union Congress, or the Monday Club.'

If he detected a note of irony in my remark, he gave no sign of it. 'Shells, atomic shells!' He obviously hoped that this distinction would bring about a change of my attitude. 'I wouldn't get involved in nuclear *bombs* – not accurate enough. But atomic shells are tactical, Charlie.

They can be put into a vehicle park, or a dump – no fall-out, and very tight destruction pattern.'

'You've been reading too many of those Staff College appreciations, Champ,' I said. 'Save the rationalization for your memoirs: what are they paying you?'

'They'll cross my hand with silver,' he admitted.

'Thirty pieces?'

'Thirty *billion* pieces, if I ask for it. And every currency in the world, Charlie. When we needed money to fight starvation, disease and poverty, Europe couldn't be bothered. But when they had to start walking to the railway station . . . then they put their hands in their pockets!' All the time the airship moved restlessly, rearing up suddenly to the limit of its mooring ropes, and then being hauled down again by the ground crew at each end of the quarry.

'You know how it works, Champ,' I reminded him. 'I didn't come out here without leaving a forwarding address. They will soon find your hole in the ground.'

Champion turned away to look at the TV monitoring screens. There were half a dozen of them, relaying pictures from cameras set high on the cliff side, and facing down to the airship. Using these, the pilot would be able to see how much clearance he had, on every side, as the moorings were cast off and it floated upwards.

'Helicopters, you mean?' Champion said, without looking up from the console.

'I don't know what they will send.'

'With half a dozen cookies on board with me, I don't care what they send. They are not going to shoot me down over mainland France. Not with a cargo of nuclear explosive aboard, they're not.'

'And over the sea?'

'A civil aircraft, registered in Cairo? We do sixty, perhaps eighty, miles an hour in this bladder. By the time they get permission to shoot, I'll be over Tunis!' His mind went back to Billy, or perhaps he had never stopped thinking about his son. 'How could Billy adapt to Cairo? Answer me truly, Charlie. How could he?'

'You mean you're frightened that he might adapt too well. You're scared in case he becomes the chief assassin for the Palestine Liberation Organization.'

'Perhaps I am.'

'But you'd give them the means by which to bomb themselves to power.'

'Not the PLO . . .' he waved his hand wearily, as if deciding whether to enlighten me about the distinction between the government in Cairo, and the terrorists who throw bombs into airport waiting-rooms and set fire to jumbo-jets. He decided against it. 'Billy stays in Europe where he was born – he's vulnerable to smallpox, malaria, cholera and a million other things.'

'You'd be separated from him?' I couldn't believe it. 'The judgement of Solomon, Champ.'

'You didn't say "You can't get away with it,"' he complained. Then we both looked up at the great black shape of the airship.

'But you *can*!' I said. 'That's what I don't like about it.'

'You can't see it, and even with the engines running the only sound is a faint hum, like a distant car. People just don't look up.'

'Radar?'

'We're keeping well clear of the air traffic lanes. The military radar is mostly facing seawards: the stations at Arles and Digne can read inland, but we keep behind high ground.'

'Flying low.'

'Yes. One hundred metres or less. There's no risk: even if some radar operator did see us . . . a huge blob,

247

moving at no more than sixty miles an hour? . . . he's just going to log it as what radar men call "an anomalous propagation" and everyone else calls a machine failure.'

'You're flying it?'

He shook his head. 'We don't take risks,' he said. 'An airline captain, qualified on 707s. He went to America and did the course, said he was going to fly it for advertising.'

'How soon?'

He looked at his watch. 'We'll start cutting into the explosives store at Valmy sometime within the next hour.'

'From the mine?'

'We've dug thirty kilometres of gallery,' said Champion. 'We are now underneath the nuclear explosives store. Some of the most experienced mine engineers, from all the Arab states.'

'Brought in as waiters?'

'. . . and labourers, foundry workers and garbage men. All they need is an Algerian ONAMO card, and the French immigration can't stop them.'

'Suppose you hit an alarm system?'

'From under the earth?' said Champion. He laughed. He knew it was a perfect plan, and he was enjoying this chance to tell me about it.

From some tiny ledge, high up on the side of the quarry, birds began to sing: not one but a whole chorus of them.

The stars were bright, and cold air coming over the lip of the quarry was striking against the warmer airship and causing it to rear against the mooring ropes: superheat, they call it. This was the time of maximum lift.

Champion smiled.

Only the inevitable is tragic. Perhaps Steve Champion's tragedy was born out of his obsession about providing money for his son. Perhaps it was a need to provide for his son a future at least as affluent as the boy's mother could have supplied. Or perhaps it was simply that Steve Champion was the same romantic, desperate man that he said his father had been.

'The money's safe,' said Champion. 'Billy will never want.'

'Wouldn't you have chosen your father, rather than any fortune, Steve?'

'No!'

'Too emphatic!' I chided him. 'Top marks for self-deception.'

'Well, it's a pretty poor liar who can't even deceive himself,' said Champion, and, like an elderly soprano defying the critics, he gave me one of his famous coloratura smiles, and held it long enough to deserve a round of applause.

It was the smile that was his undoing. Until then, I had been listening to Steve Champion, and making excuses for him. I was trying to understand his concern about Billy, and struggling to believe that he'd spend the rest of his life separated from his son. But now somewhere far behind his eyes I saw, not bonhomie, but bravura.

I looked down to where the ground crew was standing by on the moorings. As each completed his task, he looked towards the platform where we were standing – they were looking to Champion.

Champion's story about cutting into the bomb store within the next hour was nonsense. They must have done it already. The shells must be aboard, and the airship ready to go. Champion's last laugh was in keeping me talking until a moment before take-off.

No one intended to stay for another hour, or even another few minutes, if the bustle around the gondola was any indication. The mooring ropes were hitched into quick-release hooks, and the covers were now being clamped over the engine casings.

The canvas screens that extended around the rim of the quarry, to protect the airship against rock-falls, were now fully retracted. Champion leaned forward and tapped the wind gauge, but the needle didn't move.

Champion got up and walked outside, to the open balcony. I followed him. He leaned forward to see the tall vegetation that grew along the edge of the quarry. There was no movement in it. 'The wind is always a worry,' said Champion.

'There's no wind,' I said. I was watching him carefully now.

'No.' He sniffed the air. 'You can "free-balloon" up on a night like this . . . start the engines when you're in the air.'

'Is that so?' I said. He was thinking aloud. They would need to 'free-balloon' up if they were to go, without someone controlling the ascent, from this console.

'You'll look after the boy?'

I didn't answer him.

'Good,' he said, and patted my arm.

Perhaps if I'd been listening to him more closely, or remembering old times, I would never have hit him in the sudden and impulsive way that I did. He reeled against the rail. I followed the straight right with an uppercut from my left. It wasn't anything to write to *Physical Fitness Magazine* about, but Champion was already off balance. It sent him down the staircase: backwards. Even while my left was connecting, I was bringing the P·38 out of my belt. Champion landed at the bottom of the steps in a heap. He groaned, and dragged his arm from under him, but it carried no gun. Champion was too damned Sandhurst to brandish pocket guns, and his sort of tailor can't set a sleeve to hide a shoulder holster. And anyway, Steve Champion had no trigger finger. He fixed me with a look of hatred and despair, but pain closed his eyes.

I offered a silent thanks to Schlegel for the P·38. The well-oiled safety slid to fire. There was no time to thumb the hammer back; I pulled hard on the trigger and felt the double-action. I fired, and put the whole magazine of bullets into the gas bag. The Walther twisted in my hand, as all big pistols do, but I wasn't trying to win a prize at Bisley; I wanted only to puncture the envelope and let the hydrogen gas escape near the engine. I pushed the magazine catch, and shook the gun hard enough to bring the empty magazine out. It clattered to the floor. I banged the full magazine into place and brought it up two-handed style. These were the ones that had to hit. There was only the faintest glimpse of light on the foresight, but as it came up the engine nacelle, I squeezed the trigger. I'd known old P·38s, with worn trigger bars, to rip off a magazine like a burp-gun, but this one was a gentleman's pistol. It was too dark to see what my grouping was like, but inside the engine cowling, ricocheting bullets were playing close-harmony tin, like a drunken steel-band at Mardi Gras.

As the hammer nose clicked on the firing-pin, I threw the gun aside, and ran for the mine entrance. I already fancied I heard the gurgle of petrol running from the punctured fuel tank. I pictured the hot engine that it would fall upon; the thought propelled me head-first through the doors. They thudded shut behind me and the sound of the fans was in my ears, until the beat of my pulsing veins drowned it out. I stumbled in the darkness but fear beats any after-burner as a means of propulsion, and I was at the far end of the main gallery when the airship's hydrogen ignited. I knew that, in theory, an atomic shell could not be exploded by fire, but did that extend to the temperatures at which hydrogen burned?

The bang ripped the doors from their hinges, and the end of the mine gallery became a red glowing rectangle. A giant breaker of hot air picked me up and slammed me to the floor, and then did it again. I twisted my head to see what was chasing me. The patch of light was boiling whiteness. It was like staring into the sun through a square telescope. I screwed up my eyes as the main blast of heat hit me. This time the smell hit me too; not only the carbonized rubber, and the stink of hydrogen and scorched dust, but the awesome smell of burned hair and flesh. I clamped my hands over my face and found that some of the burned hair and flesh was my own. I rolled over, shouting some incoherent mixture of prayers, oaths and promises.

With the roar of the great furnace I'd created still in my ears, I crawled towards the shaft landing. Each movement was painful and the dust had been sucked up into a blinding black storm. After the first few tottering steps I knew I could go no farther.

But it wasn't going to end like this, I told myself. A man doesn't spend a lifetime working for that damned department, and die in a mine, without pension or gratuity. But a few minutes' rest . . . that was different: a man must be allowed a moment's rest.

30

'And do you know what I say?' said Schlegel for the tenth or eleventh time.

'You say "crap",' I replied. I was tired. As I wiped a hand across my forehead I smelled my scorched clothes and my scorched hair. And I looked at the burns on my hand.

'Don't go to sleep on me,' said Schlegel. 'There's a whole slew of paperwork for you to finish before you sack out. Yes, that's right: I say crap. And if it wasn't for Dawlish being so soft, I'd have your arse in a sling.' He nodded to me, and scowled at the same time. 'I wouldn't let my own mother come out of the other side of this one unscathed.'

'I believe you, Colonel,' I said.

'Well, now we can see why the girl sent that picture postcard of the Zeppelin. She got on to it too early for Champion's liking. But how could you be sure it was filled with *hydrogen*? No one fills blimps with hydrogen any more.'

'Helium is too difficult to get.'

'Helium would have left you looking pretty damned stupid, fella,' said Schlegel. 'Non-flam helium would not have burned. That would have left you with egg on your face. It would have given Champion a big laugh, and you a tail filled with lead.'

'You would have preferred that, perhaps,' I said.

'I would have preferred that. No perhaps about it.'

He picked up a newspaper that had just arrived by messenger. The headline said, 'Gas Leak Kills Twelve', with a subhead that said it had happened at a 'remote chemical plant' owned by Tix Industries. Schlegel held the paper up and flicked it with the back of his hand, so that it made a loud noise. 'A lot of trouble went into getting us that newsbreak the way we wanted it,' he said.

Schlegel opened a new box of cigars and selected one. He didn't offer them to me. 'Atomic shells!' said Schlegel. 'Would it interest you to know that Champion had not even *tried* to dig a passage to the artillery school?'

I didn't answer.

'You pleading the Fifth Amendment?' said Schlegel. 'Or did you just go to sleep? The whole thing was a bluff. And you fell for it . . .' He shook his head sadly. 'Do you realize what you did?'

'OK,' I told him. 'It was a bluff. But let me tell you what kind of bluff it was. Champion was going to fly that blimp to North Africa – there's no doubt about that.'

'So what?'

'He would have claimed to have stolen atomic shells.'

'And the French would have denied it.'

'And which of them would we have believed?' I asked him.

'I would have believed the French,' insisted Schlegel primly.

'Well, the Israelis might *not* have believed the French. And if you were the Israeli negotiators at the treaty talks, perhaps you'd have had your doubts, too.'

'And lost out in the negotiations, you mean?' Grudgingly, Schlegel conceded an inch to me. 'Champion wouldn't put his head on the block just to provide psychological advantages for those goddamned Cairo politicians.'

'He wasn't putting anything on the block,' I said. 'It was an aircraft, registered in Cairo, flying over France without permission. Who was going to press the button?'

'Nukes in French air space . . . and the Quai d'Orsay in a panic . . . ? Champion would be taking a big risk, I'd say.'

I said, 'Champion knew they'd phone the artillery commandant and find that there were no atomic artillery shells missing. They sign those things in and out, every shift: a thirty-second response.'

Schlegel didn't answer.

I said, 'All along, I was puzzled by the way that he let us know it was going to be a nuclear device. I wondered why he didn't try to disguise the *object* of the operation as well as the *method*.'

Schlegel nodded. It was beginning to get through to him. 'He did it so that you would strong-arm me into alerting every damn official in NATO. When the Egyptians claimed to have got a nuke, there were going to be a lot of our top brass saying where there's smoke there's fire.'

'It was a neat idea, Colonel,' I said. 'And since we were going to keep on denying that any kind of bomb had been stolen, Champion could come back and live in France, get Billy again, and even go to London for his stamp auctions.'

'Knowing that any attempt to hit or hassle him would look like a confirmation that he'd got the damned thing.' Schlegel nodded a grudging concession to Champion's cleverness. 'The only thing he didn't figure was that the Melodie Page kid would put the boot in.'

'And that I would put the boot in, too.'

'Umm,' said Schlegel. He rubbed his chin. He'd not shaved for forty-eight hours and his suit was filthy from poking around in the embers of the fire.

Out of the window, I could see Nice railway station. It was dusk, and the lights were on. Facing it was the Terminus Hotel. Once this had been a fashionable place to stroll and to sit, but now the great hotel was dark and empty, its windows dirty and its fine entrance boarded up. I remembered the café, with outdoor tables and fine cane chairs. I'd been sitting there, that day in that war so long ago. I'd waited for Champion, and seen him arrested by the Germans as he emerged from the station. He knew exactly where I would be, but he didn't look in my direction. Steve was a pro.

Now Steve was dead. The hotel was dead, and the café was gone. The chairs and tables were replaced by a corrugated iron hoarding. Upon it there was layer upon layer of posters, advertising everything from Communist Party candidates to go-go clubs and careers in the Foreign Legion. Across them, someone had daubed 'Merde aux Arabes' in red paint.

'Are you listening?' said Schlegel.

'Yes,' I said, but I wasn't.